**Also by
Soraya Lane**

The Devil Wears Spurs

Cowboy Take Me Away

Soraya Lane

St. Martin's Paperbacks

This is a work of fiction. All of the characters, organizations, and events portrayed in this novel are either products of the author's imagination or are used fictitiously.

COWBOY TAKE ME AWAY

Copyright © 2016 by Soraya Lane.

All rights reserved.

For information address St. Martin's Press, 175 Fifth Avenue, New York, NY 10010.

ISBN: 978-1-250-06009-9

Printed in the United States of America

St. Martin's Paperbacks edition / January 2016

St. Martin's Paperbacks are published by St. Martin's Press, 175 Fifth Avenue, New York, NY 10010.

10 9 8 7 6 5 4 3 2 1

For Yvonne Lindsay. I don't even remember when we started doing this together, but our daily writing sprints mean the world to me. Thank you!

Acknowledgments

You only have to read a few of my books to realize that I thank the same people every time, but I have a core group of people in my life that deserve ongoing thanks! Firstly, I would like to acknowledge my editor on the Texas Kings series, Holly Ingraham. Working with you has been a very positive experience, and I hope you love this series as much as I enjoyed writing it. I also owe my gratitude to the St. Martin's Paperbacks cover designers—all I can say is Wow! The covers look even better than I imagined they could.

I would also like to thank my literary agent, Laura Bradford, for always answering my e-mails so promptly, being available for general hand-holding when required, and being all-around fabulous. I'm so pleased I went to the New Zealand Romance Writers Conference back in 2010—I met Laura there, ended up seated beside her at dinner, and the rest is history!

Thank you also to my mother, Maureen. I'm feeling very fortunate to be an only child right now, because it means I can have her all to myself! That translates to having super-gran look after my kids all the time . . .

I also have to thank my husband, Hamish, who is

endlessly supportive of my work. Of course he's hoping one of my books hits #1 on the *New York Times* list, earns us millions, and gets made into a top-grossing movie!

Natalie Anderson and Nicola Marsh, you are both an incredible source of encouragement and support, and I admire you both. I love that I have you both to chat to whenever I need you. Thanks also to Yvonne Lindsay, for being there every day of the week. I can't believe how motivating it is to know that you're writing with me, making me accountable for how many words I write in our 30-minute sprints!

One of the hardest parts of being an author is other people thinking you have an easy job just because you work from home. Writing is tough, and creating an entire book is an exhausting and hard-going process at times. The three authors I mentioned above are all busy mothers, and we all often work very long hours. We love what we do, but damn, it's not easy even at the best of times! It's nice knowing that we're all there for each other when we need support.

Cowboy Take Me Away

Chapter 1

"Are you guys sure this isn't one of you trying to prove your dick's bigger than the other's?" Nate asked, arms folded across his chest as he surveyed Ryder's new house.

Chase laughed and slapped his younger brother on the back. "Hey, I win that contest hands down." Ryder shrugged off his hand and scowled at him. "Besides, I think you'll find he's had no say in the size of this place. That's all Chloe's doing."

"Ha-ha, very fucking funny," Ryder said. "At least I have a wife."

Chase held up his hands. "You got me. No ball and chain attached here."

Nate shook his head and walked around the house. "For all the shit we give you about Chloe, you know we love her, right?"

Ryder glared at them both. "Oh, I know. Haven't you noticed that's why I never let her see you guys without me around?"

"Damn," Chase teased, raising his eyebrows. "Guess I'll have to stop having coffee with her every morning. Your bedroom's so sunny late morning . . ."

Ryder shrugged, but Chase could tell he'd pissed him

off. The only thing Ryder was sensitive about now that he'd given up rodeo was Chloe, and they loved to tease him. After being on his back for years about giving up his career as a bull rider, they didn't get many excuses to boss him around anymore.

"Enough," Nate scolded. "I need a shower then I'm off to Houston for a few days."

"You taking the jet?" Chase asked.

"Yeah." Nate stretched his arms above his head, flexing his muscles. None of them were wearing shirts after their early morning run, the air a refreshing blast of cool now they'd caught their breath. "I'll be back to kick your ass again on Saturday."

"If we can move our legs by then," Chase said with a chuckle.

"I ain't running with you guys again. I prefer my mornings nice and lazy with Chloe, if you get my drift," Ryder told them.

Chase and Nate both laughed. When they ran together, neither he nor his big brother wanted to come last, which meant their early morning jogs always turned into a competition, one that Nate had won today. Chase grinned. Next time he'd beat him—he'd train every morning he was gone to make sure of it. Ryder hadn't even come close to keeping up with them.

"So you guys do like the place, right?" Ryder asked, leaning against the timber framing, eyes trained on Chase.

"I think it's awesome," Chase told him, all jokes aside. "The difference between you and me is that you're building a home and I'm building a house. You'll be hearing the pitter-patter of little Ryders before you know it."

Ryder raised his eyebrows but didn't say anything. Chase loved Chloe and he was looking forward to being an uncle one day, but there was no way he was settling down any time soon. His brother getting hitched was one thing, but it wasn't for him.

"You manage to get an appointment with the new artificial insemination specialist?" Nate asked, taking a swig from his water bottle as they all made the short walk back toward the main house, the homestead they'd been raised in on the sprawling King estate.

"Yeah, she's heading here this morning. A new vet based in Dallas, someone they've just recruited to join the team." Chase tucked his T-shirt into the waistband of his running shorts. "We're gonna have the best damn organic beef cattle in Texas, just you wait and see."

"I thought we already did." Nate grunted. "Anyway, I'm counting on it. You'd think we were breeding cows made from gold at that price."

"I'll catch you guys later. Have fun in Houston," Ryder called over his shoulder, walking back toward the small guesthouse he was sharing with Chloe until his new place was completed. "Chase, I'll come down and meet the new vet later on."

Chase nodded and followed Nate. He grimaced as he stretched out his legs. "I might have to postpone that ride I was planning on today."

Nate laughed. "You going soft in your old age?"

"Me, old?" Chase shoved Nate and sprinted up the stairs ahead of him, howling in pain when he reached the top ahead of his brother.

"Calves burning?"

"Like a motherfucker," Chase groaned, collapsing against the wall.

"I'm gonna hit the shower. See you Saturday."

Chase headed for his room and stripped down to take a quick shower in the adjoining bathroom. He reemerged with a towel slung around his waist, his entire body aching as he found underwear, jeans, and a shirt. Training with Nate six days in a row was pure punishment—they'd always run, then do burpees and crunches until they were almost crippled. He got dressed, rolled his sleeves up to his elbows, and made his way back downstairs again, stopping in the kitchen to grab a coffee and something to eat.

"Morning."

He glanced up, smiling when he saw Mrs. T, the housekeeper they'd had since he was a little boy. Nate still had her coming over every few days to keep the house tidy and food in the pantry, and they loved her like she was family.

"Morning." He grinned when she pointed to the kitchen counter. "Have I mentioned how much I love you lately?"

She laughed and flapped a hand at him. "Don't try to flatter me, Chase. I've known you since you were in diapers and you can't fool me with that nonsense."

Chase pressed a kiss to her cheek as he passed and grabbed a bagel, slicing it open and slathering cream cheese all over it. He grinned when she turned on the coffee machine, knowing she was about to make him the perfect espresso.

Nate appeared as he took his first sip, dressed in an open-necked shirt and suit pants, and shrugging into a jacket.

"And you wonder why you can't keep up with me," Nate muttered, raising an eyebrow and trying to smack Chase's bagel out of his hand.

"I don't care. I'd rather eat cream cheese than beat you." It was a lie—he hated Nate kicking his butt, but he did love his food. Hell, if he wasn't living here he'd be frying up eggs and bacon every morning like he usually did before heading out for the day. Nate, on the other hand, wouldn't dream of scoffing down half the stuff his brothers did. They were only living together temporarily—up until recently he'd been living in a little place near the front of the property, which he'd pulled down to make way for something new.

"You need to kick the coffee habit, too," Nate told him. "Start drinking green juice."

Chase almost choked on his mouthful, swallowing down a piece of bagel and staring at Nate. "You've got to be shitting me? Ain't no way anyone is ever gonna convince me to drink kale. Or eat sushi for that matter." He laughed. "We could put in a crop and cash in on the whole green juice revolution but that's where I draw the line."

Nate grabbed a bagel and stared at it for a few seconds. "Aw, what the hell. It does look good. Mrs. T, can you do my coffee in a to-go cup?" He laughed quietly. "And for the record, sushi is freaking amazing. Pity you're such an old school douchebag."

Chase finished his bagel and started another as Nate wolfed half of his bagel down, before he grabbed his coffee and took the other half to go. His brother could call him all the names in the world—it was like water off a duck's back.

"I'll see you later," Nate said. "And yeah, none of that green shit for me, either. The juice I'll pass on, but one of these days I'm taking you out for sashimi at that new place in the city."

Chase laughed. "Not a chance. But you do realize I might never move out of here, right? I never realized how good you had it."

Nate held up his bagel in the air in a wave. "Later."

Chase surveyed the kitchen now that he was alone, and smiled when he thought about how many mornings they'd all sat around together when they were kids. There were a lot of things that had been crappy about their childhood, but they'd been damn lucky, too. He never tired of hanging out with his brothers, even if they did give one another a hard time. Maybe losing their mom so young, then their dad walking out and leaving them with their grandparents had brought them closer together, but he had a feeling they'd have always been close regardless.

Chase finished his breakfast, gulped down the rest of his coffee, and headed for the back door to pull on his boots and head out to the barn. He checked his wristwatch; the specialist veterinarian would be pulling up in less than half an hour, and he wanted to get his foreman over to listen to what she had to say.

Damn. A cloud of dust in the distance told him that she was way ahead of schedule. The last guy they'd sent out had kept him waiting for an hour, so he hadn't been expecting early.

Chase jogged to the barn, calling out to Randy. He ducked into the feed shed, had a quick look around the yards, but didn't see him. The shiny white pickup had pulled up now, and he wiped his hands on his jeans and headed over to meet her. From everything he'd read in the company's latest brochure, there was no one more qualified with modern artificial insemination techniques, and he was looking forward to meeting the new recruit from Dallas AI.

He raised a hand to shield his face from the sun, squinting as she pushed open her door and stepped out. *Wow.* He hadn't expected the vet to have long blond hair or be dressed in skin-tight jeans and cowboy boots.

"Hey," Chase called out, dropping his hand and walking closer to the vehicle.

"Morning!" The blond vet turned around, a big smile

on her face that quickly turned into a look of surprise. "Chase?"

"Hope?" *Holy mother of God.*

"I, um, well . . ." she stuttered, and he just stared, speechless for the first time in his life. "I can't believe it never clicked that this was your ranch."

Chase clamped his jaw shut instead of letting it fall to the ground, and closed the distance between them, opening his arms and giving Hope an awkward hug. "Howdy, stranger," he managed, stepping back and staring down at her. "This is . . ."

"Crazy," she said, shaking her head and leaning against the driver's door of the pickup. "You look good, Chase."

He laughed, dragging his eyes slowly up then down as he looked at her. "Straight back at you." She looked a whole lot better than good.

Hope's face was flushed, her cheeks a pretty shade of pink. He hadn't seen her in years but she was just as gorgeous as she had been back then—blue eyes that danced when she spoke, full lips that framed a wide mouth, and a blond mane of that never looked too perfect to touch.

"So you've been busy these last few years, huh?" he asked, folding his arms and watching her, staring at Hope and wondering how the hell she was standing in front of him. He should have been able to come up with something witty, but seeing Hope had fried his brain. "When they said the new specialist was Hope Walker, it didn't exactly send off alarm bells."

She grimaced. "Married name, sorry."

Chase shrugged it off, not even wanting to think about her being married. She was the one who'd gotten away, the girl he'd never gotten out of his system. And somehow she'd ended up on his property without him even realizing it. Not to mention she was taken, which meant he needed to stop thinking about how good she'd look in his bed. He glanced down, noticed she wasn't wearing a ring. "So you've moved out this way for good?"

She nodded. "Yeah. I know I should have looked you up, but . . ."

"No need to apologize," he said, shrugging. It ticked him off, but he got it. They'd been out of touch a long time. "I'd have only given your husband a grilling to make sure he was good enough for you, so it could have turned nasty."

The look in her eyes made him feel like a complete prick. Hope turned away and opened a container in the bed of the pickup, sorting through some things. The girl he'd known had been able to take a ribbing—they'd teased each other mercilessly their entire time in college—but he was pretty sure he'd gone and said the wrong thing just now.

"I'd say I was kidding, but I kind of wasn't." He folded his arms across his chest, gazed down at her. "Hope?"

Hope turned back around, her smile sweet but not hitting her eyes like it used to. "I'm not married anymore," she said, her tone somber as she told him. "And believe me, you'd be all fists blazing if you met him, I can promise you that."

Chase's fists balled at his sides when he unfolded his arms, his jaw tight as he stared at Hope. They might not have seen each other in years, but they'd been best friends all through college and there was nothing he wouldn't do for her, even after all this time. They'd been through a hell of a lot together and it wasn't just something he could forget.

"You need me to teach the asshole a lesson?" Chase asked, trying not to grit his teeth as he fumed inside.

"No," she sighed, attempting a smile that did anything but convince him she was okay. "What I need to do is stop talking about my failed marriage and come see your cattle."

Chase watched her long and hard, trying to read her face. She was brave, he knew that already, but something told him that she'd been to hell and back and then some.

"You want to talk work, let's go," he finally said, stepping closer to her and taking a metal kit she was carrying. Hope made a face like she was about to protest, but he took it off her anyway. "You're not in Canada anymore, sweetheart. You've forgotten what good manners southern men have?"

She laughed, her head tipping back as she walked. "I've missed you, Chase. Man, have I missed you."

He grinned back at her, wishing it hadn't been so long since he'd seen her. It had only taken one night to ruin their friendship, and they'd hardly spoken since. She'd been his best friend for years, and now they were as good as strangers, although he could see how easy it'd be to fall back into step like no time had passed at all.

"So tell me what it's like working with sperm all day."

Hope scowled at him. "You haven't grown up a bit, have you?"

"Nope."

He matched her stride, not taking his eyes off her. She'd been beautiful back in college and now she was a knockout. Chase glanced around, checked they were alone and Ryder wasn't about to come ruin their reunion. He'd fucked it up with Hope once, and if he had his chance, he'd make up for every second.

"So who's Randy Smith? I have his name on my sheet."

"Foreman," Chase told her. "I had him book and confirm the appointment."

"Ah," she murmured. "Although if I'd looked farther down my chart instead of rushing to get here on time, I'd have noticed the words *King Ranch*. My bad."

He stopped walking, locked his gaze on her when she turned. "Would you have come if you'd known it was me?"

Her expression didn't change, her eyes warm as she stared back at him. "Of course I would have."

Chase smiled and started walking with her again, even though he didn't believe her for a second. Something had changed, something was different about her, and it wasn't just the fact that they'd grown up. But if there was one thing he was good at it was being persistent, and if he had a chance to get Hope back in his life, then he'd make damn sure he didn't miss the opportunity. If she were happily married he would have accepted the fact, but she wasn't.

"That was a lie," she suddenly said.

He raised an eyebrow as he turned to look at her. "What was?"

"If I'd seen your name I would have tried to get someone else to cover for me."

He nodded. "Nothing beats the truth."

She stopped and stared at him, her eyes locked on his. They weren't touching, but she was standing close, her perfume filling his senses, strands of her hair being teased by the wind and blowing toward him. He was recalling exactly why he'd found it so damn hard to keep things platonic between them.

"How did things end up like this between us, Chase?"

He shrugged. "We really screwed up, didn't we?"

"Yeah, we did." She blew out a breath. "For what it's worth, I'm sorry I never stayed in touch. If it's any consolation, I've missed you a lot."

"Me too," he grunted. "All these years and I've never found a drinking buddy half as fun as you." The reasons he liked Hope were a whole lot more than having someone fun to drink with, but he was pretty sure she knew that without him having to spell it out.

Chase chuckled and slung an arm around Hope's shoulders. She tensed slightly, shoulders bunching under his touch, like she'd stopped breathing for a beat, but he didn't care. Before they'd slept together, they'd touched all the time, buddies but on the verge of flirting every time they hung out. Then after they'd been between the sheets, they'd barely touched again. Well, he was taking charge now and he wasn't going to pussyfoot around.

"I might just take you up on that kicking-ass offer, you know," Hope muttered, her body finally relaxing.

"You have my word," Chase said, pleased to be talking instead of picturing her naked, because the moment he'd seen her he'd started thinking about their night together. "I don't care how many years have passed. An enemy of yours is an enemy of mine. You say kill him, he's dead."

As they reached the barn, Chase reluctantly removed his arm, set the kit down, and hitched a boot against the nearby railing. He had a small herd of heifers waiting in the round pen for Hope to look over, and the sooner he got his mind on cows instead of the woman standing beside him, the better.

"So these are my girls," he said.

He recognized the change in her face as she leaned over the railings to look them over. When they'd been studying she'd played hard and studied even harder, which was why his grandfather had always thought she was such a good influence on him. Now, he got the feeling that he was the only one getting time to play—the tiny lines around her eyes told him she was nothing short of exhausted.

"You've got quite the harem of ladies," she joked.

"Best organic purebred cattle in the state," Chase told her. "Now I just need to get them pregnant with the New Zealand sperm that cost me a small fortune."

"And that's why you called in the big guns."

Chase laughed with Hope, but what he really needed was for them to stop talking about sperm. And sex. And insemination. His head was already in the gutter without any encouragement.

"I'm guessing you must be pretty good if you managed to get a green card," Chase said, still leaning on the rails but watching her now instead of the herd.

"I've worked my butt off," she told him. "But yeah, seems that I managed to specialize enough to be of value, and it didn't take long for me to get approval to move."

Chase nodded. He'd never doubted she would succeed at whatever she set her mind to, not for a moment.

Hope held up a hand to shield her eyes from the bright sunshine. Keeping it together in front of Chase wasn't easy, and it was taking every ounce of her energy. Staring into his eyes was like . . . She clamped her jaw down, teeth grinding. Her problem was that she'd mentally left Chase in her past, and she sure as hell hadn't been expecting to see him today. Or any other damn day for that matter.

"So did you ever practice?" she asked, ducking through the railings to get a closer look at the heifers. They'd graduated together after training as veterinarians, but he hadn't been sure about his exact career plans when they'd parted ways.

"For a short time," he said, following her into the yards. "After I graduated I came straight back here and started working alongside our foreman whenever I could, but I also worked with our local vet for a while to get some practical training in. Granddad liked the idea of me having a backup plan career wise in case ranching wasn't profitable for our land one day, but the truth is all I've done since hearing him say that is come up with ways to make sure I can keep the ranching side of our business booming."

She cursed as he moved near, wishing he'd just back the hell up instead of coming into her space. Having him so close—smelling him, seeing him, looking into his dark eyes as he spoke—it was too much. After trying to forget him for so long, suddenly every memory, every touch was rushing back so fast it was almost impossible to breathe.

Hope inhaled deeply, the smell of cow dung way more calming than the citrusy scent of Chase. She glanced sideways, noticed the wayward curl of his dark hair. He'd kept it shorter in college, and now it was more unruly, but it suited him. Just a little too long at the back and around his ears, almost black, and so hard not to touch.

Enough. She hadn't thought about Chase in a long time and she didn't need to start now. She was here for work and that was it.

"What I need to do today is give them a work-up, make sure everything's in order, then we can go about getting them in calf. You know the drill."

Chase cleared his throat. "I don't want to sound like a jerk, but we only purchased a modest number of straws. Are we looking at a pretty high take rate?"

Hope met his gaze, but she kept her body angled so she hadn't turned her back on the cows. She had enough experience to know how easy it was to land a sideways kick.

"Understood. Each insemination has to count, and I'll only inseminate the ones that fit the criteria perfectly." She nodded as she glanced over them all again, pleased with how they looked from the outset—a healthy herd of big young cows. "Although from looking at them I doubt we'll find any obvious problems from the outset."

"Nate's riding me big-time over this so I need to prove it was the right decision," Chase said. "He'd turn this whole place into an oil field if it wasn't for me riding his ass to keep our stock numbers high."

"Nate's your oldest brother, right?" She was only making conversation, there was nothing about Chase she'd forgotten.

"Yep, that's him." Chase took a step back and leaned on the railings, his elbows pushed down, legs relaxed as he kicked them out, one ankle crossed over the other. "My granddad's stepped down from the day-to-day running now, and Nate's handling the business side of things with me in charge of the ranches. We have a couple other places nearby, too."

"So you're living the dream, huh?" she mused, ducking beneath the timber so she was no longer in the yard.

"I guess, yeah." Chase followed her back through, frowning when she turned to look at him. "What about you? What the hell are you doing living and working so far from home anyway?"

Damn. She'd walked into that question all on her own. "Ah, things didn't work out quite as planned." Hope tried to look unconcerned, her natural reaction to make up an excuse and get the hell out of dodge to avoid Chase's questions. But he didn't know, *couldn't know*, any of it, which meant she just needed to avoid the topic for as long as she could. If not forever. She could tell him about her ranch one day if she had to, but that was it. She'd moved on, dealt with what had happened, and what he didn't know wasn't doing him any harm. Hell, he'd probably forgotten all about her the day they graduated—she was a quick blast from the past for him and that was it.

"So your family . . ."

"Chase, have you thought about how many heifers you want me to do in the first round of inseminations?" she interrupted, desperate to get the topic off her and back on work. "We could do a few first, monitor the results before continuing on? Then we could let Nate see for himself how good these New Zealand straws are. I'm guessing that quality is more important than speed given what you've told me."

If Chase was surprised by how rudely she'd changed the subject, he didn't show it. "Whatever you think. I want to leave this up to the experts, but we don't need to be overly cautious. I just want to make sure we're focused on the end result."

"Good, sounds like a plan. I'll talk to my boss, discuss the results from my prelim work-up with the girls here, then we'll get them in calf as soon as we can." She laughed. "You'll have unruly calves to worry about before you know it."

"Yeah, ones that owe us so much money we'll be keeping an eagle eye on them twenty-four-seven." He grinned at her. "Just give me one good bull calf and I'll be indebted to you forever. It'll make all this worth my while."

She looked from the yards back to Chase and saw his face change, his jaw go from soft to hard as stone as he scowled past her. When she turned she saw who he was staring at—a man as blond as Chase was dark, a big smile greeting her when she locked eyes with him. It might have been a long time, but she recognized Chase's little brother straight away.

He grinned when he reached them, holding out his hand for her to shake. "Man, you're an improvement on the last vet."

"I'm not sure whether to be flattered or offended," she replied, laughing more from the look on Chase's face than the joke.

"He was about seventy and bald, so yeah, take it as a compliment."

"Hope Walker," she said, taking her hand back when he released it, his eyes never leaving hers as what she guessed was recognition flickered in them.

"Ryder King," he replied, shaking his head as he folded his arms, like the penny had slowly dropped. "And you're . . ."

"Hope, just like she said," Chase interrupted. "As in my old friend from college. Ryder, Hope. Hope, Ryder. We've got some business to attend to, so if you don't mind . . ."

"No fucking way," Ryder swore, completely ignoring his brother.

"Small world, huh?" she said.

"So do you mind my asking what the hell you're doing here? When Chase was all miserable and pining for you, I'm sure he said there wasn't a chance of you leaving your ranch in Canada and heading back to the US."

Hope fought the grimace threatening to take over her face. She glanced at Chase but decided to focus on Ryder—it was easier looking at his brother. Maybe she hadn't been the only one missing what they'd had.

"My family doesn't own the ranch anymore," she said, keeping her voice as devoid of emotion as she could. Hope worried the timber behind her, digging her nail in so hard that it hurt. "To cut a long story short, I wanted a fresh start, and I was recruited by Dallas AI. It was too good an offer to turn down, so here I am."

"Your dad sold the ranch?" Chase asked, his gaze so intense he could have burned a hole through her skin.

"Not exactly."

Hope smiled at Ryder and bent to take some things from her kit, purely for something to do, wishing Chase would stop staring at her and change the subject. When she looked up, both men were watching her, but neither pushed her further.

"So instead of being the beautiful heiress to your family ranch, you're staring at semen through a scope and inseminating unsuspecting heifers? Sounds like fun."

She had to give Ryder credit—he'd made her laugh when she'd been about to burst into tears only moments before.

"Let's just say that I'm better off on my own." *And with my son.* The silent words echoed through her head, her eyes dragging toward Chase and seeing the familiar dark-brown gaze meeting hers. Only it wasn't Chase's chocolate-hued gaze she was used to seeing on a daily basis, it was her son's. "So you boys going to help me put these ladies in the crush?"

Ryder shook his head, holding out his hand and clasping hers. "It was lovely to meet you, Hope, but I'm off to see a man about a horse. I'll leave you two to reminisce and sort out the cattle."

"You still riding rodeo?" she asked.

Ryder went to answer before Chase nudged him hard in the side, making him grunt.

"That was in the days before he was whipped," Chase said. "My baby bro is all grown up and married now."

Hope smiled. "Congratulations." Just because she was cynical about marriage herself didn't mean she couldn't be happy for someone else.

"She's fucking amazing," Ryder said, giving her a mischievous wink and slapping his brother on the back before starting to walk away. "I'm one lucky son of a bitch and I damn well know it."

A shiver trawled Hope's spine as she turned to face Chase, his mouth smiling but his eyes still creased with concern. She knew he'd have questions, it wouldn't be natural for him *not* to, but she didn't want to go there. Not without thinking through what she would tell him first, figuring out how much to say. It wasn't like she'd been expecting a reunion with him.

"So how do you want to do this?" Chase asked.

She sighed and squared her shoulders. "Can we just focus on work today?"

He flashed her his gorgeous dimple, the one that always creased when he grinned, a dimple that had made almost every girl in her dorm swoon on a daily basis, including her.

"I was talking about using the crush," he told her.

A warm flush worked its way up her neck, but she refused to let the blush hit her cheeks. He'd always known how to get under her skin, how to reach her like no other guy had, and being around him now was scaring her. Because it was dredging up thoughts long forgotten, memories she'd forced away so many times they'd almost completely disappeared from her mind. But the fantasy had never died, and being with him, here and now, she wished she'd chosen Chase over everything else. It had been the stupidest decision she'd ever made, and one day maybe even her son would find it hard to forgive her.

Chase touched her arm when she walked past him on her way toward the cattle again.

"You don't want to talk, we don't need to," he said, his voice husky.

"Okay," she managed, refusing to glance at him, her gaze firmly ahead on the first glossy black Angus heifer in front of her.

"But you do owe me dinner," he said, raising one eyebrow as he stared at her, making it impossible for her not to look back into eyes the most delicious shade of milk chocolate in the sunlight.

"I . . ."

His hand squeezed over her forearm, the heat in his

touch making her flush. His face showed how serious he was, eyes boring into her, the hint of smile crossing his lips the only attempt he made at concealing his determination.

Hope took a deep breath. "Only if I can find a baby-sitter on short notice."

Chapter 2

"A babysitter?" Chase was close to choking on the words, his tongue stuttering. He narrowed his eyes, stared hard at Hope to see if she was just giving him shit. But she wasn't. The flicker in her gaze, the way she met his stare, then looked away told him it sure as hell wasn't something she was joking about.

"I have a son," she said, walking away from him. "But, ah, let's get this done and I'll get back to you later about tonight."

He ground his teeth together. So her deadbeat husband had left her *and* their child? What an asshole.

"You did mean tonight, right?" she asked.

"Yeah," he muttered. "I did."

Chase couldn't recall the last time he was actually rendered speechless, but he was finding it damn well impossible to figure out what the hell to say to her today. He blew out a breath and rolled his shoulders back, standing up tall. What he did know was that he wanted to know more, and that meant not letting her say no to dinner. If she didn't commit now, he had a gut-deep feeling that he'd never see or hear from her again—she'd get another specialist to do the inseminations. They might not be in college any longer, but she'd damn well disappeared without a trace then and he wasn't going to let it happen a second time.

His phone buzzed in his pocket and it distracted him, took his focus off Hope. He glanced at the screen. *Damn.* He'd forgotten all about Sarah, aka his date for tonight. They'd had fun a few times, but he had no problems extracting himself from drinks with the cute brunette. He silenced the call and pushed it back into his jeans.

"You can take it," Hope said, glancing across at him from her safe distance a few meters away. "I'll just do my thing here."

Fuck that. Chase shook his head, over the shock of seeing Hope after so many years and ready to launch into full-on offensive mode. They'd been young when they were friends, had had fun, but he'd learned a lot since then, and one of those things was not taking no for an answer.

"It's not important," he told her. He'd let Sarah down gently, and it wasn't as if they were exclusive. They had fun some times, and sex most times, but he wasn't even remotely interested in getting anyone between his sheets except for Hope now that he'd seen her in the flesh again.

"Well, if you want to help, come and get these lovely ladies ready with me."

Chase followed her, taking in the curve of her ass as she walked, her long legs impossible not to notice, the denim of her jeans tight to every inch of them. Her T-shirt was plain, fitted but not tight, and it showed him that her figure had hardly changed over the past five years since graduation.

He groaned, his mind going back in time, fingers clenching into fists as he remembered the weight of her full breasts cupped in his palms as she'd sat astride him.

"Chase?"

Damn it. "Yeah?"

"I thought you said something."

He grinned and shook his head. "Not me." *Because that groan was about you, not for you.*

"So tell me what you've been up to these last few years. Wishing you were a vet or damn happy to be on your ranch?"

"Damn happy," he answered truthfully. "I wake up every day with a smile on my face. I wanted to get my qualifications to prove myself to Granddad, and prove to myself that if I didn't have this ranch I could carve out a career without any help from anyone. But the truth is there's nothing I'd rather be doing than hands-on running this place."

"So do you have a blonde rolling around beside you when you wake up with that smile?"

Chase chuckled. "And there she goes."

"What?" Hope's smile was as innocent as a fox about to steal a hen.

"That girl who used to give me more shit than any of the guys and get away with it."

"Ha, only because you were too chickenshit to call me out."

"Or the fact that I couldn't punch you because you were a girl."

"Mmmm, there was that."

Hope turned around before ducking under the railings, eyes flashing. He'd missed her so bad without even realizing it.

"You must be the new vet?"

Chase reluctantly turned away when Randy approached them from behind. He wanted his foreman close at hand—he liked him to be briefed about everything involving their stock, and this was no exception, no matter how bad he wanted to keep Hope to himself. He might be Randy's boss now, but he still valued his opinion.

"Randy, this is Hope. She'll be handling everything from start to finish."

"Pleased to meet you." Randy stepped forward and held his hand out.

"Pleased to meet you, too," she said. "I'm going to check them over individually and mark them, make up some charts, and then come back for another visit when they're closer to being ready for insemination."

Chase's phone buzzed in his pocket again and he pulled it out to check the caller ID. Damn, it was his granddad, which meant he had to take it.

"I'll check back on you shortly," he told them. "I have to take this."

Hope nodded and he answered the phone, walking away to the sound of her soft voice as she chatted to Randy.

"Granddad," he answered. "Everything okay?"

"Just calling in for my daily report," the aged yet strong voice said down the line.

"Don't tell me you're sick of playing dominos and bingo already?" Chase teased.

He received a noise resembling a growl in response. "I'll have you know I've never played bingo once in my life, and I don't intend on starting now."

He might be in his ninetieth year, but there was no slowing down Chase's granddad even if his body was starting to give out on him.

"I have the AI specialist here now. Won't be long before I put the King name on the map for another reason."

"I have to give it to you, son, you're on trend."

Chase stifled a laugh. The words that came out of the old man's mouth never failed to surprise him.

"You been Googling again, Granddad?"

He listened to his hearty chuckle. "I've been slipping one of the younger nurses a few extra bills to teach me about Twitter and all this trending business. I'm not ready to give up the reins just yet, son. Not completely."

"Did I tell you I closed the deal on the John Deere franchise?"

His granddad chuckled. "Don't tell me you bought the goddamn place? I wasn't even half serious when I . . ."

"We own all the rights for Texas now," Chase told him, loving that he'd managed to surprise the one man he always tried so hard to impress. "I looked at how much we were spending each year, how much of our ranching profit went into those stores, and Nate agreed. He'll have the paperwork for you to sign next week." Chase paused. "We'll make a ton of money off every other rancher in the state, Granddad, and we won't have to pay retail for any of that damn machinery ever again."

"Now that's why I trust you boys," he said, his voice gruff. "You're a chip off the old block, Chase. I'm proud of you, son."

"Thanks, Granddad." His praise meant a lot to Chase, it always had.

Chase walked a few more paces, then turned, scuffing his boots into the dirt before letting his eyes wander back to Hope. She was laughing at something Randy had said, helping him to guide one of the cows in before running a practiced hand down the animal's gleaming black coat.

Chase grimaced when he heard his granddad saying his name.

"Sorry?"

"I said I'll let you get back to it," his grandfather repeated.

"Yeah, sure. I'll, ah, come by and see you later today."

"When you boys gonna learn I'm just fine without all this pandering?"

"We love you," Chase said, his voice gruff. It didn't come naturally to him to talk about his feelings, but they'd almost lost Granddad once already and he wasn't going to let the old man die without knowing how much he appreciated him. He'd raised them all when their mom had died and their dad had given up and walked out, and everything they had was because of him. "So you're just gonna have to learn to deal with it, okay?"

Chase chuckled at his grandfather's grumbling and said his goodbyes, ending the call and staring at the blank screen for a second. He blew out a breath and scrolled through his missed calls, touching his thumb to the number he'd sent to silent only minutes earlier. He didn't mind doing it, but he'd be an asshole if he didn't feel bad for canceling on any woman for another.

"Hey," he said when she answered.

He listened to her chat for a moment before consciously changing the tone of his voice, talking more quietly and in a deeper register.

"I hate to do this to you, darlin', but I'm not gonna make it tonight," Chase said. "Something's come up."

She sounded annoyed but he continued, undeterred. He didn't care if Hope couldn't find a babysitter—there was no way in hell he was going to sit through a night with one woman and be thinking about another.

"Baby, I'm sorry. There's nothing I can do about it, but I'll call you, okay?"

Chase cringed. He shouldn't have said that, although *technically* he might call her. Maybe if Hope skipped out on him and he needed someone to take his mind off the fact they hadn't had a rematch.

He uttered a final apology and shoved his phone back in his jeans, standing stock-still for a moment and indulging in watching Hope again. She was bent forward, her long hair tucked behind one ear as she studied something he couldn't see. It had only been one night. One night that had started out as a drunken tumble and ended up as hours of pleasuring each other, sweaty bodies and tangled limbs, then even longer lying awake and talking until it was morning. And then they'd woken late, and everything had seemed different somehow when reality had hit.

For all those reasons, he should just be happy to see an old friend and forget all about that night. Sleeping together had ruined everything and it would only make things awkward all over again. But he wanted her. Chase wanted one night with her again, to hold her in his arms as he licked and sucked every part of her, rocked into her until she moaned. His memory often let him down, but there was nothing about that night that hadn't stuck to his brain like glue.

"Why did this take us so long?"

Chase chuckled, lazily stroking Hope's arm. "Because we didn't want to complicate things."

"Or maybe because we were both too stubborn to be the first to make a move."

Chase leaned over to kiss her, staring down into Hope's eyes. They were naked and sweaty still, lying on top of the bed, sheets strewn around them.

"You sure you won't stay?"

"Would you leave your family and ranch behind and come to Canada?"

He sighed. "No."

"Then you know the answer."

"So this is good-bye?" He didn't know why he'd asked when he already knew the answer, but he still wanted to hear her say it. Part of him hoped she'd eventually cave

*in and decide to stay in Texas, but then Hope didn't do
anything she didn't want to do.*

*"This is good-bye," she whispered back, pushing him
down, then straddling him, leaning down to press a hot
kiss to his lips.*

*"We better make it count then, huh?" he murmured
back, fisting a hand in her messy long hair.*

"Yeah, that's exactly what we're gonna do."

"So what do you think?"

Hope jumped at the sound of Chase's deep, husky
drawl. She pushed her hair out of her eyes, a few strands
having escaped the rough ponytail she'd hastily tied it in.
She rubbed an arm over her face and tried not to squint
into the bright sunshine.

"They're all in fantastic condition."

Chase laughed and before she could ask him what was
so funny, he'd closed the distance between them, his big
body way too close to hers as he reached out and brushed
his thumb gently across her cheek. Her lips parted until
she forced them shut, her skin tingly all over at having
Chase so up in her space. He smelled hot, like he'd been
working out in the sun, the masculine scent of him doing
nothing to quell the desire flaring within her. Even after
all these years, the pull she'd always felt toward him hadn't
eased any.

"You had dirt on your face," he murmured, brushing
another spot on her forehead this time before stepping
back.

"Thanks," she managed.

Hope smiled back at him, wishing to hell he hadn't just
touched her. She didn't need to remember what it was like
being close to Chase, and those eyes of his . . . *enough.*
She dug her nails into her palm to push the memory away,

the other hand hanging at her side as she watched him use his shirtsleeve to wipe his own face. One of the things she'd always loved about Chase was that he wasn't scared of rolling his sleeves up and doing hard work himself. They'd both grown up with more money than they could count, but they'd been determined to prove themselves no matter what when they'd been in college.

"How is it that you can look so damn gorgeous out on the job?" Chase asked her, blinking those gorgeous thick black eyelashes that framed eyes the color of the darkest brandy.

Hope swallowed, glancing back at the cows for something to do. "So you've had these girls organic for how long?" She decided that changing the subject was the easiest way to handle Chase—flattery wasn't something she was used to dealing with. And that sure as hell wasn't the kind of thing he'd have said to her in college.

"All their lives," he said, pushing his hands into his pockets and taking a step closer. "A good percentage of our pasture is certified organic now, and I've been raising this herd myself, away from the rest of our stock. It's been a long-term plan of mine for years."

"Why's it taken you so long then?" she asked, surprised.

"Because it's taken all this time for Nate to believe that organic is worth the investment. It was one thing giving me some pasture to dedicate to it, but he's always been too tight on the purse strings to indulge me in buying a few hundred organic weanling heifers."

"So this is you proving him wrong?" she asked.

"Yeah, something like that." Chase laughed. "It's a no-brainer, but that old saying that if it ain't broke don't fix it? That was kind of the mentality here for a bit, and besides, Nate's always been more interested in oil than cows. But he couldn't exactly stop me spending my own money, could he?"

Hope smiled. "How about you? What do think about oil?" She knew a lot about his family—it would have been weird for them to have been best friends for so long and for her *not* to have known about them, but he'd never talked much about oil.

"Oil has made our family more wealthy than my grandfather could ever have imagined, so it's always got to come first." He pushed his shoulders up, shrugging at the same time as he raised an eyebrow and glanced over at her. "But I still love cattle beasts, and ain't nothin' gonna change that."

She nodded. She got it—ranching was in her blood too, and even though she'd never turn down oil money, she couldn't imagine not having animals in her life.

"So tell me, Hope, when did you become so adverse to flattery?"

Hope almost choked on her own tongue. "Excuse me?"

"Don't get me wrong, I love talking ranching with you, but we both know you avoided what I said." He waggled his eyebrows at her, a brazen smile kicking one side of his mouth up. "All you needed to say was thank you."

Hope couldn't help but smile back at him. "Thank you," she muttered.

His dimple caught her eye, the expression so sexy it made her hot all over, shoots of desire firing through her body no matter how hard she tried to stamp them out.

"So are we doing dinner tonight?"

Hope stepped back again to put some more distance between them, not needing his body so close, his smile beaming down on her, his eyes like flashes of chocolate—chocolate that she was drawn to like a honeybee to pollen. She bent to collect her things.

"Can I let you know later?"

Chase nodded, but from the way he glanced away she was wondering now if he even wanted her to say yes. *Stupid.* If Chase didn't want her to say yes, he wouldn't have asked her.

"We can catch up any time, Hope," he said, nodding to his foreman as he passed. "You say when and I'll be there."

"Sure."

Chase handed her a card, the King logo emblazoned across it. She knew his personal details would be on the other side.

"My email's on there for sending me the results when you have them," he said, before dropping his voice an octave. "And there's my number for confirming dinner."

It was on the tip of her tongue to ask him if it was a date, but she didn't dare. Instead she stared at his card for a second before pushing it into her pocket.

"Give me an hour or so and I'll let you know," she said, knowing full well that she was going to get straight in the truck and try to figure out how the hell she was going to find a sitter. And then second-guess herself the entire drive back about whether she should have even thought about saying yes to dinner in the first place. She'd ask a friend, only she didn't want to tell anyone that she was going out with a man, let alone an old flame.

The difference between her and Chase was that he thought they were old friends catching up, but she knew they were a lot more than just former college buddies.

"You need a hand with getting anything into the truck?" Chase asked.

"Thanks, but I'm good," she replied, smiling back at him. In all the time that had passed, she'd never forgotten his grin; that infectious tilt of his lips and flash of his eyes that made everyone around him feel like the most special person in the world.

"See you soon," he said, raising a hand and heading for the barn.

"Uh-huh," she murmured, knowing that come hell or high water, she'd no doubt be seated across from him over dinner in only a few hours' time.

Chase checked his messages to make sure he had the right address and pulled up outside Hope's place. It was a modern-looking two-level house, lights illuminating the front door and garage in the almost darkness. He turned the engine off and pushed open his door, stepping out onto the concrete and crossing the grass to walk up the pavers to the front door. There were large trees surrounding the property and he guessed it backed onto the woods.

He knocked at the front door and took another look around. It was a nice place, nothing too flashy, but it wasn't what he'd expected. Although he hadn't exactly picked her for being a mom, so a suburban place with a yard was probably a whole lot more appropriate than a condo.

Chase knocked again, wondering if she either hadn't heard him or had changed her mind and wasn't going to come out at all.

"Just a minute!"

He smiled at Hope's call and stepped back, seeing the blur of her silhouette through the small squares of glass on each side of the front door. It was ridiculous feeling nervous, but if he wasn't careful his palms would be sweating and he'd have to wipe them on his jeans. This wasn't a first date and he wasn't a kid. This was just two friends reconnecting. His trouble was that he hadn't been on a proper date since . . . *forever.* He met women, had fun with them, took them back to his town apartment or their place, and rarely saw them again. Hope was different and she always had been.

"Hey." Hope swung the door open, her cheeks flushed, breathing hard like she'd just finished at the gym.

"Hey." Chase grinned back at her, fighting to keep his eyes on hers instead of flitting down her body. She was wearing skin-tight dark jeans and towering heels, her legs long as a filly's, but they were friends and he was trying to behave . . . *To hell with it.* He looked her up then down, raising an eyebrow when he finally met her gaze again. "You look fantastic."

She rolled her eyes, something she'd done back in college a lot but that looked kind of hilarious now she was all grown up. "You don't look so bad yourself, cowboy."

Chase was wearing jeans, his favorite boots, and a clean checked shirt—hardly noteworthy. But he took her compliment with a smile.

"You ready to go?"

She was holding onto the doorframe, leaning into it, and she kept one hand on it as she pulled back, blocking the way.

"I just need to double-check everything with the sitter," she said. "And double-check Harrison one last time."

Chase went to walk into the house, to follow her, but she never took her hand off the door. "Can I come in?" he asked.

She made a kind of grimace, like she was about to deliver a blow of bad news and didn't know how to package it. "Would you mind if I met you at your car? It's just, I have him settled and I'd rather check him one last time, then slip out."

Chase held up his hands. "No problem." Maybe she didn't want the kid to know she was going out with a man, he got that. "I'll see you in a minute."

Hope threw him what looked like a grateful smile and

shut the door, leaving him standing outside alone. He chuckled and walked back to his car. It was like being a teenager sneaking around with a girl all over again, only this time it wasn't a dad he was nervous about running into, it was a child.

Hope's nerves were frazzled. The last thing she'd wanted was Chase coming in and seeing Harrison, but she'd been running so late from work and she'd wanted to take time getting ready. Just because they'd been friends for years didn't mean she had any intention of going out without making an effort, and she hadn't had a night out in . . . months. Maybe longer.

She ran back, grabbed her purse from where she'd discarded it earlier on the bed, and looked at herself once last time in the floor-length mirror. Her jeans were tight, the stilettos a pair she'd bought on a whim and never worn before. She shrugged into her favorite leather jacket, pushed some big gold hoops through her ears, and leaned over to squirt some perfume into her hair. She'd read somewhere that a Victoria's Secret model did that before every date, and if it worked for her then Hope was happy to follow her lead.

"Bye, sweetheart," she called out as she hurried into the living room again, dropping a kiss into Harrison's hair. Hope stopped, noticed how happy her son seemed to be with the sitter. She'd asked her to come over an hour early, just in case, but it seemed the agency she'd used had given her a good one—the young woman was snuggled up on the sofa with Harrison watching a DVD, happily chatting about the characters like *The Lego Movie* was her favorite, too. "I won't be late. See you soon."

She mouthed *thank you* to the sitter when she turned around and grinned at her, before opening the door, stepping out, and locking it behind her. Hope took a deep breath, stuck her purse under her arm, and turned toward the driveway. Chase's throaty engine rumbled to life and the headlights flicked on. It was time to put on her game face. So she did exactly that, forcing a smile and squaring her shoulders like going out for dinner with her old college buddy was the most normal thing in the world.

Chase appeared and walked around the front of the vehicle, opening her door. "All set?" he asked.

"Yup. All set."

She moved past him and jumped up into his SUV, her smile easy when he went to close her door. "Thank you." Her husband hadn't opened a door for her once, and it wasn't something she'd even thought about before. "I'll have to make sure I teach my son some good southern manners."

Chase nodded. "Yes, ma'am, you will."

She burst out laughing and scolded him once he settled into the driver's seat. "Just don't be calling me ma'am. I hate that."

"Anywhere in particular you want to go?" Chase asked her.

She couldn't help but glance around the inside of the vehicle, running her hand over the black leather as she relaxed back into her seat. There was luxury, and then there was Chase's SUV. It even still had that delicious new-car smell.

"Is this new?"

"Yeah, I picked it up a couple months back." He smiled over at her before putting it in reverse. "It's the new Mercedes GL, AMG model. Best vehicle I've ever had."

She sighed. This was the kind of car she'd been used to, and now she was driving a plain old Toyota. Hardly the epitome of luxury. Tears prickled her eyes, but she blinked them back—it was stupid to get emotional over a car, but it was just another reminder of what she'd lost, of the lifestyle she'd let slip away from her like it had never existed in the first place.

"You okay?"

She blinked and quickly looked up. "Of course," she murmured. "My dad had one of the earlier models, so it just reminded me of him." It wasn't a lie, but it also wasn't the reason she'd become upset.

"So, dinner?"

"I don't believe that you haven't booked anywhere already."

"Maybe I have." Chase threw her a wink that made her stomach fall through the floor. If it wasn't for that damn dimple . . . ugh. Who was she kidding? It wasn't just his dimple that made her knees knock, it was the glint in his eyes when he smiled, the self-assuredness that as good as oozed from him, his broad shoulders filling the seat and then some. Chase was God's gift to women and he damn well knew it.

"So where are you thinking?"

"Just one of those places that always makes space for us."

"Huh." She'd forgotten what that was like, too. Although Chase's family and her family were kind of different. Her parents had had money, but Chase's family had the kind of wealth that made the Forbes list every year. "Do you take a different girl there every other night?"

Chase braked at the end of the driveway before he reversed out into the street. "No."

"Bullshit."

"I don't want to sound like an asshole, but I don't usually take them out for dinner."

"Ugh!" She made a face and went to play punch him, just connecting with his arm before pulling back. It was the kind of thing she'd used to do to him, but suddenly it didn't seem such a good idea any longer.

"Sorry, just trying to keep it real," he said with a shrug.

"Yeah, I always had to put up with your sleazing. I don't need to hear about it." It was true, she'd heard from just about every girl on campus about how great Chase was in bed, or how badly they *wanted* to get into his bed, and all she'd been able to do was bristle and tell herself that she'd meant more to him than some one-night stand. Although she was the one who'd had a one-night stand and ended up pregnant, so maybe she shouldn't have been so quick to judge.

"I never so much as looked at another girl when I was out with you."

"Yeah, true." She settled back into the comfy-as-hell leather seat and angled her body so she was watching Chase. "Although it didn't stop them looking at you."

"What happened between us? Chase started, glancing across at her, then focusing his eyes back on the road again.

"Don't," she replied, cutting him off before he could say more. "Let's just be old friends catching up, okay?"

He made a noncommittal kind of noise, but he didn't say anything else on the matter.

"So this place we're going to?" she asked, making sure the subject was closed and firmly off-limits.

"You'll love it. Nothing too fancy, good food and even better wine."

"Since when do you drink wine?"

He laughed and touched her hand, his big palm covering hers, warm against her cool skin. Her heart skipped a beat and she didn't dare to look up, didn't want to be trapped in the web of his eyes that caught her *every single time*.

But she didn't have to worry. Chase removed his hand as fast as he'd touched her, just like she'd withdrawn from the play punch.

"A lot has changed these past few years," he told her in a low voice.

Tell me about it. "I know. Believe me, I know."

"But it doesn't mean I don't still like knocking back tequila shots every now and again."

This time she wasn't scared of looking at him, her instant reaction to grin straight back at him. Hope angled her body again, happy to reminisce so long as they didn't talk about that final night they'd had.

"I don't think I could stomach one," she joked. "One whiff of lime and tequila and I'd probably be sick just thinking about it! I don't even know how we used to do it so often."

"I drag Nate and Ryder out every now and again and insist we knock a few back. But our poison of choice is usually whiskey these days."

"Whiskey sounds far more sophisticated than tequila shots."

Chase laughed, one hand on the wheel, the other resting on his thigh. "I think I've just developed the same taste in liquor as my granddad. Nothing beats a bottle of JD or Wild Turkey."

She chuckled to herself and dragged her eyes away from his profile. All this time she'd never forgotten how handsome he was, how strong and commanding his presence was, and he didn't disappoint in real life. It was like he hadn't aged a bit, although his skin was a shade darker, golden from all the hours he probably spent out under the sun.

"It's just around the corner here," he said.

"Valet parking?" she asked wryly.

"I'm not Nate," he muttered. "And I haven't changed that much. Since when did you ever see me getting someone else to park my vehicle?"

She raised her eyebrows. "Don't get all offended, I was just joking."

"You know how it is, that's all."

"You mean I used to," she corrected him, holding her smile even though she was crumbling inside.

She played with the clasp on her purse as Chase parked, watching as he jumped out of the truck and came around to her side, opening her door. It was almost comical to her that he was being so chivalrous, simply because she wasn't used to it, but she wasn't going to complain at being treated to some good old-fashioned manners.

Chase held out his elbow and she tilted back a little to look up at him, catching the humor in his gaze. She hesitated a moment before slipping her hand through, leaning in to him closer than she needed to.

"You remember doing this?" he asked, voice gruff as he pushed his hand into his jeans pocket and started walking, meaning her hand was dragged even closer to his body.

"Yeah." How could she forget? "Everyone always thought we were dating, which meant that virtually every attractive girl in school hated me."

"Hey, it worked to keep the guys from pestering you."

"Hmmm, but not quite so well with you," she said with a laugh. "You still managed to get passed phone numbers even with me sitting beside you at the bar."

They both laughed. Going down memory lane was fun, to a point, so long as they didn't delve too deep into the past. Shots at dive bars, lying out under the stars and talking shit, studying together and getting in trouble for laughing too loud. They were fun memories that she'd never forget.

"Hold up. Is this the place?"

Chase bent down closer to her, his breath warm against her face as he spoke into her ear. "You didn't really think I'd gone all fancy rich boy on you, did you?"

Hope burst out laughing. They both stopped and she stared from the restaurant to the man standing beside her. "The Rodeo Bar & Grill? You're screwing with me, right?"

"Hey, I wasn't lying," Chase said with a cheeky grin. "They always find a table for me, and I'm definitely a regular!"

Hope took her hand from Chase's arm and pushed him ahead of her. "Go on then, cowboy, open the door for me."

The noise assaulted her eardrums the second he swung the heavy timber door back, the place already busy even though it was still early. It had been a long time since she'd been out in a bar, but she hadn't forgotten that good old feeling of being sucked in by the music, the high of being about to have a drink and let her hair down. It was perfect.

"Thank you," she said, squeezing Chase's hand as she walked past him, waiting a step ahead for him to catch up.

"For holding the door?"

She met his gaze head on, knowing she'd done the right thing in saying yes to dinner. The last few months, hell, the last couple of years, had been all work and no play. "For getting me out of the house," she told him. "It's been a while since I had some fun."

"Well, it just so happens you're out with someone who hasn't forgotten how to have a good time."

Hope followed him to the bar, trying to match his stride. She was tall, close to five-nine, but even with heels on she wasn't a match for his six-foot-three frame. All three brothers were the same, tall and built with the faces and bodies of Greek gods. How the hell she'd managed to stay out of his bed until graduation was a mystery even she didn't understand. She'd started out plain stubborn when it came to Chase, and then they'd just started having too much fun for her to want to ruin it with sex, even though she'd wanted him so damn bad. And there was also that factor of loving the flirting, but loving the fact that she was the only woman to turn him down even more.

"What're you having?" he asked.

"Surprise me." She pulled out a stool and sat, dropping her purse onto the bar and dragging herself a bit closer to Chase as he ordered.

"I thought we'd prop up the bar for a bit before grabbing a table."

She glanced around. "If we can find one." The place was kind of packed. There were people standing around, the booths looked full, and there were a few vacant spots around the bar. She loved the way the beer was stashed in ice behind the counter, mustard and ketchup bottles sitting alongside jars of peanuts on the worn wooden bar. She couldn't have chosen a more perfect spot to spend an evening if she'd tried.

"We're getting that little one in the corner over there," he said, sliding some bills toward the bartender as two beers headed their way. "And the best thing about this place? They have a tequila bar."

Hope reached for her beer, holding it up to see what it was before clinking it against Chase's. "I thought we were being all sophisticated and having wine tonight."

He took a sip then grimaced. "I have a confession to make."

She raised her eyebrows, waiting.

"I was taking you somewhere different, but then when I started driving from your place, I decided it was all wrong. Wrong for us, anyway."

"Wrong how?" she asked, deciding the beer wasn't half-bad when she sipped it again.

"Fancy, expensive, and . . ." He shrugged. "We were never about all that shit, were we? It was just two great friends hanging out and rolling with the punches. But we can still drink wine. If you want."

"Beer's fine," she said, her shoulders relaxing, her body no longer tense just because she was sitting close to Chase. "In fact, this place is perfect."

Chapter 3

You're perfect. It was on the tip of his tongue to just say it, to man up and tell her what a jackass he'd been, that he should have called her, should have tried harder to stay in touch. But she'd had a phone, too, and she'd been the one to slip out of the motel room that morning and disappear. Damn. *To hell with it.* They were hanging out now and if she was going to be staying in Dallas then they had plenty of goddamn time to forgive and forget.

"They do mean grilled burgers here," he told her, draining almost half of his beer in one long pull. "And their Tex-Mex is damn good, too."

"A burger will do me fine," she said, scooping her long hair up and dragging it to rest over one shoulder. Her neck was exposed on one side now, golden skin so soft he was aching to cover it with his mouth. She licked her lips, so unaware of the effect she was having on him.

"So how're you liking your new job?" he asked.

"Hey, it pays the bills and I'm doing what I trained for. I've dedicated the last few years to honing my skills and becoming as specialized as I can."

She was saying all the right words, but he could tell she wasn't happy, that she wasn't telling the whole truth.

Hope had never been good at keeping things from him, and it seemed nothing had changed.

"But you'd rather be putting it all to practice on your own ranch, right?" He didn't want to push her, but whatever the hell had happened with her ranch was like the elephant in the room

"I was hoping to start breeding quarter horses, actually. My dad was always interested in it, and after he passed away I wanted to do it even more. For me and for him. We'd always talked about crossing them with European Warmbloods to produce top quality, sensible sport horses." She sighed. "It was one of those things on my bucket list for the future, after I'd made a name for myself."

Chase put down his beer and reached for Hope's hand, the sight of her eyes tearing up enough to jolt something deep within him. The urge to protect her went into overdrive. He hated to see her in pain.

"Hope, you should have said." He tucked her fingers beneath his. "I'd never have asked if . . ."

"My dad passing wasn't the reason we lost the ranch," she said matter-of-factly, her voice devoid of emotion even if her eyes gave away her pain for all to see. "He left everything to me. I was his only child and he knew that I was capable of running the place." She made a noise that was half laugh, half cry. "Hell, he'd groomed me for it my entire life."

"And your mom?"

Hope's hand moved beneath his, as she turned her palm over and linked their fingers for a moment before wiggling them apart. She raised her eyes.

"My mom passed away eight months ago," she said, her gaze so haunted it made him wish to hell he'd never asked. He watched her take a very slow, steady sip of her beer. "She saw everything start to crumble, she knew

something was wrong, but I managed to keep it from her."
Hope sighed and leaned forward, elbows on the bar. "I'm
just pleased she didn't see me lose our home. It would
have broken her heart and then some, and the last thing
she needed on top of cancer was to know the truth."

Chase knew he had to tread carefully here, didn't want
to push her too far. He took a sip of his beer, finishing
it, and waved with two fingers in the air to the bartender,
pulling out his wallet and putting the bills on the bar.
"Unless something's changed between now and when I
knew you better than I knew myself, you weren't exactly
the kind of woman to take risks. Not risks that'd end up
with you homeless and with no ranch to your name."

Her smile was obviously forced, her lips forming a
tight line that gave away her true feelings. When Hope
smiled and meant it, her eyes lit up like they were dancing, her lips turning up into a beamer that changed her
entire face. He knew that look well because he'd always
worked his ass off to make sure he got to see it all the
time, and the look on her face right now was nothing like
that.

"Sweetheart, tell me," he said. "You're breaking my
heart here."

She took the second beer he'd offered, plucking at the
label, her eyes downcast. "I made a bad decision, Chase,"
she told him. "We were so careful not to let anyone close
in college without being sure they weren't after us for our
money, and then I went and let this happen."

"Who hurt you, Hope?"

"Let's just say my husband wasn't who I thought he
was, even though I'd known him since I was a kid, and it
cost me everything," she said. "I don't have a ranch, I had
to sell everything. So what you see," she said, gesturing
to her body, "is what you get. I screwed up and I'm paying the price now."

His body tensed, the hand not holding his beer instantly fisting. "You gonna tell me what he did so I can do something about it?"

She braved a smile, finally looking up and sipping her beer again. "No. I shouldn't have said anything."

"You would have told me eventually." He couldn't take his eyes off her, was so mesmerized by the way she kept pulling her hair over one shoulder, biting her bottom lip when she wasn't sure about something. She might be one of the top AI specialists in the country, but right now it was like they were college kids again, like she was the same young woman who'd made him so damn hard all the time just from being around her and trying to keep things platonic that nothing, not even the most gorgeous goddamn cheerleaders, had been able to take his mind off her. "You know I'd do anything for you though, right? You want my help, you'll get it, no matter what."

"Can we just talk about something else?" she asked, looking forlorn as she slumped over the bar. "I don't want to talk about everything I've done wrong, and I sure as hell don't want you doing anything about it. Everything that could have been done is done."

Chase whistled to the bartender, then handed over some cash with a generous tip. "Your best tequila. Two shots."

"Chase . . ." Hope cautioned.

"What?" he asked, throwing her a half smile as he took the two shots placed in front of him. "If you don't want to talk about it then the only thing to do is drink tequila, right?"

She shook her head, not taking her eyes off him as she held up the tiny glass. "I'm going to regret this in the morning."

"We're both gonna regret it in the morning, but since when did that stop us?"

She laughed as he winked. "Bottom's up then, I guess."

Chase swallowed down the shot, trying not to laugh at Hope's burning-eyed choke.

"You okay?"

"Damn, we were either really drunk when we used to order these or I was a more seasoned straight liquor drinker."

"Both," he said, grimacing for her as she finished it and slammed the glass down on the bar.

"Whoa. That burned out all the cobwebs."

"Another?" Chase asked.

"I think we need to eat first. If I drink any more on an empty stomach you'll regret asking me out."

Chase nodded to the bartender again and smiled his thanks when he saw the small booth tucked away in the corner was free. It might just be a burger and beer joint, but who the hell said it couldn't be romantic?

"Come on, let's go," he said, stepping off his stool and holding out a hand to her. It was a genuine gesture, something they'd have done without thinking when they'd been more familiar with each other, but she surprised him by pressing her palm to his and bumping into him as they walked.

Hope's head was spinning and it wasn't just from the alcohol. Being with Chase again was like finding a favorite pair of jeans and realizing that they still fit like a glove. Only Chase was no worn old pair of jeans. The weight of his hand in hers, the strength of his big body beside her, the flash of those dark eyes as he gave her a glance—only Chase could have that effect on her. Everything about him screamed masculinity, even the too-long hair that should have made him look scruffy but instead had the reverse effect—he looked like a Roman gladiator with his curly locks falling past his ears.

They settled into the booth, her going one way and

Chase the other, only to end up side by side, thighs brushing. She tried to ignore the sensation of his jeans-clad leg against hers and found it impossible.

"So what'll it be?"

Hope flipped open the menu and studied it, tipping her head to the side as she considered her options. "Let me guess. You're having the Rodeo Burger. There's no chance you'd turn down a Black Angus burger."

"Am I so predictable?" Chase asked with one eyebrow raised.

Heat flooded her body, those words taking her back in time. She was certain he'd said something like that before she'd ripped off his shirt, popping every button before covering his skin with her mouth. And her tongue. And her . . . She took a deep breath. The truth was she'd missed a lot about Chase, but it was the physical element of their relationship that flooded her memory banks.

"I think I'll have the Rodeo Tortilla Salad," she murmured, ignoring his question.

"What, no fries for you?"

There was a twinkle in his gaze that made butterflies dance in her belly again. "Can't I steal some of yours? Or don't you like sharing anymore?"

They were seated side by side but Chase's body was angled just enough so he could stare at her, and she didn't let him have the upper hand, matching the heat and intensity of his gaze with her own. There was no point ignoring it or pretending it wasn't there—the sexual chemistry between them was palpable and she doubted anyone could spend time with them and not notice it.

As if on cue Chase's thigh became firmer against hers, pressed from her knee to her hip, his hand leaving the menu to slide down the table, his fingers nudging hers.

"Hope . . ."

"*Chase?*" The connection between them was broken

as a shrill, drunken voice echoed out. Hope saw the change in Chase's face, watched his eyes go from open to wary to downright pissed. She finally looked away from him and at the woman standing in front of their table, her long, manicured pink nails drumming a beat on the timber top.

"Well, well, Chase King. This why you cancelled on me tonight?"

Hope sighed. This was definitely their college days repeating themselves all over again.

"Hi, Sarah."

"You gonna introduce me to your friend here, sugar?"

Hope watched as the other woman slid into the booth beside Chase, reaching those long nails out and dancing them across his arm. He moved closer to Hope and she had to hide a smirk. Some things never changed.

"Sarah, this is Hope."

Hope raised her eyebrows and forced a smile, but she was being thoroughly ignored.

"You wanna have a drink after you finish up here? Or how about you just swing past my place later?"

Chase cleared his throat, moving even harder up against Hope.

"Ah, I don't think so," Chase told her, his voice firm.

"But Chase, *baby* . . ."

He threw Hope an apologetic look before turning his full attention to the woman he'd obviously let down tonight to come out with her.

"How about we go outside for a moment and talk in private," Chase said. "I think there's been a misunderstanding."

Suddenly things turned nasty. Like clockwork, Chase's calm words seemed to have the absolute opposite effect.

"Chase, baby, you gonna choose"—the other woman

glared at her, eyes traveling up then down—"*this* over me?"

Chase's arm went rigid against Hope's, his hand closing possessively over her thigh. "Enough," he growled out, like a bear disturbed from hibernation. "It's time to go, sweetheart. What we had was fun, but that was it. All fun and no commitment, remember?"

The look on her face was one of pure shock and Hope couldn't help but feel sorry for her. Women flocked to Chase like bees to honey and she couldn't blame them—he was handsome, he was loaded, and he had charm to boot.

"Asshole," Sarah spat out, raising her hand to slap him.

But Chase was too fast, intercepting it and shaking his head. "Uh-huh. Don't even think about it."

"You're a bastard, you know that, Chase King?"

"I never promise what I can't deliver, and I made it clear from the start that we were only casual," he said, voice as calm as ever, like he was talking a jumper down from a ledge. "I'm sorry if I hurt you, but it is what it is."

Hope was at least impressed with how the other woman sucked it up and left, not saying another word. Mind you, she'd seen the routine before and it often got nasty. Although she had to give Chase credit too—he'd always made it clear back in college that he was a one-night wonder, but women always seemed to think they'd be the one to keep his attention for longer. Which was one of the reasons she'd always said no to him.

"Well, that was awkward," Chase muttered, seeming embarrassed as he looked up from beneath his thick black lashes. "Sorry you had to see that."

"Looks like some things never change," she murmured, trying to make her expression stern.

Chase opened his menu again. "I did cancel on her, but what we had was only casual. You know how it is."

She knew the drill—he had an embarrassed look on his face, but she doubted he was the least bit worried. "You still haven't found anyone to tame you yet?"

"Believe me," he said, leaning in close, way too close for comfort, "there've been plenty try but none succeed."

She gave him a shove, half-playful, half just wanting to get him out of her space. She couldn't breathe with his body up hard to hers, could barely think about anything other than the big, strong, gorgeous man sitting beside her.

"One day you're going to have to settle down, you know that, right?"

"Would you believe me if I said I'd tried?"

It was a conscious effort to keep her jaw from dropping. "You have? You're not in a relationship now, are you?" she asked. Surely not after the woman he'd just admitted to seeing casually, but still . . .

Chase nudged her before leaning back into the leather booth seat. "Why? We haven't done anything wrong."

Maybe they hadn't physically, but the way they'd touched, the way they were behaving, was not okay if either of them was in any kind of a relationship.

"You just had some floozy wanting a booty call with you. Call me crazy but I don't actually think you'd be the kind to cheat if you were actually with someone."

Chase smiled as a waiter approached them, and he glanced at her as he ordered, raising his eyebrows then ordering for her when she nodded. It was funny how they could just switch back into the comfortable way they'd always been.

"God, we need more alcohol," he muttered. "But you're right, I might like to love 'em and leave 'em, but I'm not a cheater. Never have been, never will be."

"Glad to hear you haven't changed," she told him, pleased when a glass of wine arrived at their table barely minutes after he'd ordered.

"It's an award-winning Willamette Valley pinot, so it should be good. Or at least it sounded good on the wine list." Chase held up his glass and clinked it softly to hers when she did the same. "To old friends."

"To old friends," she repeated, holding his gaze as he took a slow, steady sip from his glass. His eyes were burning into her, not giving her a moment to escape, holding her captive. The red was smooth and silky, just how she liked it. "So tell me. Who was she and how did she almost tame you?"

"You say it like I'm some kind of a wild animal," he muttered good-naturedly.

"Um, when it comes to the opposite sex? Sorry, but that's exactly what you're like."

Chase stared at his glass for a long moment before finally raising his eyes. "I'll have you know that I was pretty easy to capture in the end. She was beautiful and smart and funny, and I didn't give a damn about not being able to play around anymore."

Hope swallowed, hard. "What happened?" If he'd felt like that about a woman, then why had it ended?

"Turns out she was putting on a pretty good show. She lied to me about her past and she was just another gold digger wanting to catch herself a rich husband."

"Oh, Chase, I'm sorry." She bit down on her lip, fingers itching to reach out to his, so they could connect like before, but scared of what it might mean if she let herself be the one to initiate something.

"So you're not the only one with a few romantic wounds." His voice was lighthearted now, the darkness gone. "I'm just pleased I figured her out before things had gone too far. Man, if we'd have been married or had kids . . ." He paused, his face falling. "Fuck, sorry. I didn't mean . . ."

"It's fine," she said, fixing a smile even though she was breaking inside. "Harrison's the best thing that's ever happened to me." Her heart was pounding, betraying her calm thoughts. She'd never wanted to be a single mom, never wanted to lie to anyone about her child's father, but she'd done her best and Harrison had had the best grand-parents in the world to help raise him. She couldn't have asked for a more supportive family if she'd tried.

"It must be pretty crappy having to bring him up on your own though. We sure know how to pick 'em, huh?"

She nodded, her breath coming in short rasps. Was it lying if she just wasn't telling him the whole story? *Or the truth?*

"So how did you figure her out?" she asked, avoiding the topic of her being a single mom entirely.

Chase grunted. "Nate didn't like her, thought there was something just not quite right, so we decided to put her to the test. See if she actually was as head over heels in love with me as she claimed to be." He shrugged. "I thought Nate was full of bullshit, but I went along with it to prove a point and I told her that Granddad had barred us all from inheriting until much later in life, that we had to make our own way in the world and we'd get our third of everything when we turned forty."

"What happened then?"

"Let's just say that she was only twenty-five and she had no intention of waiting that long to see some seri-ous cash. She was gone by the time I woke up the next morning."

"Bitch."

Chase toyed with the stem of his wineglass. "My sen-timents exactly."

They sat in silence for a little while, the country-rock

music getting louder as the place became even more crowded. It was nice being out, enjoying adult company instead of being permanently in mommy mode when she wasn't at work. She had some great work colleagues, but between Harrison and work, she hadn't exactly had any time to make new friends.

"So here we are."

She laughed. "Here we are."

"You ever think what might have happened if you hadn't bolted on me that morning? Whether things might have turned out differently?"

Hope's body ignited just at the mention of their night together, like flames licking across her skin. "Chase . . ." She didn't want to discuss it, especially not now.

"No, come on. We were friends, it was years ago, surely we can talk about it."

She wasn't sure if he was just trying to get a rise out of her, or if he genuinely didn't mind dredging up the past. "For starters, I didn't bolt, I had a plane to catch and you knew it."

He leaned farther back into the seat, his body stretched out, knee locked against hers. There was no getting away from the man.

"Let's not pretend like that night didn't mean anything, Hope." His voice was so deep it was seductive, silky, and gruff. She'd resisted him for so long, for so many years, but now that she'd been on the receiving end of that voice, of his touch, she doubted she'd have the same kind of will-power ever again. Not when it came to Chase King, and the temptation was sitting right in front of her.

"Chase," she cautioned, not sure what else to say.

"It was worth it," he said, pushing a hand through his hair. One curly lock escaped immediately, springing back, and she wanted to touch it so bad it hurt.

His confidence was overpowering, but she refused to

let him seduce her if that's what he was trying to do. What had happened between them had been a mistake, that was all. A pleasurable, amazing mistake, but a mistake nonetheless.

"Chase, I wasn't one of your one-nighters then, and I'm not now," she managed, holding her glass so tight she was afraid it would break. "That was just three years of pent-up sexual attraction exploding."

"I've never mistaken you for a one-nighter, Hope, that's why I've always been waiting for a rematch."

She glared at him, needing a damn fan to cool herself from the heat surging through every inch of her. "You need another woman to try to slap you tonight?"

Chase held up both hands like he was surrendering, only he snatched her hand into his and linked their fingers before she had a chance to realize what the hell he was doing.

"How about I keep hold of this hand just in case," he asked, his grin way too infectious to let her stay angry with him.

She noticed the waiter approaching and breathed a big sigh of relief.

"How about you give me my hand back and we eat dinner."

What she needed was to call her best friend back home. Lisa had been like a sister to her since they were in pre-K, and she was also one of the only people on the planet who knew the truth about Hope's son's father. She dug her nails into her palm. As soon as she got home she was calling Lisa, even if it was the middle of the night.

"Tequila," Chase announced. "We need tequila."

He held out a hand for Hope to grab on to, grinning when she took hold. He tugged her from the booth and dragged her toward the bar.

"I really don't think this is a good idea," Hope said, shaking her head when Chase pulled out a vacant barstool for her. "I'm not a seasoned drinker like you."

"You used to be."

"Yeah, well, that was a long time ago."

"And it would be a shame not to make use of the tequila bar."

Chase chuckled and leaned forward to order, standing close beside Hope so they could talk over the loud music. He nudged her thigh as he stared down into eyes that seemed to see straight through him. Hope had always had the uncanny ability to make him tell her anything, to bring out the best in him, but it had always made him want her so bad it had taken all his willpower not to proposition her on a daily basis. And what had he done? He'd gritted his damn teeth and pretended like he was fine with them just being friends. But that was then and this was now—and now he didn't wait around when he knew what he wanted.

The shots arrived and he ran his tongue over his lips, moistening the skin that seemed to go dry every time his eyes locked on Hope's mouth. Fuck, he wanted to kiss her. Instead he slammed one palm down on the bar, grabbed the drink, and downed it, watching from the corner of his eye as she did the same.

"Not so hard, was it?"

She giggled. Hope only ever giggled when she was drunk, and it was so goddamn cute.

"No more," she protested. "My head's going to kill me in the morning."

"Take ibuprofen before bed. You'll be fine." Chase waved to the bartender that they wanted two more and spun her barstool around so she was facing him. When her knees fell apart he stepped in, knowing he was taking a risk but not giving a damn. They were all grown up now—he wanted her, and if she felt the same, then nothing was gonna hold him back.

"Chase . . ."

"Just pick up your drink."

Hope did as she was told, gingerly collecting the next tiny glass and taking a shoulder-raising breath.

"For old times' sake," he suggested, holding up his arm and waiting for her to link with him so they could drink at the same time.

They knocked glasses and he smiled at her, a long, slow smile that spread across his lips just from being near her. All this time, all these years, and he knew he'd still do anything for her, even if things were different now.

"Bottom's up," he murmured.

Hope didn't miss a beat, drinking her tequila down as fast as he did, only she was gasping afterward like she'd just swallowed fire and he was laughing. Admittedly, he and his brothers drank a lot of straight whiskey, so he was used to the burn.

"Have I told you how beautiful you look tonight?" Chase nudged Hope's thighs farther apart, just enough so that he was standing within the triangle of her legs, up close in her space. He finally gave in and reached for her hair, wrapping a long strand around his fingers. Chase bent his head so he could press his forehead to hers.

"Do you try that line on all your women?"

He pulled back and stared into her eyes. "No. Not all women are beautiful like you are."

"Too smooth, Chase. Too smooth," she murmured, only just loud enough for him to hear.

"What would you say if I kissed you?" He couldn't take his eyes off her lips now, her hair still tangled around his fingers, her lips parted and plump.

"Don't, Chase."

"Why not?" He raised his gaze, not letting her look away from him.

"I just . . ."

Chase waited, but she never finished her sentence. He didn't waste time, cupping her face with his hands as he brought his mouth closer to hers, her ragged breath only spurring him on more. Chase brushed his lips over Hope's slowly, the softest of touches to give her every chance to pull away, and when she didn't, he smiled against her mouth, their lips touching then parting over and over again. But it wasn't enough and it was taking every inch of his willpower not to bend her hard over the counter and strip her down naked. And if they hadn't been in a crowded bar, he doubted he'd be so restrained.

Instead he pushed up harder into her, tasting her mouth as he dipped his tongue against hers, his hands still in her long, golden hair as they kissed. Hope's body was relaxed into his, her mouth matching his, her fingers clenching into his hair now, tugging harder as her lips moved faster. Her moan only spurred him on more, his hands all over her, skimming her waist, resting on her hips. He'd waited a helluva long time for this, and being up close and personal with Hope was every inch as good as he'd remembered.

"Chase."

He groaned and tugged Hope back when she pulled away, planting his lips on hers again. He was so damn hard there was no way she hadn't felt it, the sensation of her wriggling up against him, her arms looped around his neck as she tipped her head back, making him bend over to keep his mouth firm to hers. But he could tell when a good thing was about to end, and in less than a few seconds Hope was wiggling out of his grasp.

"Chase." This time her tone told him not to push her.

"Mmm-hmm," he muttered, eyes on her mouth, admiring how plump and pillowy it looked. Her lip gloss was gone but her lips were even pinker than before, rouged from all the kissing.

"Chase, I'm serious," she insisted, her fingers untangling from his hair as he groaned, trying to keep his pelvis locked against hers. Hope planted both hands on his chest, forcing him back this time.

"You sure?" he asked, his voice gravelly as he ground out the words.

"We've both had too much to drink," she told him, holding firmly on to his upper biceps now as if she were trying to lock him into place. She had no chance of holding him, all he had to do was rotate forward and he could have her pinned against the bar with no chance of escape. But that wasn't what he wanted to do with Hope. *No.* He wanted her as desperate for him as he was for her, begging to be held, aching to be kissed. Forcing her into anything wasn't his style—he liked his women to be every bit as hot for him as he was for them.

"Maybe we've had just *enough* to drink?" he asked.

Hope laughed, her head tipped back again, the delicate skin of her neck on show as she tilted her body before swinging back up again and firmly shaking her head.

"No, Chase."

"How about *yes, Chase*?"

She made a delicious guttural noise when he bent and pressed his lips to her neck, opening his mouth and sucking gently, his tongue exploring as he tasted just above her collarbone.

"You wanna get out of here?" he asked when he finally raised his head. It was like they were the only two people in the room, everything else blurring out as he focused every bit of his energy on the exquisite woman in front of him.

She hesitated long and hard, her gaze flitting from his eyes to his mouth and lingering for a long, long time on the latter. "We can't go back to my place," she finally whispered against his lips, stepping in closer to indulge in another long, wet kiss like she'd rethought her decision to say no and decided on exactly the opposite.

He chuckled. "But we can go back to my truck."

Hope shook her head. "You've had too much to drive."

"Who said anything about driving?"

A memory of the two of them laughing themselves stupid as they fell into the bed of Chase's old Chevy hit her like it was only yesterday. His big body over hers, teasing her, tempting her, but still she said no. Every part of her had screamed out to let him touch her, but she'd fought the feeling, even when his full lips had been less than an inch from hers.

But that was then, and this was now.

Chapter 4

Hope was starting to think her heart was going to beat out of her chest, it was thumping so hard. Adrenaline surged through her, excitement curling like a snake in her belly as she clasped Chase's hand and hurried for the door. What the hell was she doing? The sensible part of her brain was screaming at her to stop, to dig her heels in, stop walking, and get a cab back to her place. Alone. But the heat flooding her body, the ache deep inside her at the thought of having Chase's hands all over? That part was telling her to hold him as damn tight as she could. The past few years had been rough and forgetting everything and giving in to him was tempting.

Chase let go of her hand and slipped his arm around her waist instead, tugging her close, their hips bumping together then sticking like glue. Chase glanced down at her, eyes like flames for all the heat his gaze fanned through her. His dimple, the confidence in his stare—it was no wonder so many women fell into bed with him. Every inch of him, from his big, strong frame to the way he ran a hand through his hair—he didn't give a damn what anyone thought of him and he was sexy as hell. But he'd always given a damn what she thought of him, which was why they'd kept their clothes on for so long. And here she was desperate to peel them off now that she had the chance again.

"Hey," Chase murmured, stopping abruptly and sliding his other arm around her so his hands were locked around her waist.

"Hey," she whispered back, pleased she had so much alcohol surging through her. Without it she'd never have been so bold, brazenly staring back at Chase and sliding her hands under his shirt, eyes half closing as she ran her fingers over his toned, taut abs.

"Come here."

Hope went to hesitate but Chase didn't give her a chance to breathe, let alone change her mind. His body was hard up against hers, pushing her to his Mercedes, her back against the cold metal as he worked one of his legs in between hers. She wrapped her arms around his neck, wanting him closer, loving his chest against her breasts, her fingers in his hair, his stubble brushing her cheeks. The only thing she cared about was making sure his lips didn't have a second to leave hers. *Screw worrying about doing the wrong thing.* This was one night, just one night of indulging in being with the man she'd fantasized about every night for years.

"You," Chase muttered, slamming his hands onto the car on either side of her, "are incredible."

Hope grinned and reached for him again, angling her body to lock her pelvis against his. She was so hot for him, her entire body tingling, damp between her legs and ready for him to take her. *Damn.* She couldn't have sex with him in a car in a parking lot. No matter how badly she wanted him. Or could she?

Bleep bleep.

Chase managed to unlock the SUV at the same time as he slammed her up against him, scooping under her butt and lifting her, one arm holding her weight, the other yanking open the rear door of the vehicle. The look on his face was pure sin as he dipped her low and put her on the seat, his laugh a deep rumble as she scrambled backward and he pounced, his body so close to hers before he leaned back and pulled the door shut behind them. He was like a panther poised above her, ready to feast on her body.

"I knew there was a reason I ordered tinted windows." Chase's mouth was turned up into a wicked smile, one eyebrow arched triumphantly at her.

"So you could strip women naked on the backseat?"

"No." He chuckled. "So I could strip *you* naked on the backseat."

"Don't make out like I'm the first." Hope's breath was starting to come in ragged bursts as Chase straddled her, knees on either side of her hips as he shuffled forward, hands spread over her belly, caressing her bare skin as her top rode up.

"You're the first," he said simply, "and you'll be the last. No other woman will ever look as good as you do splayed out beneath me, so I'll be keeping this backseat as a delicious memory of you and you only."

Hope didn't believe him for a moment, but it didn't stop her from arching her back to let him push her top up higher, sucking back a gasp as he dipped his head and pressed a wet kiss to her stomach, running his tongue all the way up to her bra. He paused, letting her moan and wiggle, before flicking his tongue under her bra and sending a spasm of ecstasy through her when he connected with her nipple.

"Chase . . ."

"I'm not letting you say no," he ground out.

She laughed. "*More*. I was going to beg for more."

The surprise on Chase's face was priceless, his eyes crinkling at the sides as he looked down at her. "Oh, there's plenty more where that came from."

The Chase she'd known way back had been confident and cocky, but this Chase was different. He was slower, so obviously sure about what he was doing. The practiced way his hands skimmed her skin, the delicious dark glint in his eyes . . . She groaned as he lowered himself and dipped his tongue into her mouth, his lips following close behind in a kiss that left her grinding into him, digging her fingernails into his shoulders as she kissed him back.

Hope grated her nails down Chase's back, irritated that she wasn't connecting with bare skin. She'd been celibate since her marriage had ended and after not having sex for months, suddenly it was all she could think about.

"Off," she said when Chase's mouth relented for a moment. She grabbed the hem of his T-shirt and pushed it up. She couldn't stifle her groan when she ran her hands over his abs and then slid them upward, fingers closing over his nipples and garnering a sharp gasp from him. Hope tweaked, hard.

"You want to play dirty?" he murmured, licking his lips as he pulled back to look down at her, his body pushed up as he raised his arms and let her force his T-shirt up further. He finished the task for her, throwing it away.

The moment of satisfaction only lasted a moment though. Searing hot anticipation rocked her body when Chase undid his belt buckle and then the top button of his jeans. His grin was wicked as he tightened his thighs around her, not letting her lower half so much as wriggle as he pushed her top up high, somehow stripping her while she was still lying beneath him. His fingers traced a light, tickling trail across her collarbone, his head dipping slowly. Hope raised her mouth, parted her lips to accommodate him, but he just chuckled and ran a hand through her hair, his touch firm as he dipped his head to the top of her breast and sucked, softly at first and then hard, his other hand palm down on her stomach.

Chase could have stripped and fucked her right then and there. Screw foreplay—she was ready for him—desperate to have her legs locked around his waist, their bodies fused. But he had other plans, and if it hadn't felt so damn good . . .

"Damn." Chase's soft curse against her breast as he flicked his tongue inside the lacy fabric pulled her out of the moment.

"What?" she whispered.

"Phones," he muttered. "They always ring at the worst times, huh?"

Hope's body arched as Chase stopped talking and he pulled her bra down low, exposing her breast and covering it with his mouth, the attention his tongue was giving her nipple sending waves of pleasure through every inch of her, but . . .

"Chase, stop," she murmured, clenching her fingers in his hair and trying to tug him up.

He didn't stop. Instead he switched to her other nipple, her toes curling as he suckled hard, tongue flicking around and driving her crazy. But now she'd heard the phone, knew it was hers, and she needed to check, no matter how amazing Chase was with his mouth.

"Chase," she said, more firmly this time, yanking his curly hair harder.

"No." His mouth finally left her skin so he could stare into her eyes, his own glinting like he'd just been caught out doing something wicked but didn't give a damn anyway. "I'm not letting you go until . . ."

"I have to check my phone." She didn't need him telling her why she needed to stay where she was—her body was telling her everything she needed to know already.

"Screw the phone."

Chase went to dip his head again but she yanked him back up, hard. The moment was gone, for now anyway.

"I have to," she told him, grimacing at his groan. "I'm a mom, Chase. It could be the sitter."

She hadn't often seen defeat in Chase's gaze before, but she saw it now. He dropped a slow, simmering kiss to her mouth, plucking at her lips before pulling away and releasing her from between his thighs.

"I can't argue with that now, can I?"

Hope pulled her top back down and watched as Chase reached around for his T-shirt.

"I'm sorry," she said, sitting up and grabbing her purse. She unclasped it and found her phone, checking the missed calls. Damn, there had been two. She scrolled through.

"Your kid okay?" Chase asked.

"Um . . ." Hope blew out a frustrated breath and put her phone back in her purse. "Would you believe that it was just someone from work?"

Chase laughed and she joined in. He reached out and put his arm around her, both sitting side by side on the backseat. She dropped her head to his shoulder.

"You're a mom, Hope. There's more important things than making out with me in the back of a car, I get that."

She giggled, biting her bottom lip and glancing at Chase. *"Making out?"*

"Hey, it sounded better than anything else that came to mind."

Hope knew Chase would be up for it if she forgot all about the interruption and just climbed back into his lap and locked lips with him again. He was a man—his brain would be on his cock again in no time. But she couldn't. As fun as it had been before, she should never have gotten caught up in the moment and ended up in the backseat. There were things he deserved to know, things she needed to tell him, and instead she'd pretended like nothing had happened between back then and now.

"I'd offer to drive you home but I think I'll leave my SUV here for the night."

She nodded, reaching for his hand and squeezing it. The mood between them had changed, the sizzle replaced with something closer to friendship, even if her body was still tingling from where he'd touched her, her nipples still hard nubs in memory of his tongue laving over them.

"Tonight was fun," she said, not sure what else to say.

"Damn right it was." Chase turned his head and pressed a kiss to her cheek. "Any chance you want to . . ." His finger started at her other cheek and ran all the way down her neck to her chest, stopping in the hollow between her breasts.

"No," she rasped out, when what she really wanted was just to scream *yes* at him.

"If you're sure?" Chase's fingers made their way back up, stopping at her cheek and nudging her face sideways. His mouth moved closer to hers, hovering over her lips.

Hope might have good intentions, but even she wasn't that strong. She let him caress her lips, matching his every move until his mouth opened wider and his tongue touched hers. *So much for self-control.*

A loud voice from outside, muffled laughter, and a bang jolted them both from the moment. Chase looked pissed, moving sideways and flinging open the door.

"Sorry! Didn't mean to disturb ya." A loud voice and some drunken laughter followed.

"And that's my cue," Hope said, putting out a hand to stop Chase coming any closer. "You're a bad influence,

Chase King. This is me saying no a second time, and meaning it."

"Hey, I behaved myself around you for years." He was in full charm mode, one eyebrow raised as he grinned. "Now it's time to misbehave."

"No, you were *always* a bad influence," she corrected, clasping her purse to keep her fingers busy. If they weren't, she didn't trust them not to go wandering back to Chase. "I just resisted your charms."

"Our problem," he said, sliding closer, a wolf seducing its prey, "is that now we know what we were missing out on."

She shook her head and slid in the opposite direction, pushing open her door and stumbling out, trying hard to stay in control.

"Good night, Chase," she said.

He leaned over, a devilish smile kicking his dimple into life. "Can I at least get a cab for you?"

"No," she said, "because you'll only end up in it and I need to get home. Alone."

Chase held his hands up in the air but she wasn't going to fall for his smooth words, not now that she'd extracted herself.

"I'll see you soon," she said, checking she wasn't about to get run over by a car moving out of the lot as she called out to Chase. "We'll have our results in a couple of days and we can talk plans going forward."

Her head was starting to spin from all the tequila, not used to so much alcohol after so long not indulging.

"You know where to find me if you need me before then."

She gave Chase a final wave and laughed, shaking her head as she tried her hardest to walk in a straight line on her super high heels back toward the bar. Oh, she needed him all right, but the sensible part of her brain had taken over and she wasn't going to give in to any of her feelings again. Chase was a gorgeous man; he was sexy, strong, and confident. But her life was already complicated enough without diving headfirst into her past and getting tangled up with the one man she'd vowed never to end up in bed with again. The past year had shattered her dreams, put an end to the future she'd thought about since she was a girl. But just because she'd lost her family's ranch didn't mean she was defeated, and she wasn't going to let it define her. It was the very reason she'd left everything behind, to prove to herself and the world that she was someone in her own right.

Chase let himself into the apartment that Nate kept in town, kicking the door shut behind him and dropping his keys onto the hallstand. He groaned and shook his head. *What an idiot.* Since when did he make out with a woman in the backseat of his vehicle?

In college, that's when. He strode down the short hallway and into the kitchen, yanking open the fridge and staring in. Chase reached in for a carton of orange juice, checked the best before date and guzzled some down. This was why he didn't date moms—or at least it was why he wasn't going to date moms in the future. Interruptions didn't sit well with him.

A noise made him jump. Chase spluttered the OJ, spinning around as he choked and finding his big brother holding a handgun. "Fuck, Nate, I thought you were a burglar."

"Sorry."

"Dammit, Nate! Stop pointing that thing at me." He gestured at the gun now hanging causally from his brother's right hand. "What the hell are you doing here anyway?"

"This is my apartment." Nate shrugged. "I ended up

stuck in meetings all day. I'm wheels up in the morning now."

Chase grunted and put the juice back in the fridge. "You frightened the fucking life out of me." Nate kept the place because it was close to the King offices, and because he never liked to bring women back to the ranch, but they all had keys and if they drank too much he and Ryder used the place too.

"Where've you been?" Nate asked.

"Out with a friend?"

"You grab a few beers?"

"Dinner."

Chase undid a few buttons on his shirt and crossed the room, flopping down onto one of the two sofas. Nate was only wearing boxer briefs, clearly disturbed from bed, but he claimed the other couch and kicked back, too.

"Hold up, you just came home from a date on your own? Man, you're losing your touch, little brother."

"Maybe I didn't want to bring her back." Or maybe he wished he'd been a bit more forceful about them coming here instead of settling for the back of his truck.

Nate chuckled. "Did you meet her online? Was she not up to her profile picture?"

"Fuck off."

"Oh, I get it. This wasn't just a fun night out, this was . . ." Nate sat up, arms resting on his knees as he stared straight at him, eyes narrowed before he howled with laughter. "You've been hiding someone from us, haven't you? Someone so goddamn *special* you haven't even spent the night with her yet. Oh, this is good."

Chase glared back at Nate, not about to let his brother get the wrong idea and tease him mercilessly.

"This is why I don't tell you shit."

"No, this is exactly why you *should* tell me shit," Nate countered. "Now come on, spill. I can't believe you've been living in my house all this time and you haven't said a word."

"We had the AI specialist come around today," Chase said, wondering why the hell he was even talking to Nate about Hope. He still couldn't figure it out in his own head, which meant he should probably be keeping it to himself. They'd had fun tonight and he wanted her, *damn did he want her*, but she was still different. Things between them were way more complicated than they should be.

"I don't want to talk about getting our heifers pregnant, I want to know about the girl," Nate replied with a chuckle, getting up and going over to the fridge. He returned with a bottle opener and a couple of beers. "We can talk shop in the morning before I go."

Chase frowned, taking the opened beer from his brother and swallowing it down. "That's the problem. I was out with the AI specialist tonight."

Now it was Nate frowning. "You know we don't mix business with pleasure."

Chase scowled. "I know the rule, you don't need to remind me. But this was different." Their granddad hadn't been strict about a lot of things, but he never made exceptions to the few rules he did have. No screwing anyone who worked with you or for you; never raise a fist to a woman; always remember those who've helped you, and never forget those who've spurned you.

"Different how?" Nate asked.

"It was Hope. I had no idea it was her until she arrived, and we went out for dinner to catch up. I haven't seen her since we graduated from A&M."

Nate stared at him, beer bottle in his hands as he leaned forward. "So let me get this straight," Nate said, his brows drawn together. "You're talking about Hope, aka hot Hope, who you spent like four years lusting after in college? *She* was the specialist vet who turned up today?"

"We were just friends," Chase corrected, worrying his thumb across the label of his beer bottle. "And I wasn't lusting after her through *all* of college."

"Bullshit," his brother muttered. "You might have played friends but you wanted her the whole time. You'd have been crazy *not* to have wanted her in your bed."

"Yeah, well, look where that got me." Chase took a pull of beer and then changed his mind. He wanted a whiskey instead. He needed something stronger to try to get the image of Hope flushed and rumpled in the back of his car tonight out of his head. "We were good as friends." He stood and collected two glasses and the whiskey bottle.

"That still what you think?" Nate asked, nodding when Chase offered him a glass. "You going to try telling me that you'd like to be buddies with her instead of something more?"

"Fuck no." Chase grimaced as he swallowed the liquor down. "But we already screwed our friendship up. And besides, I know what she looks like naked now." The mental image of her body was like a red-hot poker burned into his memory banks. He'd never forgotten, but after tonight? He wanted her skin beneath his hands again, his mouth tasting her, *all of her*. He was getting hard just thinking about it.

He scowled as Nate sat back and chuckled. Chase hadn't thought about Hope in a long time, but now that he'd seen her she was *all* he could think about. Naked that night five years ago in the motel room. Starting to get naked in the backseat of his SUV tonight. He doubted he'd be able to shut his damn eyes without imagining her, which meant he needed to get good and drunk before he even thought about calling it a night.

"So you *did* sleep with her?"

Chase grunted. He hadn't talked about Hope to his brothers back then because the whole thing had pissed him off, that something had finally happened and then everything had fallen apart, and he wasn't exactly going to brag about it. She'd been his best friend, and he'd ruined their friendship because he hadn't been able to keep it in his pants.

"So what you gonna do about it?" Nate asked.

"Jack shit."

"Don't be an idiot. You want her, go get her."

Chase groaned. "She's different now." Besides, did he want more? Did he want to go there again? He balled his fists. Of course he fucking wanted her, he just didn't want to admit it. Or maybe he didn't want to admit that he felt bad thinking about her as just fun—he didn't want anything more than a good time, but he also didn't want to hurt her. And that's why they'd kept to just friends at college, because he didn't want serious and she wasn't the kind of girl out screwing around for fun. She was a take-home-to-your-mom kind of woman.

"Different how?"

"She's a mom, for starters," Chase told him. "It makes things more complicated."

Nate howled with laughter. "You're scared of her because she's a mom? No one's asking you to be stepdad of the year. You know that, right? And FYI, moms can have a sex life if that's what you're worried about."

Chase glared at his brother. He wasn't going to go into details about what had happened and how it had complicated things between them tonight. "She's not just some woman, Nate. She's . . ."

"The one who got away, I know."

"Fuck off." He knocked back the rest of his whiskey and reached for the bottle, then changed his mind and stood up. "I should never have said anything. Just forget it."

"You're a douchebag," Nate said, finishing his drink

and stretching. He poured himself another, then raised an eyebrow at Chase before filling his glass, too. "This is the only time I've ever seen you all het up over a woman. You want her, do something about it or shut the hell up."

Chase stalked across the room, ready to slam his fist into something to get rid of his frustration. He stared out into the darkness then marched back and snatched the glass, drinking the lot in one gulp. "It's fucking easy to say and damn hard to do." He'd tried—tonight had been fun and they'd ended up almost naked—but the way she'd left told him that they weren't necessarily going to have a repeat performance.

"There's your answer right there."

Chase set his glass back down and leaned on the table, palms open against the timber top. "I'm not following."

"She's under your skin, brother." Nate grinned, leaning back on the sofa and resting his feet on the table. "If she was easy we wouldn't be having this conversation."

Chase grunted and turned around to go. He needed sleep and he sure as hell didn't want to talk about Hope any longer. Maybe lying in bed thinking about her wouldn't be such a bad thing. "Night," he called out.

"Sweet dreams." Nate was laughing as he said the words.

More like wet dreams. Chase trudged up the stairs and tried to think of anything but Hope. Trouble was, their night together was still like a fresh memory—her long hair curled around his fist as she'd sat astride him, the fullness of her breasts, the curve of her ass when he'd cupped it with both hands. *Fuck!* Making out with her hadn't taken the edge off at all. It had only made him want her all the more.

What he needed was to get Hope out of his system, find someone or something else to distract him. Because until he did he doubted he'd get a decent night's sleep ever again. Only problem was he didn't want anyone else. He wanted Hope and he wanted her real bad, *mom or not.*

He contemplated calling some of his friends to see if they were out, but changed his mind. Going out and drinking more wasn't going to help him any, especially when he had a herd of cattle to move in the morning and he'd already consumed a whole lot more than he should have. Which meant he had a date with his pillow, whether sleep found him or not.

Chapter 5

Hope stretched out in bed, keeping her eyes shut tight as sun bathed her body. She loved having an upstairs bedroom and not having to worry about pulling the blinds, letting the sun wake her every morning. Although after being up so late the night before . . . Hope groaned and opened her eyes, staring at the white ceiling. *Chase*.

She dragged her body up, head foggy and starting to pound, but nothing changed the memories playing through her mind on fast-forward. Why had she kissed him? What had possessed her to jump in the back of his car and . . . *Oh my God*. Letting him touch her bare skin, *touching him* like she was a horny teenager.

Hope rose, dropping her feet over the side of the bed and wiggling her toes into the thick carpet before stretching her arms out again and padding quietly down the hall to peek into her son's room. She nudged the door a little and saw him lying sprawled across the covers, one of his legs hanging off the side. She stood awhile, just staring at her little man. He deserved to have a father in his life, to have the kind of idyllic childhood she'd had. She was the one who'd made the decisions, yet it was he who'd suffered, even if he didn't realize that yet. He'd liked his stepdad, but it wasn't the same as having his biological father in his life.

Hope walked quietly back to her room and stripped down, jumping in the adjoining shower. She rinsed her hair and washed it, then lathered her body and washed all the suds off. She ran one hand across her breasts, caressing them, her nipples hard nubs, the water warm and inviting against her skin. When Chase had touched her there . . . *Enough!* Hope flung her hand out and turned the faucet off, water dripping off her as she stood blinking droplets from her lashes. What she'd done with Chase was as much a mistake last night as it had been five years ago, and the last thing she needed was to start fantasizing about him in the shower.

She dried herself, dressed in jeans and a tank, and applied some makeup, leaving her long hair wet and twisting it up into a knot. She'd dry it after breakfast—if she was lucky she might get to have a coffee and read the news on her iPad before Harrison even woke up. Usually he was snuggled in her bed already, but he'd obviously stayed up late having fun with the sitter and instead of calling out to her at two a.m. had kept on snoozing.

Hope flicked her coffee machine on and opened the pantry, frowning when she realized it was virtually empty. Harrison would eat his Froot Loops like usual, but . . . She leaned back, listening. She was sure she'd heard something.

Knock, knock, knock. It sounded out again. She headed into the hall, pleased that she had a peephole that she could peer through before opening her door. No one ever just swung past her place for the hell of it, because she'd only just moved here, and definitely not at this time of the morning.

She stood on tiptoe and peered through, expecting to

find a salesman or a pesky neighbor. But it wasn't a neighbor. It was Chase.

Hope ran her hands down over her jeans, palms instantly sweaty. What the hell was he doing on her doorstep?

"Chase?" she said as she swung open the door.

He raised two paper bags and gave her his butter-wouldn't-melt smile. "You're either going to kill me for knocking on your door this early, or thank me for bringing breakfast."

Hope leaned against the door, finding it impossible not to return Chase's infectious grin. "It just so happens I've been staring into the pantry, willing some food to materialize. So you're in luck."

He chuckled and took a step forward. "So does that mean I can come in?"

She leaned back and waved her hand down the hall. "So long as you don't mind the mess."

Hope shut the door behind Chase and watched as he sauntered slowly into the kitchen. He was wearing the same jeans he'd had on the night before, a dark pair that made it more than obvious how good his butt was, paired with scuffed boots and a fresh T-shirt. Damn him for looking so good so early.

"So what are you still doing in town?"

"I stayed at Nate's apartment," he said, setting the bags down on the counter and turning slowly, checking the place out. "Then I woke up early and felt like an asshole for what went down last night, so I thought I'd come here before heading home."

"So you came bearing gifts?" she asked, reaching for one of the bags to see what it had inside.

"Yeah, something like that," he said. "I just . . ." Chase spread his palms out on the counter and leveled his gaze on her, his dark eyes like a storm cloud drawing her closer to danger. Everything about him was so impossible to pull away from, his eyes as magnetic as the rest of his damn body.

"Mmmm, cream cheese and jam. My favorite," Hope announced, ripping open the bag and taking a bite. She swallowed as Chase watched her, dabbing the corner of her mouth and feeling more than a touch guilty. "Oh my God, please tell me this one was mine?"

He laughed. "I still remember what you like," he said. "Jam and extra cream cheese for you, bacon for me, and one with just cream cheese in case your son wants something, too."

Hope stared back at him, her bagel still in one hand, a napkin in the other. Suddenly it was like she was attempting to swallow a small rock when she tried to chew and digest another bite.

"I guess we did eat breakfast together a lot," she managed, avoiding the fact he'd brought something for Harrison.

"Are you kidding?" he said, ripping his bag open at the same time as he made himself comfortable on a barstool. "Half the time we were eating breakfast before we'd even been to bed after a big night."

She chuckled, the feeling of nostalgia passing as she remembered their early years at college. "You're referring to the nights when you hadn't taken some gorgeous leggy blonde back to your dorm, right?"

He frowned, eyebrows drawing together. "Hey, I didn't discriminate. There's nothing wrong with a beautiful brunette."

"Seriously though, you definitely had a thing for blondes."

His frown faded, his expression more serious. "Maybe

I was trying to compensate for not being able to have the blonde I really wanted."

If she'd been trying to swallow stones before, now she was trying to swallow rocks. "Coffee," she muttered, realizing her machine was still on. Just her luck she'd have burned the motor out leaving it on so long with not enough water in it, and these days it wasn't like she could just go out and buy another one. "You still take it black with sugar?"

She heard him move behind her, his boots scuffing against her wooden floor.

"I'll always feel like a shit for ruining our friendship that night, Hope, but it wasn't like I hadn't wanted it for a long time."

She tried to ignore him, focused on the coffee machine, on filling it up with water and setting both cups on the tray. They'd gone over this last night, talked around what had happened, and it wasn't something she wanted to discuss when she was sober. She'd done her best to block out that night, to push away her guilt, but with Chase standing behind her, his feelings on the matter more than clear, it wasn't exactly easy.

Hope froze. Chase's hands touched her shoulders, his palms firm as his thumbs locked at the top of her back. His touch was light yet firm, making her want to lean into him and relax at the same time as wanting to escape his hold and run.

"Seeing you again, it's brought everything back," Chase said, his voice gruff as he leaned in. His breath was hot against her neck, his hand moving to gently scoop up her hair and brush it to one side so her bare skin was exposed. Goose pimples rippled across her entire body, her fingers barely functioning as she tried to continue making the coffee.

"Things have changed," Hope murmured, trying to stay focused, to not be swayed by Chase's touch. If he knew the truth he wouldn't be saying any of this to her. "I've changed."

"Yeah, but this hasn't," he insisted, his mouth closing over her neck, lips so smooth, so delicate against her that her knees were in danger of buckling. "Nothing about how much I want you has changed. Just now we don't have to worry about screwing up our friendship. We already did that."

Hope reached to flick the switch on the machine. Her brain was telling her to be sensible, but she couldn't. Instead she wavered, let her body take over, resting back ever so slightly against Chase, his chest firm against her back, his frame big and comforting as he slid his hands slowly over her shoulders and down her arms, drawing her back.

"Mom?"

Hope leaped forward, smashing her hip into the counter she moved so fast. "Harrison!" She as good as shoved Chase on her way past to get to her boy, her heart swelling as she saw him standing there in the middle of the kitchen, hair sticking up in every which direction, his teddy clutched tight against his chest as he stared at the strange man in the house.

Hope bent and placed a smacking kiss on his forehead before scooping him up into her arms. Her blood still felt like it was on fire and pumping around her body at a rapid pace, her body screaming out to her that the man she wanted was still so close, but she stayed focused on her son. When he was with her, nothing else mattered—not even Chase King. She was a mom and that was just the way it had to be.

"Sorry, sweetheart, I was just about to come back up and check on you."

"Who's that?" he asked, peering over her shoulder as she cuddled him.

Hope turned slowly, taking a deep breath and holding Harrison even tighter. His legs were looped around her waist and he leaned back to get a better look at Chase when she faced him. This was a moment she'd never imagined, not in a million years.

Harrison, this is your dad. That's what she should have been saying. Only she'd planned on keeping this a secret forever, or maybe she just hadn't accepted that this was something she had to face one day. Instead she took a deep breath and forced a smile, her heart starting its rapid beat.

"Sweetheart, this is mommy's friend Chase. Chase, this is Harrison."

"Harris," her son said, wriggling to get down. "Only Mom calls me Harrison."

Hope forced her breath out, her lungs constricted enough without forgetting to exhale. The sensible part of her knew that there was no way Chase would put two and two together, that all he'd see was a cute kid and not even think about who his father might be. As far as he was concerned she'd had a husband, and he was the dad. But another little part of her wondered if he might see the resemblance, if the deep brown eyes mirroring his would set off something inside him that told him the truth.

She watched, helpless, as Harrison took a couple of steps closer to Chase, his teddy tucked firmly under one arm now as he sized up the man in front of him.

"Hey, Harris," Chase said, dropping to his haunches and holding out his hand. "I'm a friend of your mom's from way back when she was at college studying to be a veterinarian."

Harrison eyed him, not taking his hand but watching him anyway.

"How about a high five instead?" Chase asked, holding up his hand and grinning when Harrison touched palms with him.

"Why were you touching my mom before?" Harrison asked.

Hope clamped a hand over her mouth, meeting Chase's gaze as they both tried not to laugh. She could see that he was finding keeping a straight face even harder than she was.

"That's a great question, buddy," he said, still staying at eye level with Harrison, facing his accuser. "You're pretty protective over your mom, huh?"

Harrison nodded and she moved closer to her son, dropping a hand to his shoulder.

"Chase used to be Mommy's best friend," she told him, letting Chase off the hook. "He was trying to help me with the, ah, coffee machine." She didn't like lying to her son, but it wasn't like she had another option right now. Besides, if she was honest with herself, she'd been lying to him all his life where Chase was concerned.

"How about I make that coffee," Chase said, clearing his throat and rising. His eyes were dancing with humor, the corner of his mouth tilting upward just enough to make his dimple crease. "Black?" he asked her.

Hope dropped a kiss into Harrison's hair, inhaling the sweet smell of his shampoo as she took a deep breath. "Please," she murmured.

Never in a million years had she expected to end up in Texas again, with Chase King standing at her coffee machine, in her kitchen, and her son wriggling out of her grasp to clamber up onto a barstool to watch him.

"Oh yum, bagels!" Harrison announced, not noticing the box of Froot Loops and bowl she'd put out already for him. He also didn't seem to notice it already had a bite out of it when he reached for Chase's discarded bacon and cream cheese one, tucking straight into it.

"Sorry," Hope whispered when Chase turned around.

He just laughed. "Don't sweat it, I'll just have the plain one."

If only she could just relax instead of being a jangling ball of nerves, but the simple fact that they liked the same bagels only made her feel worse than she already did.

"Was my mom out with you last night?" Harrison asked as he munched, almost impossible to understand. She wasn't going to call him out on talking with his mouth full, he'd only get embarrassed and he was having fun chatting.

"Yeah, she was," Chase replied, turning around again and putting her coffee on the counter.

She mouthed *thank you* as she slid it down toward her. He grinned back, way too at ease in her kitchen for her to be comfortable.

"Can I go with you next time?"

"Harrison," she interrupted before Chase had a chance to answer, "how about you and I go out for pizza tonight? It just so happens I've heard about a great place."

"We've only just moved here, you know," her son announced, completely ignoring her, all his attention on Chase. "We come from Canada, but Mom got a new job here."

"You've got a lot to say, little man," Chase said with a chuckle as he turned again, this time with his coffee cup in his hands. "I think you and I are gonna be good friends."

Hope's heart started its rapid-pounding-then-stutter thing, making her feel sick to her stomach. Taking the job here had been a no-brainer, but ending up reconnected with Chase was just downright dangerous. She took a sip of her coffee, grimacing as it burned the tip of her tongue.

She needed to get Chase out of her house, and, like the big bad wolf he was, not let him back in.

Chase finished his coffee and set the cup on the counter. He watched Hope as she bent down to wipe a smudge of cream cheese off the corner of her son's mouth, dropping a kiss into his hair before standing back up.

"So what's your plan for the day?" he asked, taking both their cups to the sink and rinsing them out. He checked the dishwasher and put them in when he saw it had a dirty load.

"I'm heading into work soon," she said, nodding to Harrison that he could run off. "I need to go and get the little man ready."

"Do you have a nanny during the week?"

"He goes to pre-K for a few hours each day. I drop him there in the morning, then he has a nanny in the afternoons. She collects him and has him until I come home."

"That must be tough," Chase said, noticing the flicker in her gaze when she talked about her nanny. "You guys seem pretty close."

"We are." She busied herself squaring up a pile of magazines, clearly not wanting to make eye contact with him. He knew her too well though, could see straight through it. "I guess I never expected to be a working mom. Not like this, anyway."

He nodded, taking a few steps back toward her now that there were only the two of them in the room again. "You thought you'd be chilling on your ranch, making homemade lemonade and enjoying a brood of children by now, right?"

She laughed, finally looking at him again. "Maybe not an entire brood, and I always wanted to help run the ranch, but yeah. I didn't expect to be a working single mom with a trail of debt in my wake, that's for sure." She turned to glance out the window, needing to gather her thoughts. "The dreams I had seemed realistic a few years ago, and now everything's just turned to dust."

"You ever gonna tell me exactly what happened?"

She shrugged. "One day. Right now I'd rather forget it."

Chase wanted to push her, but he knew the more he pushed the more she'd pull back, even though it was on the tip of his tongue to just ask her to tell him what the hell had happened and get on with it. Maybe she was afraid he'd go and hunt down her ex-husband. Because he damn well would if he could. Whatever had gone on was bad, he knew that instinctively. Hope had always been so focused and determined, would never let anyone take advantage of her or make her do something she didn't want to do. And yet something about what had happened at home had traumatized her more than she was letting on.

"How about you head over next weekend? Come hang out on our ranch for a bit."

Her eyebrows shot up, mouth parted as she looked back at him. "Ah . . ." she murmured, clearly not sure what to say. "I don't like leaving Harrison. I know it sounds crazy, but going out with you last night was the first time I've ever left him with a sitter in the evening. It's bad enough doing it when I have to work."

He shrugged. "You're a mom, I get it. And a damn good one."

"Thanks."

"So just bring him with you. He can bunk down when it gets late. We'll order in pizza or whatever he likes." Chase smiled. "Hell, if it means seeing you again I'll drive out myself and get him McDonald's. Is it still called a Happy Meal?"

"Yes, they're still called Happy Meals," she said with

a laugh, shaking her head. "But I'm not sure that's such a good idea."

"What? Coming over or the take-out-food part?"

"Both of us coming over," she said.

"Is it so strange? I kinda like kids, and he seems pretty cool." Chase stepped closer to her, reaching out and touching her hand, stroking his fingers over hers until she looked up at him. She stared for so long at their hands interlocked, a big breath making her body shudder. Chase just stayed still, watched her, wished to hell they were in the house alone so he could kiss that damn fine mouth of hers then jump her up onto the bench and finish what they'd started the night before. He was getting hard just thinking about it, wanting to skim his fingers over bare skin, to explore every inch of her again and get it out of his system.

"Chase, I have to get going otherwise I'll be late getting Harrison to . . ."

He cupped her chin with his fingers, holding her still as he leaned in, mouth hovering over hers, giving her the chance to move away if she wanted to. But she didn't move. Hope's lips parted, her breath warm against his skin.

"We shouldn't," she whispered.

He grunted and shuffled his body even closer. "I know."

He didn't give her any longer to think about it, covering her mouth with his, brushing their lips together, cupping the back of her head, her hair silky beneath his touch. Hope moaned, kissing him back, her hand sliding between them and clutching the front of his T-shirt as she locked him in place. Chase slipped a hand around her waist, nudging her pelvis forward so it was slammed against him, his tongue searching out hers.

"Chase," she whispered against his mouth, palm flat to his chest as she pushed him back. "Stop."

He groaned, hard as a rock and sure she'd felt it. He wanted her bad, and he wanted her now. "What if I say no?" he muttered.

She sighed and he let go of her, running his hand through her damp hair and down her back.

"You smell great," he told her, wishing she was stepping into him and not away.

"Chase, we can't do this."

Not this again. He didn't want to talk about why they couldn't, he wanted to talk about all the reasons why they *could*. "Why not? We already ruined our friendship years ago."

She stared at him, long and hard. "We're different people now. Things have changed. And it's not just me any longer."

"And some things are still exactly the same," he said. "I screwed my way through half a sorority in college, Hope, and you want to know why?" He paused, wondering if he should have shut the hell up, but he'd started now so he might as well just tell her how he felt. "Being around you all the time was torture. Not wanting to fuck up what we had meant I tried to satisfy myself elsewhere, and I can tell you now the best damn night of my life in college was the last one."

Tears welled in her eyes and he didn't know why. She brushed them away with the back of her hand, turning away from him, but he wasn't going to let her.

"Hope?" He reached for her but she moved just far enough back that they didn't connect. "Baby, what's wrong?"

"Everything's changed, Chase. We're not the same people we were back then."

"So you're a mom. I don't give a damn." Well, he had, but after talking to Nate he'd realized how stupid he was being.

"Do you remember why we got on so well in the first place?" she asked.

He chuckled. "Because I was trying so damn hard to impress you that you eventually had to talk to me?"

She smiled as she cleared away some of Harrison's things. "We got talking and we both realized we came from money. You'd been used to girls wanting you because of who you were, and I was just happy to be away from home and be a nobody for a while."

"I remember," Chase said. "I liked that there was virtually nothing I had that you didn't already have yourself, so I trusted you."

"Except for a private jet. And a status as one of Texas's most eligible bachelors."

They both laughed then and Chase leaned forward, elbows on the counter as he watched her load the dishwasher. "So what're you trying to tell me?"

"I don't even own this place, Chase. By the time I pay my rent and bills, not to mention the nanny, there's hardly anything left over. Not a penny. So when I say I'm not the same girl anymore, I mean it."

He stared at her. "You need money? Is that it?"

"No!" She slammed the dishwasher shut. "But I'm just a regular person now, Chase. I'm not the heiress from the big ranch. I'm just . . ."

"You're still just Hope to me," he said, standing up straight and not taking his eyes off her for a second. "It wasn't the fact that you had money that made us best buddies."

"I know," she muttered. "I'm just finding life tough right now. It's been a pretty big adjustment, that's all."

"Well, for the record, I don't give a damn whether you have a dollar or a million dollars in your bank account," he told her. "Now are you coming over this weekend or not?"

She glanced at her watch, eyebrows shooting up. "Shit! I have to go, Chase. I'm seriously late."

"I'll let myself out," he said, grinning as she grabbed a lunch box and madly started to rifle through the pantry.

"I'll see you on Monday to go over the results," she told him, voice muffled.

"And I'll let the guys know you'll be joining us for poker night."

Chase didn't wait around to hear her reply. He walked down the hall and headed for his SUV, grinning at how different it was seeing Hope in *mom* mode. The grin faded when he thought about what she'd said, though, knowing that no matter what he'd just told her, she was right. It did bother him just a bit that she didn't have the ranch to inherit any longer. Whatever had gone down, it had affected her big-time, and it was true he'd always trusted her because he'd known she had no motives for wanting to hang out with him. She hadn't ever wanted anything more from him than his friendship.

He steeled his jaw as he thought about Stacey, wishing to hell he could just wipe her from his memory banks. The one woman he'd let close and she'd been the gold digger from hell. Damn cunning she'd been, fooled the lot of them except for Nate, and ever since then he'd preferred one-nighters. The only women he saw more often were ones who knew it was only ever going to be casual.

But Hope was still Hope. She might not have money any longer, but she had a great career. She'd make something of herself no matter what stood in her way, he was certain of it. Just like he was certain that he could trust her. If he couldn't trust Hope, he couldn't trust anyone.

He jumped into his vehicle and grabbed his phone from the center console, texting his sister-in-law. He loved Chloe—having a woman around the ranch had been the best thing that had happened to all of them, even if they were loath to admit it sometimes.

Hey. I have a fifth for next Saturday night. Thought you might like some female company for once.

He dropped his phone back into place and fired up the engine, reversing and heading for home. It wasn't often he didn't wake up at the ranch at daybreak and head straight out to work, and he was ready to roll his sleeves up and get some dirt beneath his hands. Not to mention move a couple hundred cattle beasts.

Come hell or high water, Hope *would* be joining them next Saturday. He'd fucked it up once with her, and he wasn't going to do it again. So they'd had sex. So what? As far as he was concerned, they could do it again and again until it was out of both their systems. And if it led to something more? He groaned and tightened his grip on the steering wheel.

There was no way he wanted to settle down yet, but that didn't mean he'd mind being exclusive if it meant having Hope in his bed. He stared at the road ahead, finding it impossible not to think about her. What he wanted was her hair wrapped around his fist, locking her in place so he could kiss her and tease her, only letting go so he could clamp his hands over her butt and lift her on top of him, to feel the sway of her body as she rocked back and forward.

Fuck! He pumped the accelerator, the truck sliding up a gear. If he kept thinking like that he wouldn't make it through the day, let alone the trip home.

Chapter 6

"Should I ask if you made this?"

Chase laughed and kicked his boots off, walking through the kitchen in his socks and pausing to peer into the dish Nate had just taken the lid off. "Yeah, I knew you were coming home so I slaved over the stove all afternoon." Chase slapped his brother on the back. "Good to have you home."

"If I ever lose Mrs. T . . ."

"You'll die, I know." Chase pulled a couple of beers from the fridge. "Heads up!" He threw one at Nate and grinned when his brother dropped the pot lid to the floor with a clatter to catch the beer.

"You're fucking asking for it," Nate said good-naturedly. "You itching for a fight?"

"I'm itching for something, and it ain't a fight."

Nate grimaced. "You still haven't done the deed, have you?"

"Can we not talk about her like she's just some fucking . . ."

"Sorry, my bad," Nate apologized. "Ryder got all testy like this when Chloe had him all rubbed up the wrong way."

Chase took a long, deep swig of his beer, refusing to take the bait. If Nate was trying to rile him up, then full points to him. "Let's not go there."

"Why? Make you want to punch me?" Nate waggled his eyebrows.

"Makes me want to slam my fist into your face so hard I'd send you straight into that wall over there." Chase cracked up. "So yeah, I guess I'm in a bad way."

Nate held up his beer. "There's something in the water around here, that's all I'm gonna say." He took a sip and nodded at him. "God help me if I catch the bug."

"Unless Faith's around," Chase teased. "You seen her lately?"

Now it was Nate growling, his face darkening as he glowered. "Don't fucking go there. I've told you already that there's nothing going on and there damn well never will be."

"Touché." Chase took another swig of beer and laughed at his brother, so het up just from Faith's name being mentioned. If anyone had it bad it was Nate, although he'd never admit it, not when it came to his friend's little sister. The last time Nate had seen her when they'd all been out he'd been in a foul mood for days.

"How about we agree to disagree, huh?" Nate said, clinking his bottle against Chase's as he passed and headed for the sofa.

"Deal." He needed a break from thinking about Hope. "Although she's coming over next Saturday night and I need you to promise to stay the hell away from her."

"You invited her over for poker? With Chloe?"

Chase raised an eyebrow. "There something wrong with that?"

"Hell, I'd be worried about our darling sister-in-law giving her a grilling, not my inappropriate flirting. Chloe's the one I'd be keeping her away from."

"Yeah? Well, I'll take my chances with Chloe. You?" Chase shook his head. "No fucking way. They'll get along just fine. Anyway, how did you get on in Houston?"

"Good." Nate grunted as he flicked the TV on, surfing through a few channels and leaving it on a football game. "Seems like you're right on trend about your whole organic obsession. I reckon we can get a distribution deal directly with a handful of upmarket butcheries and restaurants. Start relatively small and build from there."

"Music to my ears."

"Mine too. So long as it starts to turn a decent profit." Nate sighed. "More work for me, but diversity is good. It'll be nice to focus on something other than property acquisitions and oil."

"So you starting to think that my actual ranching might be as lucrative as your precious oil one day?" Chase was only kidding, there was no way he could make their cattle as productive as their oil drilling, but the harder he worked to preserve and expand their herds, the less likely Nate would be to want to move away from traditional ranching.

"Your cattle will always have a place here. Ryder's bulls? Now that's something I'm not convinced about yet."

"Don't even bring it up," Chase said. Ever since their little brother had stopped riding rodeo and started breeding bulls, he'd become like a fierce mama bear over them. Whoever said rodeo bulls weren't treated well enough hadn't met Ryder yet. "You reckon he's got a few winners?"

Nate shrugged. "I reckon we underestimate Ryder way too often. He'll knock one out of the park pretty soon, just you wait and see."

"You want to head out tonight?" Chase asked, feeling like a caged lion ready to pace outside of his cage. "I could do with a few stronger drinks."

"Sorry, I'm beat," Nate said, kicking back and putting

his feet up. "Why don't we crack a bottle of Wild Turkey? That strong enough for you? Should go nice with the stew I've got ready for us."

They both laughed. It was kind of a King tradition that everything they ate went well with Wild Turkey or Jack Daniel's.

Chase finished his beer and went to retrieve the whiskey. "Yeah, sure thing. I'll head out later and see Tommy and Carter." He'd flicked his friends a text earlier in the day that he'd try to make it out for at least one beer, shoot a few games of pool. "How's that stew coming along anyway?"

"It was waiting with a note to heat for fifteen, then eat. Want some now?"

Chase nodded and followed Nate to the kitchen, standing back while his brother gave the stew a final stir then dished it up into two bowls.

"So tell me, brother," Nate said, taking the tumbler Chase offered him and nodding to the bowl he'd left on the counter. "What're you thinking about the whole child situation? You decide it wasn't such a big deal after all?"

"I hate to say it, but you were right. The kid's pretty cute, and it doesn't matter that she's a mom."

Nate frowned. "I can hear a *but* coming."

"She's broke."

Nate laughed. "She can hardly be broke. Isn't she the heiress to some massive ranch in Canada? Wasn't that why you two lovebirds couldn't make it happen way back when?"

Chase blew out a breath, sipping his drink and leaning back into the sofa. He wasn't really that hungry after all. "Something happened, but she won't go into details. It seems like her family lost the ranch somehow, something to do with her ex-husband maybe? I dunno. What I do know is that she's only just making do." It was stupid that he was even starting to worry about it, but he was.

Nate slowly sipped his drink, swinging his legs down and sitting up so he was facing Chase. He watched as his brother put down his drink and collected his bowl. "Since when do you care about whether someone has money to their name or not? It's not like any of your good friends are loaded."

Chase grimaced. "Have you forgotten about Stacey? That gold digger was after one thing and one thing only." His brother was right, he didn't give a damn about money under normal circumstances—they'd been raised better than that. But with women it was different. When it came to relationships, they had to be careful. All of them.

"I think you're being a bastard comparing her to that girl," Nate said, raising the bottle and pouring them both another nip. It seemed he wasn't that hungry either, although Nate had at least taken a few mouthfuls. "This is Hope you're talking about. She has her own career, and besides, you know her. She's not some gold digger, Chase. You know I'm always skeptical, but not about her."

Chase sighed. "I know. But it's like as soon as she told me about losing the ranch I became wary. Maybe not at the time because she had me kinda distracted, but the more I think about it? Fuck, I don't know." He shook his head. "We knew we could trust each other in college because of our backgrounds, that we weren't using each other for money or anything else. But then I got to thinking about how she's pushing me away, and that maybe it's some weird reverse psych bullshit . . ."

"I'd go back to worrying about her being a mom," Nate said with a chuckle. "Now that was stupid, but not nearly as stupid as worrying about her not having money or her trying to dupe you. So what if she's going through a rough patch right now? She'll be earning great money in her new job and she'll be back on her feet before you know it. It's not like she's some no-hoper or con artist or anything. She's a highly skilled veterinarian with a great career ahead of her."

Chase knew Nate was right. Now that he'd actually said his thoughts out loud they did sound stupid—insanely douchebag-paranoid kind of stupid. Maybe he was just overthinking the whole thing.

"I think I'm gonna head out. Clear my head a bit and catch up with the guys."

Nate reached for the remote. "I'd join you if I wasn't so tired. Have fun."

Chase knocked back the rest of his drink and left his glass and unfinished dinner in the sink on the way past, heading for the stairs to pull on a fresh pair of jeans and a shirt. His phone buzzed in his pocket and he fished it out, expecting it to be Tommy wondering where the hell he was. He glanced at the screen. *Wrong.* It was Ryder. He answered at the same time as he dropped to the top step to sit. "Hey."

"You guys up?"

Chase glanced at his watch. "It's not even ten yet. Of course we're up."

"You might want to sit down."

"Who died?" Chase's heart starting racing and he jumped up and ran down the stairs. "Is it Granddad? Has something happened?" He hadn't visited the hospital today and . . .

"It's Chloe."

Chase slowed down, dropping into a chair. Nate hadn't moved, but he did take his feet off the coffee table and lean forward when Chase gestured at him.

"It's Ryder," Chase told Nate in a low voice, hand over his phone. "Is everything okay?" he asked.

"Do I fucking sound okay?" Ryder hissed, his voice low like he didn't want anyone to hear him.

Chase hit speaker and put his phone on the table, exchanging looks with Nate.

"She's pregnant," Ryder said in a low voice. "I'm gonna be a dad."

Chase glanced back up at Nate and burst out laughing at the same time as Nate's face broke out in a grin. "Damn, Ryder. I thought you were about to tell me she'd been in a car crash or something."

"Don't sound so terrified, brother," Nate called out. "Congrats."

"Yeah, awesome news," Chase said, thrilled for his little brother.

"Did you guys hear me? I'm going to be a dad. I can't be a dad," Ryder muttered, sounding like he was about to tear his own hair out. "I mean, I . . ."

"You're scared, that's all. But you're gonna be a great dad," Nate said. "Calm the fuck down and breathe."

Chase scooped up his phone, rising to reach for the whiskey bottle. "You want to come over and celebrate?"

"Chloe's in the bathroom. I gotta go," Ryder said. "She'll kill me if she finds out I've ruined the surprise. She wants to tell you guys in a couple of weeks once we've had the first ultrasound."

Chase and Nate laughed again. "If anyone would make a great dad it'd be you. You and Chloe will be awesome. And don't worry, we won't say a thing."

"I know, it's just . . ." Ryder's voice trailed off. "I'm shit scared, that's all."

Before Chase had time to answer, Ryder clicked off and he was left staring at a black screen. When he did glance up, Nate was still grinning.

"You know I'm gonna be the favorite uncle, right?"

Chase knocked back his shot and slammed the glass

down on the table in front of him. "Oh, it's on, *brother*. There's only going to be one favorite, and that'll be me."

They both laughed and Chase got up and headed for the sofa, crashing into his favorite worn leather one. Screw going out, he couldn't be bothered making the effort, not tonight. He sent Tommy a text that said he'd catch them next time.

"Make it something good. I need the distraction," he muttered.

"Maybe we should go out," Nate suggested.

"Nah. I'm good here."

Chase had no idea what was going on, how their baby brother had ended up married with a baby on the way, but he was happy for him. Chloe was a great girl and they deserved to be happy. But a dad? It sure as hell wasn't something he was ready for, not anytime soon.

The idea that Hope had a child was enough for him to deal with.

Chapter 7

"Stop staring at me."

"I can't."

Hope burst out laughing. "If you don't I'll give you a black eye."

He came closer, his voice lower this time. "I don't believe you."

She held up her fist and grinned. "I might." He'd been watching her too long, staring at her from the other side of the bar, and she wanted to wipe the all-women-love-me look off his face.

"How about I buy you a drink?"

"I'm not going home with you."

She received a wink in reply, but instead of giving him what he wanted she made a sad face and leaned over to pat his arm. "Poor baby. Haven't you ever had a girl say no to you before?"

"No," he replied, pulling out his wallet.

"I'll have a drink with you if we buy our own," she finally said, not immune to how handsome the guy was even if she had no intention of sleeping with him. She'd seen him around, and watched him take home way too *many girls, and she wasn't going to become a notch in his belt.*

"Darlin', I think you should give me a chance."

She refused to be seduced by his silky drawl. "Darlin' "—imitating him with a fake southern drawl—"this is me giving you a chance."

He burst out laughing, pushing away from the bar and walking back a few steps. Hope wondered if she'd been too rude, too standoffish, but he spun around, then walked straight back toward her and held out his hand.

"Let's start over," he said, a glint in his eye telling her he could be a hell of a lot of fun. "I'm Chase King. Mind if I sit here?"

She took his hand and shook it. "Hope," she replied. "And sure, pull up a chair."

They smiled at each other, ordered their drinks, and started talking. Chase had her laughing so hard within minutes that her sides felt like they were going to split.

"You do know that I'm still not going to sleep with you, right?"

He grinned. "You know what? I actually don't care." Chase winked. "I mean, don't get me wrong, I'd love to rip your clothes off, but you're fun to hang out with. So if drinking and talking is all I get, so be it."

Hope sipped her drink, trying to think of something witty to say and failing. He was dangerous, and saying no to him wasn't easy, but she'd already had more fun tonight than she'd had all semester.

"You like guitar?" he asked, one eyebrow arched.

"Maybe. Why?"

He knocked back the rest of his drink, winked, then headed toward the stage. The band was taking a break and his grin was wicked when he glanced back at her. She followed, watching him, wondering what the hell he was about to do.

"I'm gonna play guitar and sing you a song."
She shook her head. *"No way. Get back down here."*
"Darlin', when I decide something, there ain't no one who can change my mind."

"Hey, gorgeous."

Hope glanced up, memories interrupted as the man she was thinking about appeared in front of her. She'd once thought she was immune to Chase's charm, but now she knew that was a lie. His big frame was braced against the entrance to the barn, shoulder pushed into the door-jamb, arms folded firmly across his chest. Somehow he managed to look casual as hell, like he didn't have a care in the world, while at the same time looking alpha enough that she almost wanted to run in the other direction. It was like she was a flight animal trying to tango with a predator, her instincts all messed up.

"Hey, Chase."

Hope held her head high as she strode toward him, meeting his gaze head on. She wasn't prey, she was just as much the predator as he was. Or at least that's what she needed to tell herself. She was a professional woman here to complete a job. So what if her current client happened to be a hot-as-hell guy from her past? She gulped. Trouble was, he wasn't just any guy, he was Chase fricking King.

She was only a couple of feet away from him and he still hadn't moved.

"Outta my way, King." What she needed was to act like they were still back in college. She'd never had a problem dealing with him then.

"Or what?" His wolfish grin sent a lick of anticipation through her body that made it almost impossible not to step up into him and show him exactly what she wanted to do to him.

Hope swallowed, returning his trick of one arched

eyebrow, something she'd practiced in college so she could tease him if he ever tried to pull a move. "Or I'll make you," she said, remembering just how fun it was to be feisty back to a man who was used to women dropping around him like flies.

"And how you gonna do that?" Chase was loving every second of this, she could tell. His grin had turned into a full dimple-bearing smile, the kind that was capable of making her insides turn to mush.

"It just so happens I have a few good tools in here," she said, trying not to grin as she held up her box of work implements. "I don't always work on heifers, you know. Sometimes I'm called out to do things like, oh, I don't know, castrate bulls."

Chase's stare hardened. "Is that the best you've got?"

"No," she said, one hand on her hip. "I've also got a great handheld electric cattle prod."

Chase just continued to stare at her, still not moving. She responded by flicking the clasp to open her kit.

"Hey, if you're prepared to take a chance . . ." she started.

He grunted and moved to the side, only just enough so that she could squeeze past. She put her kit in front of her and turned sideways to maneuver her way past, keeping her eyes slightly downcast. But it wouldn't have mattered which way she was looking when Chase's hand caught her arm. Her instant reaction was to raise her chin, which only made her eyes collide with Chase's.

"You know what I'm thinking?" Chase said, his voice sounding like it had been dragged over gravel.

"What?" she forced out.

"That it would be pretty unusual for a vet specializing in artificial insemination to carry anything related to castration."

Damn. The handsome rancher was smarter than she'd

given him credit for. She didn't say a word, just focused on breathing. It had been bad enough before they'd gotten all hot and heavy in his truck, but now she knew exactly what she was missing out on. Her body was on high alert, nipples like hard nubs aching to be pressed against his hard chest.

"Gotcha," he whispered.

Hope cleared her throat and made a quick move sideways, desperate to put some distance between them. Where had the easygoing Chase from the other morning gone?

"I've got work to do," she told him, forcing her voice to cooperate and sound businesslike. "And I'm only here for a few hours."

"So stay longer," he said, following her.

"I've gotta do what I'm told these days, Chase. Keeping the wolf from my door and all that." She grimaced when the smile disappeared from his face, replaced by a more serious straight line. Being around him was like existing in a fantasy world—when in fact being around him should be reminding her of everything she'd done wrong. If she'd only told Chase the truth and come back to Texas with him instead of going home, she'd never have married her husband and ended up without her ranch.

"Come on then," he eventually said, pointing toward his office. "How about we go over those results and then you tell me what you need."

It felt like a truce of sorts, but she was smart enough to know that Chase would always be one step ahead of her when he wanted something.

Chase was pissed off. He hadn't seen Hope since Friday morning at her place, and now that she was here . . . he'd just expected things to go differently. And he sure as hell wasn't used to women doing everything in their power to steer clear of him. What he needed to do was stop laying it on so thick, give her some breathing space.

"So how did all the bloodwork come back?"

"Great. Sorry it's taken me so long to get back here," Hope replied, setting her things down and taking an iPad from her vet kit. "I have them all on here to go over with you. I don't usually show clients but I figured you'd actually know what you were reading."

He nodded, moving closer so he could see the screen over her shoulder. Chase reached out to tilt it forward a little so he could see it better, his fingers brushing across hers. It had been unintentional, but he heard her sharp intake of breath at the same time as her body stiffened. If he shuffled forward the smallest of steps his chest would be pressed to her back, but he didn't. Instead he slowly removed his hand and stood still.

Hope didn't miss a beat, launching straight into a dialogue about the blood results, talking fertility and timelines. If he hadn't been so damn interested in what they were doing he would have found it impossible to concentrate, but he ground his jaw shut tight and listened, making all the right noises so she knew he was paying attention.

When she finished she moved sideways and glanced up at him. "So we're in agreement that they're all ready to be inseminated?"

"Your practice was pretty clear that they thought you were the best, so I'm taking a backseat," he told her. "I trust your judgment."

He thought he saw a flicker in her gaze, noticed that either what he'd said or something else had rattled her. Or maybe he was just overthinking everything to do with his gorgeous vet.

"So have you been monitoring them to see if they're

in estrus? I'd hate to miss this cycle and have to wait another three weeks until the next."

"No signs yet, but I've been monitoring them a while to work out their cycles, ever since I decided to import the sperm. I think we're a few days away at least."

"You know, you could always train to be an AI tech. It wouldn't take much, then you could do all this yourself. I know you did that degree so you could manage everything to do with the livestock here yourself."

"But that's why I have you," he quipped, not letting her think for a second that he was going to let her walk away. "I called in the big guns to make sure this went off without a hitch."

"Well, remember to call me the minute you see any signs. I want the herd kept close to the pens, so get ready to have them in the squeeze chute. I don't want to worry about the weather, and I want to make it as stress-free as possible for them, too." She blew out a breath. "You might think I'm crazy, but I firmly believe that the less stress the animals experience, the more likely they are to end up in calf. I treat them well, make sure they're calm, and the results usually speak for themselves, bring my percentages up above most of my peers'."

Chase folded his arms across his chest. "Any particular music you want me to play for them? Classical, or a little Beyoncé-style girl power perhaps?"

She positively glowered at him. "I knew you'd be an idiot when I told you that."

"I'm just being a douchebag. You're probably right about the whole stress thing."

"Oh, I'm right," she said, hands on her hips.

Damn, she looks good angry. Chase held up his hands, trying not to laugh. She'd always been fun to tease and it seemed that some things never changed.

"Have you thought any more about Saturday night?" he asked, edging closer as she backed away. Hope seemed more interested in getting outside than staying trapped in the office with him.

"Uh, not really," she said. "I meant to ask if you'd discussed what we're doing with your foreman? It might be good to have him prepped to help if we need another set of hands."

Chase stood back and let her gather her things. She was acting weird, all in a flutter over something. But he sure as hell wasn't going to let her wriggle out of answering him about poker night.

"You let me worry about keeping Randy informed," Chase told her. "Now back to Saturday night. I've already told my sister-in-law and she's pretty excited about having some female company." It was only half a life—Chloe hadn't said otherwise, and she was probably sick to death of having to hang out with the three of them anyway.

"I don't like getting a sitter for Harrison, so I think I'll have to say . . ."

"You're worried about Harrison? Hell, the more the merrier. Bring the kid with you, I thought I told you that already?" He *knew* he'd already told her that. "I'm looking forward to hanging out with the little man."

Hope looked like she was wavering, finding it hard to say no to him.

"You're sure?" she asked, looking as uncertain as he suddenly felt.

"Positive." Chase grinned at her. "We'll order in pizza, have a few beers, make sure we've got some lemonade or something for Harris. It'll be fun."

He didn't give a crap whether she was a mom or penniless anymore. He wanted her and this time around he wasn't scared to make it clear.

"And your brothers won't mind?" Hope asked, still looking like she wasn't convinced about the whole thing.

"Hey, your kid probably misses your ranch like hell, right?"

Hope shrugged, but he could see her smile was strained. *She* no doubt missed it like hell herself, so having to console her son, who'd lost both his grandparents and the home he loved, wouldn't be easy.

"He can have some fun, play around, do whatever he wants. And if you want to drink then you can both crash here for the night."

Hope's face went from uncertain to alarmed. "I, uh, Chase, I'm not sure how to say this but I'd never let my son see me with another man. It's just . . ."

"Gotcha," he said, interrupting her to put her out of her misery. "There's no need to explain. I just meant that we've got a lot of space so if you want to stay, don't over-think it." A platonic sleepover hadn't been exactly what he'd had planned, but he'd agree to anything right now if it meant getting her to commit to coming over.

"Thanks," she muttered.

"We tend to drink a lot, talk a lot of shit, and Chloe always beats the pants off us." He laughed. "Sometimes literally."

Hope collected her gear and nodded toward the door. He followed, giving her a little distance.

"I'm not into any kinky strip poker," she said, "just to make that crystal clear."

"That's just Chloe's way of teaching us a lesson when we think we can beat her," Chase said with a chuckle. "I promise you won't see any of us naked around the poker table." Naked in his bedroom maybe, but not in the living room. "When Ryder met Chloe, she turned out to be an ace player, and she's still teaching us a few lessons."

"Okay. So long as it's PG rated, we'll come. Harrison will be super excited."

"He seems like a good kid. Super protective of his mom."

"He is. It's been hard on him, the whole moving away and divorce."

"He misses his dad?"

Hope raised her eyes, stared at him like she could see straight into him. "He misses a lot of things."

Chase watched her, waited for her to elaborate, but she didn't.

"So Saturday night," he said. "Come over early, just whenever. We'll kick off about seven with pizza and then poker once we've had a few drinks."

"Sounds good. Call me before then if you think the girls are ready though, okay? We need to time this perfectly to get results."

"Hey, Hope," Chase said, reaching out and catching her hand.

She spun around, face flushed, lips parted as she stared up at him. Every part of him was on high alert, wanting to crush those goddamn pillowy lips to his, shove her up against the wall and have his wicked way with her, but instead he fought his instincts and kept a soft hold on her hand, not pushing her.

"You sure you don't want to stay for a while? I'd love to show you around."

She hesitated, glanced at her wristwatch. "I have to be somewhere in about an hour."

"Sounds like just enough time for us to grab some lunch and go for a walk." Chase stood his ground, boots locked into place on the concrete floor as he watched her face.

"Okay, that'd be nice. I'll just put my stuff in the truck so I don't forget anything."

Chase slowly released her hand and watched as she walked away from him. There was something different about Hope, like she was holding something back, more reserved than she'd used to be. Or maybe she was just confused about whatever the hell was going on between them. For God's sake, she'd lost her ranch, the parents he knew she'd adored and been incredibly close to, and left her husband—what the hell did he expect? Of course she was wary, and she had every right to be. Especially when it came to men.

"Problems with the insemination?"

Chase tore his eyes from Hope when his foreman spoke from behind him. "Hey, Randy. We're all good here, how about you?" He nodded to one of the younger ranch hands standing beside him.

Randy shrugged. "I think one of Ryder's new bulls is a little pissed off with the world, but other than that everything's fine."

"Great. Hope's just been going over the latest results with me."

"The girls all in good shape?"

"For sure." Chase turned back to see Hope shutting her driver's door and heading back in his direction, wiping her palms down over her jeans, eyes downcast. "The sperm's been checked and it's all good to go. Hope tested the sample they sent and we have the rest of the straws arriving by courier in the morning. We're gonna have the best goddamn breeding program in the state by the end of the year."

"Sounds good, boss. Let me know if there's anything I can do to help."

"Thanks. And shout out if there's anything you need me to look at. I'll be around for the next couple of hours before I head down to ride the boundary and check the fencing."

"Hey, Randy."

The foreman tipped his hat as Hope passed him. "Mornin'."

"Come on, Hope. Let's go by the house and grab something to eat, then we can go for a wander and I'll show you what I've been working on these last few years."

Hope needed her head checked. She'd already decided to try to distance herself from Chase, to come on-site, do her job, then get the hell out of dodge. And then he'd gone and asked her to hang around *and* come over on Saturday night, and her resolve had just blown straight past her in the wind. What she needed was to just keep their conversation nice and neutral. Instead of dredging up the past and second-guessing herself over the secret she'd kept from him these past five years.

"You haven't talked about your granddad."

Chase glanced at her as they walked. "We've had a rough time with him lately. Seeing his health decline has been tough."

"It's never easy seeing them fade away in front of you." When her dad had died, it had been like a knife stuck into her heart, twisting every hour and making the pain even worse. Growing up an only child she'd spent so much time with her parents, riding up in front of her dad in the saddle since she was tiny, helping her mom tend to orphaned animals and work in the garden. It had been an idyllic childhood and she'd adored her parents until the end.

"You're speaking from experience?" Chase's gaze struck a chord within her, his dark eyes full of such intensity it sent a shiver down her body.

She hadn't told him exactly what had happened, how she'd lost her folks, because talking about it still didn't come easy to her. "Your granddad was always like a father to you, and I know what it was like losing my dad to an illness. It's like your heart being ripped clear from your chest, over and over again." Tears pricked her eyes. "Just promise me that you've told him how much you love him. Don't leave anything unsaid. I watched my dad get sicker and sicker, but I still left some things too late."

Chase's arm was around her in seconds, slung across her shoulders as he pulled her in tight. It was impossible to resist him when they were close like this, when every single part of him seemed to envelop her. His scent was a heady mix of cologne and pure, hot male—not sweaty, just a musky smell that was all his. And the feel of being against him was something she'd never forgotten. Chase had been the guy who made her feel safe when they'd been out together, the man who'd have been able to take out any threat with his bare fists. She was no helpless female, but that didn't mean she didn't appreciate the kind of guy who could protect her in a dark alleyway at night. No one would ever have guessed he was a trust fund kid, because he got along with everyone he met no matter where they were from or what their background. There was nothing that had ever seemed to intimidate him, either. He dealt with his own shit, no matter what.

"We're not big on feelings, but we've always told Granddad we love him. That's one regret I won't have."

Hope nodded, giving in to the feeling of Chase against her, leaning into his frame. She was just short enough to tuck in under his shoulder, bumping against him as they walked. If she didn't feel so guilty about what had happened between them all those years ago, she probably wouldn't have been so reluctant to connect when he was making his thoughts so damn obvious.

"You remember when I met your dad that first time? I was sprawled out on the bed in your dorm, you were down the hall in the shower, and by the time you came back he was giving me an absolute grilling. Your old man was all ready to march down to security and have me thrown off campus. I thought he was gonna knock me out."

She grabbed Chase's arm as they walked, howling with laughter at the memory. "Oh my God, that's right! My mom walked in on him about to pin you against the wall."

"I tell you, he was ready to have me whipped for being in his baby girl's room. And that was one fight that I was not going to be a part of."

"Hey, I was his only daughter. What did you expect?"

"What did I expect?" Chase chuckled, drawing her even closer and laughing into her hair, a too-familiar gesture that took her straight back in time. "If I'd spent the night with you, it would have been worth it. But I'd been a fucking monk where you were concerned and I was still shitting myself."

Hope had tears in her eyes again, only this time they were tears of happiness. "Don't act like you were Mr. Fricking Innocent," she joked. "You would have been in my panties in a flash if I'd shown you any interest in that department."

"Damn straight! But the fact is that I didn't, and I still wanted to hang out with you all the time."

She sighed, shaking her head. "So tell me about your granddad. What's actually happening with him?" She still hadn't told him about her mom, about how one minute she'd been fine and the next she was diagnosed with cancer and gone within a few months. That wound was still too raw.

"He's going through radiation again, and it's fucked him. He's still this tall man, but he's not imposing anymore, you know? He's lost so much weight."

"Does he still live here? When he's not having treatment, I mean?" She could tell how hard it was for Chase, talking about the man who'd raised him, his easygoing smile long gone.

"When he can be home he's here, with a live-in nurse, but he's been staying at the hospital for a while now. Hopefully we'll have him back soon, but I know damn well that it's probably wishful thinking on my part." He blew out a breath. "I think the last time he was really himself was when Ryder brought Chloe back here when they were first together. It was like everything was back to normal, him having a whiskey and laughing, but that seems like a lifetime ago now."

"Hey, if we don't have faith, what are we left with?"

Chase sighed. His body moved against hers and suddenly he pulled away. "Come on, let's grab that something to eat."

She followed him into the house, taking her boots off when he did and walking across the polished timber floor in her socks. She might get away with wearing skinny jeans and cute shirts despite her profession, but her socks and boots were the same as every other rancher's and vet's. She wiggled her toes when Chase looked over at her, flashing her his dimple but not saying a word.

"This place is amazing."

She'd never been inside the house, and it was stunning. Different from her family's home, but similar in plenty of ways, too. The photos that crammed the hallstand showed the three boys at every age, and as she bent to take a closer look she could see that in most of them they were either riding horses or climbing trees—never sitting still. She moved across to look at another set of photos, only this time she gasped.

"You okay?" Chase called out.

Hope straightened and hurried after Chase. "Me? I'm fine. Just looking at how cute you used to be." Her heart was racing. Looking at those toddler photos had been like looking at pictures of her son. Guilt hit her like a fist to the gut.

"As opposed to how I look now?"

"Don't go fishing for compliments. It's doesn't suit you."

Hope peeked into the kitchen when Chase disappeared, wondering who'd spoken. A lady with gray hair pulled back into a bun was waving a finger at Chase and it soothed the panic inside of her to see him being told off.

"Hope, meet Mrs. T. As in the one woman in the world who can keep us boys all in line."

"Nice to meet you, Hope."

"You too. And I sure don't envy you having to keep this guy in order."

Hope shook hands with the older woman, who smiled as she stood with her hands on her hip, apron covering her front. There was a softness about her that was appealing, that made the kitchen seem warm and welcoming, but she was obviously no-nonsense, too, where the boys were concerned anyway.

"Let me tell you, they were little rascals when they were young. It's the reason I've got all this darn gray hair."

They all laughed and Hope relaxed. She'd overreacted before, that was all. Her secret was safe. If Chase had so much as suspected something when he'd met Harrison she'd sure as hell know about it by now.

She ran a tongue over dry lips, pleased that her heart had stopped racing. "I'm raising a little rascal myself," she told her. "He's four years old and already making me turn gray."

"We just need to grab some lunch on the go," Chase said, dropping a hand on Mrs. T's shoulder as he passed, his smile as warm as the gesture. "Enough for two?"

"There's always enough for two," she said with a chuckle. "Especially for a lovely lady like this one. Besides, I'm not expecting Nate back for a bit."

Hope smiled her thanks and was about to say something when a deep, commanding voice boomed down the hall to them.

"Nate won't what?"

Chase groaned, and she glanced at him before turning to see Chase's older brother walk into the kitchen. He was the spitting image of Chase, just as tall and with unruly black hair, although he seemed slightly bigger if that was even possible. Chase was lean and muscled from working on the ranch every day, but his brother looked like he spent time in the gym. He also looked like he could chew up and spit out anything that got in his way.

She instinctively moved a little closer to Chase. *Better the devil you know than the one you don't.*

"Oh, hey." His brother's face broke out in a big smile, his eyes softening when he saw her. He came over and held out his hand. "You must be Hope."

"And you must be Nate," she replied, shaking hands with him. His grip was firm but not too hard and he was still smiling, his eyes not leaving hers for a second. Someone had sure taught the King boys about holding eye contact, and she bet every woman they ever came across appreciated it.

"I think we met way back," he said, leaning against the counter as he chatted with her. "Back when Chase was . . ."

"Okay, so we're off now," Chase interrupted, glaring at his brother. Hope glanced at Mrs. T and saw she was struggling not to laugh, turning her back to chuckle as she finished up with whatever she was making.

"Hey, I was just getting to know Hope," Nate protested. "You know I have a ton of questions about the AI work she's doing here."

"Fire away," Hope said, deciding that it would be way easier to spend the next thirty minutes with the eldest King brother than be alone with Chase. He was easy to talk to and even though he was one of the most gorgeous damn men she'd ever met, it seemed that only Chase had the ability to twist her all up in knots.

"You can talk Saturday night, isn't that right, Hope?"

She tensed as Chase's hand brushed hers as he spoke, their fingers linking before she had a chance to protest. His palm was warm to hers, fingers firm as they locked on either side of her digits.

"Don't tell me you actually said yes to poker night?" Nate's face broke out in an even bigger grin as he pushed off from the counter and reached for an apple. "You can always change your mind, we won't hold it against you."

"I'm sure it'll be fun. Unless you guys are scared of another girl joining the table?" she asked innocently.

Now it was Chase howling with laughter. "Ouch! Yeah, that's our Nate, hates that Chloe can beat his ass every goddamn time and doesn't want another woman to take him down."

"Hey, she's a professional fucking player," Nate growled. "There ain't a man alive who'd find it easy to beat Chloe."

"You're serious?" Hope wasn't sure what they were talking about or if it was some kind of an inside joke.

"Language," Mrs. T muttered from behind them.

The boys looked vaguely guilty but continued on ribbing each other.

"Chloe is the master poker player," Chase explained, still keeping his grip on her hand. "Nate's pissed because he can't screw with her head and beat her *or* flirt with her."

"It's not for lack of trying." Nate made a face. "Besides, my problem is that she has no fucking tell. *None.* It's just not natural."

"Yeah, well, she settled a pretty major gambling debt of Ryder's by being her amazing goddamn self, and even though she showed us all her tricks when we were in

Vegas, we're still nowhere close to beating her." Chase grinned. "We love her like a sister, but we still hate that we'll never be able to win."

"And yet you keep on playing?" Hope asked dryly. "Sounds to me like you boys are just sore losers. Either that or you like being whipped."

"Hell yes," Chase replied, laughter shining in his eyes as he met her gaze. "We're not used to losing and it damn well hurts."

"Especially to a woman," Nate muttered. Then he held up his hands, looking guilty. "Sorry, that came out all wrong. I just . . ."

"Want a shovel?" Chase joked. "'Cause that hole you're digging is just getting bigger and bigger."

Nate grimaced but Hope just laughed. "I'm not offended. It's fine. You're used to winning and you're sore losers. I get it."

"For the record, I'm all for girl power. You know, Beyoncé put a ring on it and all that."

"Oh my God." They both raised their left brows at her when she cursed, as alike as twins. "I thought only Chase could be such a complete douchebag, but now I know who he learned it from."

"I deserved that," Nate said, taking a bite of his apple. "Kick me in the balls and leave me on the ground awhile as punishment."

Chase nudged her in the side. "Come on. Now that we've wasted time on Nate, we're outta here." He let go of her hand, leaving her to stand facing Nate on her own and trying not to laugh at the almost embarrassed expression on his face. "Thanks for lunch, Mrs. T."

"Oh yeah, thanks for lunch," Hope called out, remembering her manners. When she was around Chase she seemed to forget everything else.

Hope walked out of the kitchen with Chase and headed

for the front door again to retrieve their boots. She took the sandwich he passed her, feeling like a kid again. It was times like this that she had to remind herself she was a grown woman—a mom and a specialist veterinarian—because so often she went straight back to feeling like a college kid in her early twenties again. Time had flown, and she'd had to grow up fast.

"I think Nate's already looking forward to Saturday night."

"Ha-ha, I doubt it." Hope straightened after pulling her boots on and unwrapped her sandwich. She glanced at the filling before taking a bite.

"Mrs. T's famous turkey and homemade cranberry chutney," Chase told her as if he'd read her mind. "We always tell her we'll have everything, but hold the lettuce and tomato and anything else that resembles a vegetable."

She took a bite. "Yum," she murmured. "Tastes like home." Her mom had always been amazing in the kitchen, only Hope hadn't inherited her skills despite all the hours she'd spent leaning on the counter waiting for cookies to come out of the oven. "My mom made everything from scratch. We had jars of sauce, pickles, and jams everywhere in our kitchen."

"We were pretty lucky with Mrs. T. She was like a mom to us in plenty of ways. Still is, I guess. She's the only one you'll ever hear us saying *sorry ma'am* too. But back to Nate, he's a big softy. Don't let him get to you."

Hope finished chewing, hand over her mouth before she spoke. "He didn't offend me, if that's what you're worried about. He's just like you. I get it. Some men like to win, and some men *really* like to win when it comes to showing off to women."

"We're nothing alike," Chase insisted, looking genuinely surprised.

Hope shook her head as they walked. "Wrong. You're

everything alike, trust me. Talking to him was just like being with a slightly bigger version of you."

"Damn, you think he's bigger than me?" Chase pulled a serious face before laughing. "But yeah, you're right. He's like the larger, badder version of me. Only a *smidge* taller though, I'll have you know."

Oh, you're plenty bad enough. And big enough. She bit her lower lip, keeping her thoughts to herself. Any badder and she'd be a mess.

"So what are we looking at?" she asked. If there was one thing she knew, it was that keeping the conversation away from dangerous territory was the safest bet between them.

"Nothing. Everything." He turned toward her, walking backward, that damn, captivating smile of his hitting her head on.

"So this was just a ploy to get me alone?" So much for keeping the conversation neutral.

"Hey, it's not every day I get to spend time with a beautiful woman."

"Bullshit," she muttered, taking another bite of her sandwich even though her appetite had long disappeared.

"Well, during work hours," he corrected, his dimple a flash of sexiness as he shrugged. "It's just nice seeing you again. Is that so wrong?"

"So what made you want to go organic?"

He stared at her, his lips twisting like he was planning on saying something smartass, but thought better of it. He spun back around so he was walking beside her rather than looking back at her. "You mean besides organic being the future of ranching?"

"Yes, smartass, besides that," she said dryly.

"Hey, it took me a long time to convince Nate that this was a good idea. Sorry if I'm a little smug now that it's all coming together."

"Your cows aren't in calf yet," Hope reminded him.

"Yeah, but I have the best in the business working with me. What could go wrong now?"

"Chase," she cautioned, not wanting him to jinx what they were working on.

His chuckle was more of a deliciously deep rumble than a laugh. "Nothing's gonna go wrong. You always were the worrier."

She laughed incredulously. "Are you kidding me? If it had been up to you, you'd have drunk your weight in Jack Daniel's each semester."

He leaned in close to her, slinging his arm across her shoulders again. The familiarity of his gesture made her uncomfortable, made her body tense. Goose pimples rippled across every inch of her skin when his warm breath touched her face.

"Thank you," he whispered, before pressing a lingering kiss to her cheek. "All these years, I've never said thank you. So there it is."

"You're welcome," Hope spluttered. What the hell was going on? One minute they were into each other, then they were back to friends, and now he was . . . She blew out a breath as she extracted herself from Chase's arm, slipping away to force his arm to drop down.

"You can take full credit for keeping my grades up. Without you I'd have been a waste of space."

"Says the guy who studied as little as possible and still managed straight As." Hope had to fight the urge to roll her eyes. She'd worked her ass off right through college, determined to make her own way in the world, and Chase had been on cruise control and still managed to ace everything. Although she knew that deep down his determination to succeed had equaled hers, he just didn't like to show it. "I reckon you would have coasted through without me anyway."

"Not a chance," he insisted, stopping when they came to a post-and-rail fence that bordered a huge field that stretched all the way down the valley. The feed was plentiful and she could see a few horses grazing, their heads dipped into the long grass. "I was so damn determined to impress you, and it was pretty obvious from the start that my bank account and my good looks weren't gonna cut it."

"So modest," she quipped. "Seriously, Chase, could your head get any bigger?"

He shrugged, clearly not embarrassed in the least. "Hey, I'm just sayin'. Other girls made a play for me without any effort on my part, and you just gave me this look." He paused, laughing. "*That* look."

"What look?" She leaned on the same section of post-and-rail fence that he was propped against, only a little farther down so she wasn't close enough for him to try to touch her.

Chase's eyes were crinkled at the corners as he squinted into the sun, making him look older but even more damn gorgeous, if that was possible. He held up his hand to shield his face from the sun, golden-tanned forearm commanding her attention, reminding her what he'd looked like buck naked, how amazing that skin of his had looked stretched over muscle beneath her on the sheets of a motel bed.

"That look that told me in one quick sweep that I was being a dickhead and needed to pull my head in," he told her. "The unimpressed stare that made me want to be a better man just to prove myself to you. Because I only cared about one person's opinion back then, and that person was you."

Her heart was starting its too-fast beat again, thumping away in her chest like mad. "All that in just one look?" She tried to keep her voice light-hearted, but she could hear the wobble in it, hoped she was at least fooling him even if she wasn't fooling herself. They'd meant a lot to each other, and maybe they still did, which made what she'd done, or what she hadn't done where Chase was concerned, so much worse.

"Yeah. All that." His voice was raspy, toe-curlingly deep.

"What do you want from me?" Hope asked, forcing her voice to comply with her thoughts, needing to ask the question.

"Isn't it obvious?" Chase's expression had turned from friendly to determined, the glint in his eyes telling her she was about to find out *exactly* what he wanted from her. "I want you."

Hope gulped, focused on each breath, not daring to look away. Like being confronted with a predator, she had that feeling that she couldn't back down, had to stay strong and show that she was just as capable of staring back at him as he was her.

"Chase . . ."

"No, hear me out, Hope," Chase said, leaning deeper over the railings, his dimpled smile like a touch straight to her heart, teasing her, making her body betray her. "What we did that night, it wasn't just some meaningless fun and I'd be lying if I said I didn't want a rematch. I think I made that clear the other night."

She was speechless. Absolutely, utterly speechless. Hope kept her jaw clenched tight. It wasn't that she didn't feel the same, but . . .

"You want to hang out as friends, well, fine, but I want to lay it all out so you know how I feel." Chase pushed back off the fence and moved toward her, his frame blocking out everything else when she turned to him, stared up into dark eyes that seemed to warm every inch of her. He raised his hand, fingers curling gently around her chin as he tilted her face up, eyes searching hers. "You change your mind about wanting something more, I'm here."

Hope was transfixed, couldn't take her eyes off the man so confidently telling her exactly what he wanted. Part of her wanted to just scream *yes*, but the more dominant side of her was immobile, knowing it was all wrong. Sober, it was obvious that she needed to steer clear of Chase romantically; the other night it had been the alcohol talking, or at least that's what she was telling herself.

"So what do you say?" Chase's husky voice commanded her attention, her gaze falling to his full lips as he spoke. It would only take a second to close the distance between them, to remind herself what it was like having that mouth moving in time with hers, but she resisted.

"I say, I'll think about it," she told him, her voice barely a whisper. If she went there with Chase, there was no way she could keep her secret, would have to come clean, and then what? He'd hate her and do what she'd always feared—want to share custody of her son, make her stay in Texas when her heart was still in Canada, with the land she was desperate to buy back one day.

"That's all I needed to hear." He grinned, fooled her into thinking he was about to pull away. She took a deep breath at the same moment his mouth closed over hers, so softly all she could do was gasp against him as he kissed her tenderly, his hand resting on the back of her head, palm against her hair.

Hope was powerless to pull away, even though she tried. The soft push and pull of his mouth on hers, the warmth of his skin, the hard planes of his body as she leaned into him—it was too good, too mesmerizing to say no to.

A loud ringing ruined the moment, broke the connection between them. It was Chase who pulled back first, his lips moving slowly away from hers, hand running the length of her hair and then skimming down her back before trailing away. Hope was numb, a chill running through her body like a gentle shudder, cold when his body left hers.

"And the phone does it again." Chase chuckled. "I think it's yours."

She blinked, broke the trance she was in, and reached for her back pocket, plucking out her phone. "Shit." She cleared her throat and took a second before answering. It was her boss.

She glanced up at Chase and wished she hadn't, not with the heat in his gaze that spelled out every kind of trouble. He wanted her and she wanted him. The only difference was that he'd come out and said it and she was still trying to deny it, even if her body had just betrayed her.

Hope focused on what her boss was saying, gazed out at the trees in the distance as she answered his questions and promised to hit the road straightaway to see a client in trouble. When she hung up, she was straight back into work mode.

"I have to go," she announced, slipping the phone back into her pocket.

Chase grabbed her hand, stroked his thumb across her palm. "Saturday night?"

She nodded, wondering what the hell she was doing but knowing it was going to happen regardless. There was no way she wasn't coming over for poker night, even if the sensible thing would have been running a mile in the opposite direction. She was in too deep to just walk away now, at least until her work on the ranch was done. *Then* she could run for the hills.

"Yeah," she muttered, taking a step back so that he eventually had to release her hand. "Yeah, I'll be here. But you call me before then if you notice any signs, okay?"

Chase nodded. "Hey, is everything all right? I mean, that wasn't about your son, was it?"

She smiled. "No. If it was about Harrison we wouldn't even be having this conversation because I'd be long gone." She pushed her hands into her pockets for something to do, and to avoid Chase grabbing hold of her again. What she needed was to *not* have his skin anywhere near hers. "It was my boss, wants me to head to the Ramsey ranch. They're having trouble with some very late calving and they want me to see if there's anything I can do to help."

"You want me to come lend a hand?"

Hope started to walk backward, shaking her head. "No, Chase, I'll be just fine. And it's not brawn they need, it's medical knowledge."

"You sayin' I'm all brawn and no brain?" He flexed his biceps and made her laugh. "I've delivered one hell of a lot of calves single-handedly, I'll have you know."

"Good-bye, Chase," she said, running the pads of her fingers across her lips once she'd turned away.

"See you Saturday night."

She kept walking, not looking back. Because the last thing she needed was to see that handsome-as-hell cowboy leaning against the fence with his sexy-lazy eyes trained on her. The memory of his kiss was more than enough to distract her for the rest of the day, especially when she had her arm elbow-deep in a heifer stuck in the second stage of labor.

Chapter 8

"So tell me about her."

"Who?" Chase looked up, beer in hand. He'd just finished helping Chloe since Ryder was still nowhere to be found.

"Who do you think, doofus?" Chloe gave him a pretend slap across the back of the head as she passed him, putting a bowl of chips and a homemade dip on the table.

Chase scowled and took a sip of his beer. "She's, I don't know, what do you want me to say?"

"I'm not going to laugh at you," Chloe said, collecting her soda from the kitchen counter, "if that's what you're worried about."

Chase arched an eyebrow. "There's nothing to say, Chlo. Seriously." He shrugged. "And I'm not into this talky, touchy-feely stuff anyway."

"Give me a break, Chase," she muttered, sipping her drink when he did. "I've known you a while now, and neither you nor Nate has ever invited a woman over to hang out with us." She laughed. "To your bed, sure, but not to meet the family."

"This is hardly meeting the family," he said. "I just

thought you'd like some female company, balance up the genders around the table."

Chloe leaned across the table, taking his hand and giving him a long, serious look. "Chase, you got it bad, you know that, right?"

He grunted. So much for coming over to hang out with Chloe for a while to relax. He would have been better off having a beer with Tommy first, or meeting up with some of the other guys who'd already be out shooting pool. "Don't be crazy." Yeah, he liked Hope, *a lot*, but Chloe was seriously exaggerating.

"And for the record, if I wanted some female company, I could ask one of my friends over." Her grin was wicked. "As far as I'm concerned, these little poker nights are more of a family thing."

"Where's your husband, anyway?" Chase asked. He was sick of Chloe baiting him and he wasn't going to engage—she was worse than his brothers!

"He'll be back in a minute. He went down to check on Bruce."

"Who the fuck is Bruce?"

Chloe took another sip of her soda and rose, wandering barefoot to the oven to check on the nachos he'd seen her put in earlier. *"Bruce,"* she said in an exaggerated voice, "is our new bull. Ryder thinks he's going to be the biggest, baddest rodeo bull around. He didn't want to say anything to you guys until he was sure, but he's sure."

"Better to call a bull Bruce than a kid, I guess."

"Hey, who's talking about my moneymaker?"

Ryder slid into the kitchen on socked feet, grabbing Chloe when he stopped and planting a smacker of a kiss on her lips. She giggled, arms looping around Ryder's neck as he dipped her back for another. If Chase hadn't known them so well he would have looked away, but he was used to it and they clearly didn't mind having an audience.

"Your better half was just telling me about your new acquisition."

"Hey, when does your girlfriend arrive?" Ryder quipped.

"She's not my girlfriend," Chase told him. "Hope will be here by six and I don't need you giving me or her any shit."

Ryder looked smug as he pulled his wife in tight, arm around her neck. "Oh, I won't be giving her any shit, don't you worry about that."

"Hey boys." Nate appeared, dressed down in jeans and a T-shirt. He was carrying a bottle of Wild Turkey, their favorite whiskey, and sporting a big grin. "And lovely lady."

Chase watched as Nate shoved Ryder out of the way to put his arms around Chloe and plant a kiss on her cheek.

"Hands off," Ryder growled.

"Wait till I get my hands on Chase's girl. Then we'll really see some fur fly, huh?"

Chase glowered at his brothers. They were both morons, and Chloe was being a royal pain in his ass, too. Maybe he shouldn't have asked Hope over after all.

"You guys are gonna have to behave, 'cause she's bringing her kid," Chase told them.

Nate and Ryder both stopped dead, staring at him. Chloe was the only one still smiling.

"Bad," she said, waving her finger at him. "Only a guy with it *real* bad would let a kid tag along."

"Hey, he seems nice." Chase shrugged. "Besides, it was the only way I could get her to come."

Ryder and Nate exchanged looks and then went to the fridge and both pulled out beers. Ryder took a long pull of his then disappeared into another room, while Nate headed over and sat down beside Chase.

"You know we love you, right?"

Chase ignored Nate. "You are gonna be nice to her, aren't you, Chlo? She's not just some woman I met at a bar, she was my best friend in college. We were like . . ." He paused. Nothing witty came to mind. "I don't know, but we were tight."

"So you're trying to tell me that I can trust her, is that it?"

"I guess I'm just saying that she's the real deal. You'll like her."

"I think she just knocked at the door," Nate called out.

Chase pushed his chair back and jumped up at the same time his brother started to laugh. Chloe gave him a guilty smile, clearly trying hard not to join in with Nate's bullshit.

"What the fuck?"

"Sorry," Nate said, "I just wanted to see that excited look on your face when you thought she was here. Kinda like a puppy . . ."

"Ha-ha, very funny," Chase muttered. "And I don't know what the big deal is. She's an old friend coming over to hang out and play some poker with us." He stopped talking when a knock sounded out. Either Ryder was playing some bullshit game or she actually was standing at the front door now. "Just think of her as one of the guys."

"Are you going to get that or shall I?" Nate asked dryly.

Chase just stared at him long and hard before standing again, taking his time. His brothers were great, but they were assholes, too.

"I'll get it," he said, talking as he walked. "And just don't go giving her a hard time. Or the kid."

"As if I was ever gonna give the *kid* a hard time," Nate called back. "Give me some credit."

Chase stalked down to the door, wondering what the hell he'd done inviting her in the first place. He knew his brothers were full of shit, but still—this was Hope and they had history. He'd be lying if he said he wasn't trying to impress her, and the thought of convincing her to stay tonight . . . Damn. She'd made it clear that she wouldn't be intimate with him in front of her son, and he got that she'd only just separated from the boy's father, but he still wanted her in his bed. If not tonight, then soon.

He swung open the door and had to look down to see Hope. She was dropped down on her haunches, one arm around her son as she talked to him, but when she saw Chase she rose.

"Hey," she murmured.

"Hey, straight back." Chase leaned in and put an arm around her, drawing her in close so he could kiss her cheek. Her hair had the same sweet-berry kind of smell it had always had, wafting up to him and making him want to hold her tight, to inhale it at the same time as touching every inch of her body.

He reluctantly let her go, conscious that her son was watching.

"Hey, Harris, how are you buddy?" he asked, holding out his hand and grinning when the boy grasped and shook it.

"Can we come in now?"

Chase stepped back. "In you come." He bent down as Harrison passed, touching the boy's shoulder. "I hope you're good at card games, cause I might need your help tonight."

The kid grinned back at him, looking like he'd just been let in on a big secret.

"Thanks for having us over," Hope said as they walked.

"Harrison was pretty excited about coming. It's been a while since we've just, I don't know, had fun, I guess."

"Come meet everyone," Chase said, letting her walk ahead of him through the door into the big open-plan lounge and kitchen. "Then you might change your mind."

"Hey, what lies are you telling the lovely lady?"

Ryder emerged at the same time they did, hair wet from his super quick shower and dressed in a clean pair of jeans and a fresh shirt.

"Harrison, this is my brother, Ryder. Harris is one of the boys tonight," he told Ryder.

"Hey, Harrison." He watched as Ryder held his hand up for a high five and touched the boy's head, grinning at him before giving Hope a quick kiss on the cheek. "Nice to see you again, Hope."

"Hi." Chloe came forward and gave Hope an impromptu hug, her warmth so genuine it made Chase smile. He should have known how welcoming his sister-in-law would be. "I've heard so much about you."

"Hopefully only good things?" Hope laughed and pushed her hands into her jean pockets before pulling one straight out and reaching for her son. "This is Harrison. And I hope at least one of you guys likes Transformers because he's stuffed at least five of them in my bag."

They all laughed, but it was Nate who called out. "That'd be me. If you've got an Optimus Prime in there, I'm all in."

Harrison's face broke out in a beamer of a smile and Hope nudged him toward Nate who was sitting sprawled on the sofa. Chase could see he was desperate to show someone his Transformers, so he put one arm around the boy and reached for Hope's bag. He wasn't opposed to reliving his childhood either.

"You mind if I take this?"

She slipped it off her shoulder. "Be my guest."

"Hey, wine or beer?" He heard Chloe ask. "I usually drink beer with the guys but I'm just as happy to not be one of the boys and drink a nice chardonnay."

"Harris, this is my big brother, Nate. Nate, Harris," Chase said as Nate leaned forward, ditching his beer and gesturing for the boy to come sit beside him.

"Who you got in there? Bumblebee?"

Harrison nodded. "And Wheeljack."

"You and me are gonna get on just fine," Nate said. "How 'bout you take a look in mom's bag and get them all out, and then you can show me how to transform your favorites."

Chase dropped to the ground with Harris, trying to figure out how to transform one of the toys he had. The boy made it look easy but Chase was struggling.

"I think you'll have to help me out here, buddy," he admitted.

Harris leaned over and transformed it in about a minute. "He's a goodie. See his Autobot patch?"

Chase nodded. "You sure know a lot about Transformers, huh?"

"I watch them on YouTube. Mom said she'll buy me a Dinobot if I'm good tonight."

"Dino what?" Chase asked with a laugh.

"Dinobot. You know, from *Age of Extinction*. The movie."

Chase was in way over his head. "I have no idea what you're talking about, but next time you come over I reckon you should bring it so we can sit down and watch it."

Nate nudged him and nodded over at Hope. Chase could have sat all night and played games, but he appreciated the chance to spend some time alone with Hope. He smiled at his brother. It wasn't often he owed Nate for helping him out, but right now he sure as hell did.

"So have you played poker before?" he overhead Chloe ask Hope.

Hope glanced at Chase and they both laughed. "Well, there was a time that I talked Chase into playing with a few of the girls in my dorm."

"Oh yeah?" Ryder passed Chase a beer as he shook his head.

"Imagine a lot of drunk girls and an even drunker Chase, having his ass whooped and ending up butt naked."

"No way!" Chloe clapped her hand over her mouth as she laughed. "I bet he's never told any of the guys about that."

Hope gave him an apologetic look, but he just smiled back at her. She could tease him all she wanted, it was his brothers who couldn't get away with it.

"I never told anyone because I was expecting to end up with an entire dorm full of seminaked women to myself, and instead I ended up bare and they were all still fully clothed."

"Ah, so my darling husband learned his poker skills from you, did he?" Chloe asked dryly.

"Why do I feel like I'm missing a really good story here?" Hope asked, looking from Chase to Chloe.

Chase touched Hope's back, his palm pressed to her leather jacket. It annoyed him that he couldn't feel her skin. "It's a long story," he told her as Chloe grinned. "My idiot brother lost a big-ass poker game, Chloe came along and saved the day, and the rest, as they say, is history."

"She also saved my ass when she convinced me to stop riding two-thousand-pound bulls for a living," Ryder pointed out, his arm looped around Chloe's waist as she snuggled in closer to him. "Sometimes it takes a good woman, doesn't it, Chase?"

He eyeballed his brother. "I wouldn't know." Whatever the hell Ryder was playing at, he wasn't biting.

"Harrison looks like he's getting on well with Nate," Hope said, touching Chase's forearm as she craned her neck to look past him. "You think I should just leave them to it?"

Chase stared at her hand where it was touching him, steeled his jaw as he remained immobile. "Nate's good with kids." He cracked up. "And women."

"I think the women part runs in the family," she said dryly, tipping her glass back and taking a sip, exposing the silky soft skin of her neck as she did so. Chase couldn't tear his eyes away, was captivated by every inch of skin he saw, every inch that he wanted to explore with his mouth. He stifled a groan.

"So how's work going?" Chase asked.

She was about to answer when Chloe called out, interrupting them.

"Hope's on Team Chloe, Chase. You guys are gonna get your asses kicked tonight. And there'll be no handicaps either, just two women against you three."

Chase made a face at Chloe, but it was Hope he wanted to watch. She was smiling, the look on her face contented, none of the tenseness he'd noticed earlier in the week. After they'd made out in his SUV, she'd been hard to read, but being with her now was like stepping back in time. It must have been hanging out with his family, not just being the two of them.

"Work's good," Hope said, turning her attention back to him, eyes shining. "I mean, I'm doing something I enjoy, and they pay me well. Once I put on my big girl panties and realized how lucky I still was, I stopped feeling sorry for myself and just started to make the most of it."

"Hey, you're a bigger person than I am," Chase said, turning around and pulling out a chair at the table. He waited for her to sit down before pulling out the adjoining one for himself. "If all this was taken away from me, I'd be a goddamn mess."

"So still no plans to ever move away from the ranch?" Hope asked.

Chase shook his head. That was something he didn't have to think about for a second. "This is where I belong. No questions asked."

They kept coming back to their ranches, their past, every time they spoke, and he hated to see her smile falter when she was reminded about the home she'd left behind. Chase changed the subject, fast.

"I hope you're hungry, because Chloe likes to feed us like we're starving."

"She seems great." Hope's smile was easy again, natural. "I can tell you like her a lot."

"I do." Chase drummed his fingers across the timber tabletop. "She's a great girl and Ryder was damn lucky to find her."

"And you? Does it make you want to find a wife, Mr. Love 'Em and Leave 'Em?"

Chase raised his gaze, stopped drumming his fingers, and closed his palm around the beer bottle instead. He studied Hope's face, her aqua blue eyes framed by thick dark lashes, fine features offset by full lips that looked even more damn kissable when all pink and glossy.

"Maybe." He shrugged. "Maybe not."

"No yearning to settle down?" she asked.

Chase was watching her lips as he listened. "Are you asking because you want to know, or are you just making polite conversation?"

A slow pink stain spread across Hope's cheeks and he fought the urge to smile. She'd been fishing, only she hadn't expected him to put out his own line instead of biting. There was something satisfying about seeing her

squirm, especially given what she'd just asked him. After
Stacey, settling down wasn't something he'd thought
about. Maybe when he was forty; maybe if and when he
ever decided he wanted kids. Right now he hadn't thought
about having a woman in his life at all, not since his last
relationship. So long as he could have a beautiful woman
in his bed when he wanted, he was a happy man. Or at
least he had been until Hope had showed up, and suddenly
she was the only woman he wanted.

Hope should have just kept her mouth shut, but then
again she could say that about everything when it came
to Chase. He was infuriating and intoxicating all at the
same time, and just like had happened before, all the will-
power in the world could be shattered in one slow second where this particular cowboy was concerned.

"Forget it," she said, refusing to even think about what
it would be like to be with Chase, to be more than just
some fun to him. Sure, she'd like a few more repeats,
but the look on his face when she'd asked him about settling down had been answer enough. It told her she'd been
right in keeping her secret all this time.

"Need another top up?"

Hope smiled at Chloe. She'd already decided she liked
her, and she admired the way Chloe could handle the
King brothers. Soft and feminine, but with just enough
sass to keep them in line.

"I thought you were having wine with me?" Hope
asked, glancing from Chloe's glass to her face and wondering why the other woman couldn't stop smiling.

"I thought I'd keep my mind fresh for the game. Start
with sparkling water instead."

Hope went to say something then clamped her mouth
shut, raising an eyebrow and grinning at Chloe. "Yeah,
sure."

Chloe burst out laughing and Ryder gave her a play punch on the arm as he joined them. "I thought we weren't telling anyone," he muttered in a low voice.

"I haven't told a soul," Chloe whispered, still smiling. "I can't help if someone guesses."

"Hey, your secret's safe with me," Hope said, shutting her mouth and making a zipping action across her lips as if to seal them then throwing away the key.

"What, that Chloe's pregnant?" Chase chimed in.

"Ryder!" Now it was Chloe angry with him, clutching his shirt and pulling him in tight. "You promised we'd tell them together."

"I, ah . . ." Ryder looked guilty as he tried to escape Chloe's hold and failed. "Come on, Chlo, they're my brothers. I tell them everything."

Chloe sighed, clearly not able to stop smiling for long. "Worst-kept secret ever," she announced. "We're having a baby, and until I reach at least the twelve-week mark, we're keeping it a secret from anyone outside this room."

"What about Granddad?" Chase asked.

"We are going in tomorrow to see him and tell him." She put her hands on her hips and glared at Ryder. "He was *supposed* to be the first to know, just in case something happened. We wanted him to know he had his first great-grandchild on the way."

Hope studied Chase as he held up his glass. There had always been something about him, some *thing* that made him different from every other guy she'd ever met. He'd been a womanizer, a naughty influence on her, but he'd also been the nicest, most caring guy in the world to her. Which was why she'd never wanted to burden him after their one night together, knowing that on the one hand he couldn't think of anything worse than settling down, but also that his sense of honor and duty would have forced his hand. And what could have been worse than knowing a man like Chase had settled because he had to, not because it was what he wanted? There was also the fact that she hadn't wanted to leave her ranch behind and return to Texas once she'd found out, too. And there would have been no way the King family would have let her son grow up without being part of the family, without being in Texas.

"To my gorgeous sister-in-law and my pain-in-the-ass brother," Chase announced. "You guys are gonna be the best parents, and I can't wait to meet the first little King baby."

"Hear, hear," Nate called out from the other side of the room.

Hope tore her eyes away from Chase's strong, angular face, and looked at her son. He was still happy hanging out with Nate, although she was sure he'd be getting hungry by now.

"Harrison, you want to come grab some fries?"

"And nachos!" Chloe chimed in. "I've got beans and plenty of cheese on them, so they should be good."

Harrison left his toys behind and jumped up, heading over to her. "Help yourself, kiddo. I'll grab you a drink."

"Here's a soda," Chase said, passing Harrison a can. "There's more in the fridge and help yourself to anything. The pizzas should be here soon, too, so eat your heart out."

They all pulled out chairs and sat around the table. Hope reached over and took a nacho, bumping arms with Chase, pleased that he was being so nice to Harrison. She didn't look up. This whole scene seemed so familiar, and then there was Chase. He was familiar and tempting and seductive all rolled into one, enough to make her want to scream with frustration.

"Has Chase taken you over to see his new place?" Chloe asked.

"No." Hope sat back, finished her mouthful, and watched Chase. "Where is it?"

Chase shrugged. "About five minutes' walk from here, on the ranch," he said, like it was no big deal. "I was going to take you there the other day but we kinda ran out of time."

Nate chuckled and she turned to see what was so funny. "Don't let him pretend like it's just some modest little guesthouse. It's insane. I think he's planning on either lots of guests or a football team of kids one day."

Hope glanced at Chase. "How about a grand tour later on?"

"You betcha." The heat in Chase's gaze spread through her like wildfire.

"So when do we play poker?" she asked.

"After pizza," Ryder told her. "And more drinks. Plenty more drinks."

"One more and I'm switching to soda," Hope said, smiling as Harrison tucked into the nachos like he'd never eaten before. "Otherwise I won't be able to drive home."

"So stay," Nate suggested, like it was the most obvious solution in the world.

Chase was still watching her even though it was his brother who'd spoken. The question lingered. She felt like everyone in the room was watching her even though she knew they weren't. Ryder and Chloe had already started chatting about something else, but the intensity of Chase's gaze was spellbinding.

"What I meant," Nate continued, leaning across the table and pouring some more wine into her glass, "is that we have plenty of spare rooms in the main house. You and Harrison are welcome to stay over."

She let out a low shudder, a breath that she hadn't even realized she'd been holding. Chase had mentioned it the other day, but she hadn't really let herself think about it again, even if she had packed some things just in case. "Thanks. Maybe I'll take you up on that."

Nate might be a hotshot rancher tycoon, but he'd sure as hell stepped up not to make her feel uncomfortable. He grinned and pushed back his chair, and she couldn't help but wonder whether he would have been so kind to her if he'd known the truth. At the time it had seemed like the best thing for everyone, but now being with the King family and seeing how close they were firsthand was making her wonder if she'd deprived her son of more than she'd ever realized.

"Hey, Harrison, what do you say to a sleepover?" Chase asked.

His head snapped around, eyes flashing with excitement. "For real?"

Everyone laughed. Hope ran a hand through his hair when he came closer. "For real. Maybe we can take a look around the ranch in the morning before we go?" She glanced at Chase to check if it was okay.

"It just so happens that we still have a pretty awesome old pony here. How about a ride in the morning?" Chase asked him.

Harrison jumped up and down, hands balled into fists.

"That means yes," Hope said, "in case it wasn't obvious."

"That's what you used to do," Nate said to Chase with a chuckle, watching Harrison. "I still remember you getting all excited over stuff and jumping all crazy."

Cold washed over Hope, a shiver coursing through her body. She didn't know what to say, hoped no one was watching her.

"I thought he was a cool kid, now I'm certain," Chase said, waggling his eyebrows at Harrison and making him laugh. "If he's anything like me then he has to be, huh?"

Hope smiled, pleased she hadn't overreacted. She *was* going to tell Chase, she owed it to him, and tonight was plain evidence that she didn't have any other choice, she just had to figure out how. Maybe once her work on the ranch was done, so she could walk away if she had to without there being professional repercussions for her. She couldn't afford to be fired, and if the King family threw their weight around, her boss was hardly going to choose her over the biggest ranchers in Texas.

A knock at the door echoed down the hall.

"That'll be the pizza." Ryder jumped up at the same time as Chloe did, but he set her straight back down again. "And you, my darlin', aren't moving an inch. Don't forget you're carrying my little baby in there." Hope watched as he put a protective hand over her belly, dropping a kiss to her lips. "I'll be back in a minute."

Hope wasn't jealous, but she was envious. All the years she'd been married, it had never been like that even when it was good.

"You don't have to stay," Chase said, surprising her. His hand closed over her thigh, his touch as warm as his breath. "Nate didn't mean anything by it, and just so you know, I didn't put him up to it."

"I know," she replied, guilt mixing with anticipation as she angled her body to face him. "But it'll be fun, right?"

He moved his fingers, sending goose pimples down her leg. They were facing, so close but so far apart, and if Harrison hadn't been nearby she wouldn't have hesitated to give in to her desires. Maybe it was the alcohol making her more confident, making it easier to push the deceit from her mind—it was almost painful *not* to act on it.

"Don't," she whispered as his mouth moved closer to hers.

"Sorry. I have to keep reminding myself to behave around you."

She took a deep breath and pushed back, reaching for her wine and running her fingers down the stem for something to do. "Maybe later," she murmured, knowing that it would *definitely* be later if she was given half a chance.

"How about we go for a walk down to my new place and I show you around, once Harrison has crashed."

Hope let Chase link their fingers together and she watched them, intertwined. "He likes to stay up pretty late," she cautioned.

"It just so happens I'm the night owl from hell," he said, flashing her his dimpled grin. "So is that a yes?"

She wondered what the hell she was agreeing to. "Yes," she muttered.

Chase looked like he'd just won the lottery. "It's a date then."

She had the shivers back, anticipation building in her belly. All these years she'd wondered *what if*, and now here she was ready to have a rematch with the only man who'd ever truly made her feel alive. There wasn't a bone in her body that didn't want Chase, even if it was just for one night again, before she finally told him what she'd kept secret for so long.

Chase ran his hand down her thigh this time and she stifled a gasp, distracted only when Ryder reappeared with enough pizza boxes to feed a football team. "Let's eat and then we can get this card game started."

Hope's heart was still pounding, her pulse racing as Chase gave her one last, slow lazy smile and removed his hand, reaching for a slice of pepperoni. She took a sip of her wine to calm her nerves before doing the same, finally regaining her equilibrium when her son climbed back onto the chair beside her and started to eat.

Coming to the King ranch with her son had been dangerous business, and being within any kind of close radius to Chase? That was almost the worst goddamn mistake she'd ever made, because there was no walking away now, not yet, anyway.

"So tell me, anything else you like apart from Transformers?"

The table fell quiet as Harris pushed up onto his knees, reaching for a piece of pizza and answering Chase.

"Yeah, Spiderman's pretty cool."

Chase laughed. "How about Batman?"

Harrison's nose wrinkled. "Not as cool as Spidey."

"You know how to shoot a web?" Chase asked, glancing at Hope and making her smile.

"Sure do," Harrison said, dropping the slice of pizza to his plate and pretending to blast Chase.

They all laughed and Hope took a big gulp of wine. The night was going so perfectly that it terrified her.

Chapter 9

"You make this look so easy," Hope said, leaning in close to Chloe to see her hand.

"It is!" Chloe grinned at her as she hid her cards. "I was hustling at card games when you were probably playing with Barbie dolls. It's second nature to me."

Hope laughed, sipping her beer. She'd ditched her wine earlier and decided to drink with the boys. "So Chase wasn't joking when he said you could beat the pants off any man?"

Chloe giggled and leaned into her, like they were old friends. It was nice, just hanging out and having fun, relaxing. She hadn't done this sort of thing in a long while—first her parents had fallen ill and she'd been alongside them as they both battled treatments, then her marriage had started to crumble, the ranch had slipped out of her grasp . . . There hadn't been a lot of time for just having fun for longer than she could remember. And Chloe was right—she'd been the little girl playing Barbie and Ken, make believing cute little romances and expecting to have a husband and family of her own one day, on her ranch.

"One day I'll tell you my story," Chloe said, raising the

stakes of the game they were playing without breaking for a pause. "And maybe then you can tell me all about how you managed to keep Chase all hot under the collar over you for a decade."

Now it was Hope's eyebrows shooting up in surprise. "Don't be silly."

"Oh, I'm not," Chloe said. "I've never seen him all rubbed up the wrong way like this before."

"We have history, that's all," Hope told her. "And things didn't exactly end great between us." She wasn't sure how much Chloe knew, or how much she wanted to tell her.

"Hey, it's none of my business," Chloe said, grinning at the boys as they stared at her, her voice low. "But one thing I do know is that when you're dealing with a King, you have to tread carefully. It's way too easy to put your heart on the line, even when you're least expecting it." She sighed. "I never thought I'd feel like this, but Ryder came along and everything changed. *Everything*."

Hope nodded. Oh, she knew all right. She doubted she'd ever feel the way she had about Chase with another man, so she completely understood that when Chloe had fallen for Ryder, she'd fallen damn hard. But at the same time, she couldn't let things get that serious between them, because then her lie would seem even bigger.

"You do well managing these boys on your own," Hope said. "One King would be handful enough for any woman and you've got to put up with all three of them."

"You know what? They were intimidating when I first met them, but they're all gorgeous. And I don't just mean to look at. They'd do anything to look after me, all of them, and there's not many guys out there in the world like that."

"Don't I know it," Hope muttered. "Chase is about as far removed from my ex-husband as is humanely possible."

She'd known her ex since they were kids in elementary school, but the older he'd become the less she'd actually *known* him.

"I'm out," Chase said, standing up and winking at Hope across the table.

"And just like that he's got you in his web," Chloe whispered, nudging her with her elbow. "I think they practice that sexy wink."

Hope laughed at Chloe, but her eyes were trained on the man standing across from her. His shirt was all crumpled now, sleeves pushed up to his elbows, and a beer bottle was hanging casually from his hand. If he was the only man left on earth, she'd be damn lucky to be the last woman.

He drained the rest of his beer, left the bottle on the table, and walked around to her, dropping a hand to her shoulder. She shivered at his touch.

"You see the little guy fell asleep?" His words were soft, low as he bent toward her.

Hope looked over her shoulder at Harrison, saw him flopped face first on the sofa, a Transformer still clutched in one hand.

"He's had a great night."

"I know. He's pretty fun to hang out with, and he seemed to like showing us all up when it came to Transformers." Chase raised an eyebrow. "And you? Have you enjoyed your night here?"

The husky, deep notes of his voice sent a delicious rush of anticipation through her. She licked her lips, suddenly aware of how painfully dry they were. "Me too."

He edged closer. It was like they were the only two people left in the room, the only sound reaching her ears the echo of his breath. She raised her eyes so she was staring into his, no longer nervous of being so close to him, or of seeing the blatant desire in his gaze. She'd consumed more alcohol than she'd planned on, but she wasn't drunk—just enough was coursing through her body to give her the kind of confidence she'd had the last time they'd been together.

"Why don't I show you my new house?" He reached for her, his fingers colliding with her arm. He didn't move straightaway, but then he ran his hand down her arm, not stopping until his fingers caught hers. "What do you say?"

"Yes," she murmured, her lips parting as he leaned in, waiting for his kiss. *Screw saying no. To hell with being sensible.*

Chase bent lower, but he passed her lips, his mouth falling closer to her ear. "Let's go then. Harris will be fine here with the others."

Hope let out a breath she hadn't even known she was holding. She kept her fingers looped with Chase's as he turned, facing the table they were only a few feet away from. Reality came crashing back when the others all glanced up at them, still consumed by their card game.

"I'm taking Hope over to see the house," Chase said. "You guys all right to keep an eye on the little man?"

Chloe looked straight at her, her smile genuine. "Go for it. He's safe here with us."

Hope returned the smile. "Thanks. I don't think we'll be long. But call Chase straightaway if he wakes up."

Chase tugged her along tight to his body as they walked. He let go of her hand and slipped his arm around her instead, and she didn't hesitate to tuck under his arm, her head to his shoulder. He was warm against her, his abs taut where her hand rested against his side.

"How far away is it?" she asked.

He pulled open the front door and she went just ahead of him, settling back against him once it was closed.

"Not far."

They walked in silence, the moon illuminating their

surroundings. Stars filled the sky, the only disturbance to an otherwise black canopy overhead. Hope kept her head tilted as she walked, admiring the night and trying to stop her heart from hammering so hard it jumped out of her chest.

"Hope," Chase said, slowing down, then turning her around to face him. He still had his arm around her, only now it had slid partway down her back, and he'd raised his other to cocoon her even closer to him.

She watched him, raised her hands to his chest, palms flat to his T-shirt. She grasped the fabric, ready to tug him in, only Chase didn't need to be told what to do.

He bent, his body accommodating for her height, head dipping as he sought out her mouth. Chase's lips pressed to hers, so gently at first that she moaned in his mouth, desperate for more, wanting to strip him right then and there.

But Chase wasn't letting up. He kept his lips soft, brushing against hers; even when she tried to yank him closer he held his ground, his body immobile, a statue made from stone. Hope was desperate for more, wanted every inch of him against her, his mouth hard, his body tighter to hers.

"Slow down, tiger." His deep whisper against her mouth drove her wild.

"Maybe I don't want to go slow," she muttered. After trying not to think about him sexually or any other damn way all night, she was ready to jump him. She wanted him here, right now, on the grass if she had to. So long as every part of her was touching every part of him, she'd be happy.

"Come on."

Chase grabbed her hand again and started walking. She had half a mind to throw a tantrum and refuse to move, but she didn't. Whatever the hell he felt for her couldn't be anything like the way she was attracted to him, because if it was, there was no way in hell he'd have been able to just stop like that.

Hope followed along blindly, no longer giving a damn about how pretty the sky looked or what they were passing. She was like a doe in heat, desperately following the scent of a stag up ahead.

"It's just there," he said.

Hope stopped walking and looked at the big two-level house up ahead. Nate hadn't been joking when he'd said it was massive.

"It's huge." The others hadn't been lying when they'd said it was fit for a family of ten.

"That's what all the ladies say."

Hope thumped him hard on the arm, grinning when he howled with laughter.

"The house. I was talking about the house, you idiot." And just like that she was no longer so hot under the collar she was incapable of speech.

"Ah, Hope, you never did like my jokes, did you?"

"Screw you," she muttered.

"Funnily enough, that's exactly what I'd like you to do."

Hope glared at him, ready to call him out. Only when her eyes met his, bathed in moonlight, all sense fled her brain again. Chase went to say something, his lips parting, but instead of uttering a word he lifted her up in his arms so fast she didn't have a moment to protest.

"I thought . . ."

"What?" he asked gruffly, marching at a rapid pace, his arms locked tight around her. "That I didn't want you because I didn't strip you naked just now?"

"Mmm, something like that," she responded.

"Sweetheart, I was trying not to push you."

Damn, push away. "You don't have to go easy on me."

"Fuck, Hope, I'm trying to show you that you're different."

"What if I don't want to be different?" She had no idea why she was saying what she was saying, why she wasn't just keeping her thoughts to herself.

"You want me to treat you like a one-night stand, is that it?"

Chase barged the door open with his shoulder, backing into the dark house. It was all framed up with some of the walls completed, although it was hard to see in the half light. But what she could see was Chase as he stared down at her.

"Yeah," she told him, her voice barely audible. "Maybe I do."

"You should have fucking said so before," he muttered, dropping her to her feet and backing her up against a wall. She barely had time to register what was happening before he had her pinned, his big body not giving her an inch of wriggle space. He pushed his forearms against the timber wall, bracing himself in front of her, his mouth dangerously close to hers.

"Tell me what you want,'" he ground out.

She gulped. "You," she mumbled. "I want you, Chase." Her voice became more confident as she spoke, her eyes trailing their way up his chest until she met his gaze.

"Well, that's good." His voice was as sexy as a shot of whiskey thrown over ice. "Because I want you, too."

Hope sucked back a breath as Chase took one arm off the wall and stroked a finger down her cheek, caressing her lower lip before dropping his mouth to cover hers, his hand sliding around her. The moan that escaped her was deep and guttural, responding to the heaviness of his lips, the decadent way his tongue slid into her mouth and teased against hers, sending spasms of pleasure through her body. She wanted him so bad it was almost painful, her need for him so deep she wanted to wrap her legs around him right then and there.

"I've been waiting a long time to do this to you again," he whispered, no longer bracing his weight against the wall at all. Now his hands were all over her, relentless, skimming her waist as he shoved her top up.

Hope didn't let his mouth leave hers for a second, her hands wrapped around his neck, tugging him closer. She sucked hard on his lower lip when he tried to pull back before covering her lips with his again, over and over, gasping for breath when he forced her back hard against the wall, shoving her top up high until he could yank it over her head.

Hope's fingers fumbled with the buttons on Chase's shirt. Frustration got the better of her and she yanked hard, no longer caring about undoing them—she just wanted it off. Now.

"In a hurry?" he asked, laughing as she ripped the rest of his shirt open and forced it back, pleased when he shrugged out of it.

"Yes." She pushed up his T-shirt, annoyed he was wearing two layers. His damn cowboy getup was way too hard to get out of. When he was finally bare chested she took a second to admire the man in front of her, ran her hands down his chest, sliding them around his waist. Her eyes had adjusted to the almost darkness, could make out his body. It was then, when Chase gave her a wicked grin, that she realized she was almost naked from the waist up, her lacy bra the only thing left covering her.

"Pretty," Chase said. "But it'd look better off."

Hope gasped when Chase expertly flicked the clasp at the back one-handed, her bra falling forward. He pulled it away, discarding it, his eyes fixed firmly on her bare breasts.

"As kissable as I remembered them," he growled out,

dropping lower, his mouth covering one of her nipples as he ran his tongue around her delicate areola before closing harder over her skin and sucking, first soft then hard.

Hope dug her nails into Chase's shoulders, her back arching as he continued to pleasure her. But as much as she wanted him to keep going, she also wanted his skin beneath her fingers, to be exploring him at the same time.

"Chase . . ."

"Hmmm," he murmured, switching his attention to her other breast.

She tangled her fingers in his hair, loving that it was long enough for her to grip. Hope let him continue, toes curled, pleasure building in her belly like a fast burning fire until it was almost too much to bear. She yanked him up, his hot mouth closing over hers the second his back was straight.

Hope kissed him back, her lips as urgent as his, her body desperate. She hadn't been with a man since her marriage had broken up, hadn't even thought about how deprived she'd been of sex, but now that she was with Chase, the desire within her was impossible to fight. She couldn't end this even if she wanted to—she wanted Chase, and she wanted him right here and now.

"Don't push me," Chase murmured against her skin, his mouth moving so fast she could hardly keep up with him. One minute he was kissing her lips, the next his tongue was trailing a hot, wet path down her neck.

"Or what?" she asked, tugging him up by his hair again and forcing his mouth to hers.

"Or I'll stop trying to be a gentleman and lose all goddamn control."

She laughed, reaching down for his belt buckle and pulling it across, freeing him of the belt and then working on the top button of his jeans. Hope was frantic, she couldn't help it—years of pent-up desire and sexual frustration were coming to a head.

Chase matched her every step of the way, fiddling with the zipper on her jeans at the same time as he tried to struggle out of his own jeans. She laughed when he stumbled, suddenly self-conscious when he moved away from her, the night air cool against her breasts without Chase warming them.

"Fuck!" he cursed, tripping over and slamming his arm against the timber frame beside him. "Damn boots."

Hope watched as Chase kicked off his boots, discarding her own shoes before unzipping her jeans. When she looked back up, Chase was immobile, staring at her as he stood in his boxers. She stifled a smirk at his hard-on, loving that he was clearly as excited as she was. Her heart was beating hard, erratic, but she was determined to give him a show now that she had his full attention.

Her breathing was hard as she leaned farther forward, tossing her long hair over one shoulder so Chase could see her breasts as she finished peeling her jeans off. Then she straightened, stretched, sliding her fingers into the edge of her panties and slowly, *slowly*, pushing them down an inch.

"Fuck slow," Chase cursed, closing the distance between them and slamming her back against the wall.

Her back protested, the timber hard against her skin, but it barely registered. It was nothing compared to the buzz consuming her body, the excitement of knowing what was coming, what was about to happen between them.

Chase kissed her—one hot, searing kiss that had her begging for more, her hands frantic around his neck as she tried to force him back again. But Chase was on his way down lower, his tongue never leaving her skin until he reached her navel. Hope's breath was sharp, her body quivering as he finally took his mouth off her only to slip his fingers inside of her panties and take them down ever so slowly. He pulled them down, his breath against her belly still as she stepped out of them, leaving them on the ground at her feet. And just as she was about to pull Chase up, to wrap a leg around him so he could enter her, his mouth closed over her sex.

Her moan was loud, guttural, but she couldn't help it. Not when his lips covered her, his tongue so gentle she could barely feel it one second, then firmer, more intense the next. His kiss was so intimate, his touch so right, and even though she wanted him inside her she . . .

"Chase," she whispered his name as her body flooded with heat, her pleasure building, fast. "Chase."

He didn't reply with words. Chase kept up the intensity, cupped her ass to hold her still, not letting her move. His mouth was relentless as she strained against him, finally giving in to the waves of ecstasy. Chase only slowed when her fingers went slack against him; she'd been gripping his hair with one hand, the other set of fingers dug into his shoulder, and now she was ready to fall into a puddle at his feet her body was so relaxed.

She looked down, her eyelids heavy. "That was amazing."

Chase gave her a long, smoldering look, his dimple as sexy as the wink he gave her. "Darlin', that was just for starters."

Heat rose through Hope's body, and it had nothing to do with embarrassment and everything to do with desire. Her body was still tingling with the high of her orgasm as Chase slowly rose, pressing barely there kisses to her skin as he straightened.

Hope leaned back, shut her eyes, and felt up and down his big body as he rose.

"I think I'm having my unfair share of the fun here," she murmured.

"Bullshit," he said with a laugh, grabbing her hands and pinning them above her head. "If this isn't fun, then I don't know what is."

Chase pressed into her, his cock hard against her thigh. She gasped when he roughly cuffed her hands with one of his own, his other stroking between her legs, feeling how slick she was for him.

Hope went to open her mouth but Chase took charge, his lips closing over hers, rough now where before he'd been more gentle. She struggled to move her hands but there was no way she could get out of his grasp unless he let her, and he was more interested in shedding his boxer shorts than letting her move. Chase was in charge, and instead of wanting to fight him, she damn well loved it.

"What a way to christen my new place," he said into her ear as he finally released her, letting go of her hands and placing his hands on her ass instead, scooping her up into the air.

"Cha . . ." His name died in her mouth when he thrust her back against the wall, her legs locking around his waist as he pushed inside of her. His eyes were on hers, his gaze open as he took her hard and fast, right there in the entrance to his new house, the cool air snaking around their hot, slick bodies. Chase pumped into her, over and over, her legs tightening around his waist, not wanting him to slow or stop.

"Fuck, Hope," he muttered against her mouth as she bit down on his lip, her arms looped around his neck.

"Don't stop," she ordered. "Don't you dare," she moaned as he shifted position slightly, "stop. Ever."

A familiar, delicious warmth spread through her as her climax began to build. Chase was pushing her so close to the edge, his body strong and hard beneath her hands as she felt him all over. He was everything she'd remembered and more.

Just as she was almost there, so close, he stopped, his breathing ragged against her cheek as he pressed a rough kiss to her lips.

"No!" she begged.

He didn't say anything, just spun her around so she was facing the wall, entering her fast from behind, thrusting back into her. His hand reached around, pleasuring her at the same time as he drove harder and harder, until she couldn't hold back any longer.

"Damn," he muttered as she clenched her muscles around him, his mouth hard against her neck, her back slammed hard against his damp chest as they both climaxed at the same time.

She smiled, eyes shut, reaching behind to cup his head as he sucked on her neck.

"That was worth waiting for," she told him, leaning back into him as he wrapped both arms protectively around her. His cheek was pressed to hers now, his touch soft where only moments before he had been rough and determined.

"You have no damn idea how long I've been waiting." His whisper was deep, an octave lower than she'd heard from him before.

Chapter 10

Chase ran his hands down Hope's body, frowning when her skin broke out in goose pimples. The last thing he wanted was to see her dressed again when he'd finally gotten her naked, but being in an under-construction house at night wasn't exactly tropical. Besides, it had gotten so dark now he could hardly see her.

"As much as I'm loath to say it," he said, keeping her wrapped in his arms as he turned her, "I think you need some clothes on."

"Maybe," she said with a laugh, "but how about we keep you bare?"

Hope ran her hands down his back, nails digging into his butt before scraping the back of his thighs.

"Watch it," he growled, grabbing hold of her hands, "otherwise there'll be a round two."

Hope tipped her head back, eyes trained on his. Even though it was dark he could still make out her face; his eyes had long adjusted and he could just see the fullness of her beautiful lips, her hair messy around her high cheekbones as she stared up at him.

"Shit," she muttered.

"What?"

"We, um, we didn't use protection."

Chase stared into eyes that had always been able to see straight through him. "Do you trust me when I say I never go without? This was a very, very rare moment of weakness."

"It's fine," she said, leaning in to kiss him. "I'm on the pill and I haven't been with anyone since that night with you except my . . ."

"Husband," he finished for her. "It's okay."

"And I do trust you," she said. "It just doesn't make up for the fact that I didn't even think about it before now."

"You're one of the only people I've ever trusted, Hope," Chase told her, bending for her panties and holding them up, grinning as he flicked them at her. He rose once he'd located her bra and top in the dark.

She put her underwear back on as he watched her. Chase ground his teeth together—it went against his natural instincts to stand by and let Hope cover up, but it wasn't like he could drag her into a warm comfortable bed.

"I've missed you, Hope." It also went against his instincts to talk about his feelings, but he'd fucked up with Hope once and he didn't want to do it again.

"It's funny how things work out, huh?"

She was dressed in her underwear now. Chase stepped into her space, unable to help himself—he didn't like the distance between them. He stroked the top of her breast, drawing her back into his arms and holding her close. Chase dropped a kiss into her hair, trying to ignore how damn hard he was getting again. There was something more fragile about Hope now than there had been years ago, something different about her that he couldn't quite put his finger on.

"Maybe things worked out just the way they were supposed to," he said.

She wrapped her arms around him, shivering as she tucked closer to his frame. Her breasts were pushed to his chest as she leaned back a little to look up at his face.

"Maybe you're right."

He kissed her, forcing himself to keep his touch light. He felt differently about Hope, wanted her to know how damn special she was.

"I know I'm right. Imagine if you didn't have your little guy?"

Her body stiffened, enough for him to notice, and she released her hold on him.

"I think it's time we went back. You know, just in case he's awake or something."

Chase nodded and turned to pick up her jeans, grabbing his boxers at the same time.

"Want to have a quick look-through with me first?" he asked. His brothers gave him shit about the house all the time; it'd be nice showing it to a woman to see what she thought. "If he'd so much as stirred I bet Chloe would have called."

"Yeah, a look around would be nice," Hope said, wriggling into her jeans and smoothing down her hair. It still looked untamed, but he wasn't going to tell her; there was something sexy about how tousled she looked.

Chase dressed quickly and took a few steps backward, remembering the temporary lights the builders had rigged up now that the roof was on. "So you've seen the entrance," he joked, gesturing to where he'd had her pressed against the wall as he flicked a switch. "Not sure if I'll ever be able to come through my front door without thinking of you naked."

"Ha-ha," she said dryly.

"Hey, it'll make the place. Best housewarming gift a guy could ask for." Chase grinned and grabbed her hand, pulling her through to the next room.

"And this is . . . ?"

"The living room and kitchen. All open plan, with big doors that open out to the view." It wasn't easy to see with shadows everywhere from the floodlights positioned on the ground, but he could still show her around.

"Wow. This place is going to be amazing, Chase. You must be so proud."

He pushed his shoulders up, shrugging. "Yeah, it will. The guesthouse I used to live in wasn't half-bad, but I'm looking forward to moving in."

"Nate wasn't kidding when he said it was a family home." Hope looked sideways at him. "You'll make some lucky girl a great husband one day, Chase."

He was about to laugh when he noticed her tears, just moist enough to make her eyes swim. Chase pulled her closer, didn't like seeing her upset.

"I can't say I've thought about it," he told her. It was the truth. It might be a big house but he'd built it all for himself—an awesome bachelor pad and nothing else.

"And through here?"

He walked a few steps to the right. "The lounge. I've got plans for a big, kick-ass screen for watching football."

"Sounds heavenly."

"Hey, your place isn't half-bad," Chase told her.

Hope gave him a wry look. "I don't want to sound like a spoiled bitch, but it's hard coming to terms with it. I know I should be grateful to be living in a nice house, but when I think about my ranch house it kind of pales in comparison."

"You want to tell me about it yet?" Chase asked.

Hope shook her head. "Do you have all the bedrooms upstairs?"

Chase took the hint. "Most of them. I have a big one downstairs with its own bathroom, just in case I'm ever some old invalid and I can't make it up."

"Or you could have just put in an elevator," she joked.

"Yeah. I thought about it."

"You're unbelievable." Hope laughed.

"I'm just lucky I have a good interior designer. She's been fantastic at telling me very diplomatically when I should rein in my stupid ideas."

"I doubt you'd have many stupid ideas." She laughed. "Or not that many of them anyway."

Chase looped his arm tighter around Hope. His head was spinning right now. There was no part of him that wanted to settle down, but he also didn't want to let Hope walk out of his life again. And now that they'd had sex it wasn't like they could go back to being friends, even if he wanted to.

"Chase?"

He turned to face Hope, smiling as she reached to touch his face, her fingertips light against his cheek.

"You're a really good guy," she said, her face impossible to read. Her smile seemed sad, her eyes moist again. He didn't know what the hell was going on with her, and she'd made it pretty clear she didn't want to talk about her troubles, so he didn't ask again. "I meant it when I said you'll make some woman very happy one day. There's not many men like you in the world, Chase."

"Oh yeah?" He chuckled, but he knew she was being serious and he shouldn't have joked. "I'll take your word on that."

She rose on tiptoes and kissed him, both of her palms to his cheeks. It was like a last kiss, her hold on him so tight, and it pissed him off. There was no way this was it.

When she finally pulled back, he caught her around the wrists, slowly letting her arms down and taking her hands in his. "Maybe there's only one woman who could ever make me settle down." His voice sounded gruff, the words coming out of his mouth so foreign he could hardly believe he was saying them. "You've always been the one, Hope."

"Don't say that, Chase. Just"—she blew out a big breath—"don't."

"Why not?" He'd said it now and there was no point in backing down and pretending like he didn't mean it. "I'm not saying I want a wife and two point five kids, but if there was one woman I'd put before anything else, it'd be you. Always has been, Hope."

Her eyes dropped, the connection broken. *Fuck it.* He should never have opened his big mouth.

"I need to get back to Harrison," she said, her voice low.

"No, Hope, I was talking to you, goddamn it." Chase was pissed off now. He stood in front of her, blocking her way.

"What do you want me to say, Chase?" she asked. "There's always been something between us and there always will be, but everything's changed. It did the second we left college."

"You're talking about your money?" His laugh sounded cruel even to his own ears. "I don't give a flying fuck whether you're as poor as a church mouse, Hope. I trust you no matter what." He might not have thought quite like that when she'd first told him, but he'd quickly realized how stupid that was. Hope would never lie to him, and if she needed money he was pretty sure she'd just come out and ask him for help.

She was silent and he was pissed with himself for upsetting her.

"Come here," he ordered, forcibly tucking her under his arm and holding her close. He dropped a kiss into her hair.

"I'm sorry," she muttered.

"For what?" He slipped his hand into the pocket of her jeans as they started walking. "The only thing you have to apologize for is if you dial me out of a rematch. Because there's no way in hell I'm gonna let that be the last time I see you naked. You hear me?"

Her laugh made him smile. Chase walked them back out into the open, heading toward Ryder's place again. The lights were like beacons in the dark, welcoming them over. He knew some people would hate living so close to their siblings, but he loved it. The ranch was his life—nothing came before family—but he was slowly starting to see that Hope had been as good as family to him, too. Because the kind of friendship they'd had had been too important to lose. He should have jumped on their plane and turned up at her ranch when she hadn't returned his calls. So they'd had sex? So what. It had been great and they'd just proved that for a second time.

Maybe there was a reason no woman had even been able to hold his attention for longer than five minutes. Maybe he'd just blamed his ex, Stacey, as a convenient excuse, because he'd never felt about her like he felt about Hope.

Maybe it was Hope who'd ruined it for every other woman he'd ever met, and he was just the stupid fuck who'd not realized what he could have had.

"You still gonna stay the night?" Chase asked as they walked, breaking the silence between them.

"Am I still invited?"

"Hell yes. My bed's been waiting a helluva long time to meet you."

"Chase," she groaned. "You know I can't."

"Even if Harris is asleep on the sofa? He won't even know what his naughty mama's up to," Chase joked.

She bumped her body against his. "I'm sleeping with *him,* Chase. Don't go getting any ideas."

"Of course you're sleeping with him," he said with a laugh. "I'll carry the little guy over to my room and you

can both sleep on my bed. It's the comfiest in the house."
His grin was wicked. "But don't think for a moment that
I'm not jealous of him snuggling you all night."

"You're sure?" Hope stopped walking, looped her arms
around his neck. He scooped her body to his and kissed
her, her pillowy, soft-as-heaven lips matching his. "That
we can have your bed, I mean?"

"Yes, just like I'm sure that I want to make love to you
again," he said when he pulled back, just enough so that
he could speak. He kissed her again. "Sweet, sweet love."

"Come on, cowboy," she whispered. "It's getting cold
out here."

He reluctantly let her step back, but he didn't let her
go. "If you change your mind and get lonely in the night,
I'll be . . ."

"You get an A+ for trying," Hope interrupted.

"So long as I get an A+ in the bedroom, too."

"Has anyone told you you're an arrogant son of a bitch
sometimes?"

"Yeah, just when you thought I was a new-age, sensitive kind of guy, right?"

"Something like that."

They walked hip to hip the rest of the way back. He
might have sunk a shitload of money into his new breeding program, but if it meant having Hope on the ranch for
the next few months, then he was ready to pray that things
didn't go perfectly to plan. Because once it was over, he
was going to have to think long and hard about how to
keep her in his life, and he wasn't sure if he was ready to
make that kind of decision or commitment any time soon.

"Hope, wake up."

Hope groaned and pulled the covers up higher, not
ready to open her eyes. She was so warm, Harrison's

little body tight against her as she pushed her face deeper into the pillow.

"Hope." This time the words were accompanied by a gentle shake.

She peeked out, diving straight back under when she came face-to-face with Chase. The night before came rushing back to her; Chase carrying Harrison over to the main house, her snuggling into his bed, sleepy and sated, and Chase kissing her good night before leaving them to sleep in the adjoining guest room. He'd insisted his bed was the nicest, that his room would be better for them, even though she'd thought all the rooms looked pretty incredible.

"I need you," Chase murmured.

Hope ran her tongue over her teeth, wishing she could use a toothbrush. She pushed the covers back and gently extracted herself from her son, making sure he was tucked in still, then swung her legs out of bed and straightened. She glanced down, saw her breasts were dangerous close to spilling out, then heard Chase's low groan.

"You're sure a nice sight to see first thing in the morning," he said, reaching for her hand and pulling her so fast toward him than she landed against his chest with a thud. His lips closed over hers, not giving a damn when she tried to protest. He kissed her long and hard, both hands on her butt. She was only wearing her underwear, and his fingers had slipped past the fabric of her panties to connect with bare skin.

"Was this why you needed me?" she asked, pushing him back with both hands and peeking behind him to make sure that Harrison was still asleep. "You know I hate being woken, right?"

"No," he said, clearly distracted as he dropped his mouth to the top of one breast.

Hope yanked him back up by his hair, not giving in to how damn good his lips felt. She was in the same room as her son and it wasn't going to happen.

"Chase!" she scolded.

His grin was shadowed with his dimple on one side. "Sorry. You distracted me."

Hope extracted herself from him. "So the reason you've roused me . . ."

"You slept in," he said. "I've already been up and done the rounds, and some of the girls are definitely getting close. I think we'll be inseminating by this evening at the latest."

"Shit, really?" Hope grabbed her clothes and hurriedly put them on.

"Darlin', I wouldn't be waking you for nothing. You looked cute all snuggled up with your boy."

She gestured for him to walk out of the room in front of her and she followed. "It's been just the two of us for a while now. We're kind of used to cuddling up in bed together."

Hope excused herself to use the bathroom, letting Chase go on without her. She quickly went to the toilet, then made the mistake of looking at herself in the mirror. On second thought, she turned the faucet on and splashed her face, trying to freshen up. She glanced up again. *Useless.* She was at least pleased she'd wiped most of her makeup off before crashing, but she still could have used some help to look better.

Ugh. She didn't have time to worry about how she looked, and besides, Chase had seen her barefaced plenty of times in college. If she was going to scare him off for not looking cute, she'd have done it years ago.

Hope turned the faucet off, ran her fingers through her hair, and headed into the kitchen.

"Oh, hey," she said, averting her eyes for a second when she almost walked smack bang into a bare-chested Nate. He was wearing running shorts and shoes, but his chest was slick with nothing but sweat.

Nate grinned. "Morning." He shrugged into his T-shirt and Hope turned to Chase.

"I'm going to head straight out. I don't want to miss an opportunity," she told him.

"You hungry?" Chase asked, palms down on the counter as he leaned forward.

"Starved," she admitted, hand over her growling belly. "Are you offering me breakfast on the go?"

His smile was infectious. "You go, I'll follow with bagels."

"And coffee?" She gave him her sweetest smile as she walked backward.

"And coffee," he promised, shaking his head.

"I'll babysit," Nate chimed in, grabbing an apple and taking a bite as he watched them. "I'm sure I can distract him with Autobots versus Decepticons."

"Thanks," she said. "I'll check the heifers, monitor them for a little while, and then if I need to stay I'll arrange a sitter and get Harrison back to my place."

Nate shrugged, like he had nothing better to do than look after a kid. "Don't sweat it. I'll feed him and then we might head down to see the pony. Is it okay if I take him out for a ride?"

"Absolutely." Hope hurried toward the door then stopped. "Damn. I don't have any boots."

"There's a pair Chloe wears sometimes at the back door," Chase said, already slicing into a bagel. "And no taking him to the pony. I'm the one who made the promise and I want to see the look on his face when I introduce them."

Nate just shrugged, but she didn't have time to hang around and listen to them banter. So long as someone was looking after Harrison, they could fight over the honors.

"Thanks." Hope might be insanely attracted to the man making her breakfast, but she was also excited about her work. And if she was honest with herself, she liked the idea of showing Chase just how good she was at what she did. She might not have a lot of money anymore, but she was a damn good vet, and she was going to make sure every single one of his herd got in calf if it was the last thing she did.

She looked in on Harrison again quickly before she left, but he was still sleeping and she didn't want to disturb him. Normally she'd never have left him to wake up without her, but he'd had an amazing night and he'd gotten on like a house on fire with Nate. With the entire family.

She pushed away a familiar, sickening feeling of guilt and squared her shoulders. *His uncle*. Nate was Harrison's goddamn uncle, and here she was keeping the truth from everyone. It had all seemed so clear when she'd decided to keep Harrison a secret from his father, but cracks were forming, and she didn't know what the hell to do to make things right.

Chapter 11

Chase spread the bagels with cream cheese and looked around for the to-go cups Nate usually kept stashed away. When he found them he flicked the machine on and put the coffee in the filter.

"I know you're gonna laugh at me, but I couldn't stop thinking last night that Harrison kinda looked"—Nate paused, coming around to lean against the counter beside the coffee machine—"like you did as a kid. Like we both did."

Chase tightened the filter arm and turned to stare at his brother. *He what?* "You've got to be fucking kidding me."

He knew that look on Nate's face, knew when his brother was going to go like a dog with a goddamn bone. Chase sighed and resisted the urge to slam his fist into something. When it came to Hope, he jumped straight into the defensive; always had, always would. But Nate was talking the same way he had when he'd suspected Stacey of being a gold digger.

"Do you know anything about the kid's dad?" Nate asked.

Chase went back to making the coffee. "She was

married and the guy turned out to be an asshole by the sound of it. I was hardly gonna ask her for details."

Nate folded his arms, expression serious. Classic Nate. "And you're certain the husband was the boy's father?"

"Fuck!" Chase swore, burning his hand on the side of the machine. He glared at his brother. "Leave it, Nate. Just fucking leave it, okay?"

"I'm just sayin'," Nate said, shrugging. "He looks a lot like you did as a kid. Just go check out some old pics if you don't believe me."

Chase finished making the coffee, stirred in some sugar, and then put the lids on. He didn't want to be having this conversation. It was bullshit.

"Maybe you should work out when you guys did the wild thing," Nate suggested, his palm closing over Chase's shoulder for a second. "I'm guessing you used protection, but you know, mistakes happen."

Chase stared at the coffee machine. They hadn't used protection. Twice in his life he hadn't, and both times had been with Hope. "I think you're barking up the wrong tree," Chase said, balancing the coffees one on top of the other and then grabbing the bagels, refusing to even consider what Nate was saying. "Hope wouldn't do that to me, and the fact the kid looks like me? Dark hair and dark eyes doesn't mean he belongs to me, Nate. This is just you being all overprotective like you always are when it comes to family."

Nate shrugged. "So ask her then."

"No, I'm not going to fucking ask her out of the blue if I fathered her kid." Chase shook his head. "Just look after him till we get back, and keep your stupid theories to yourself. And don't take him riding. I want him to like me and taking him down to the horses is gonna be my thing."

So they hadn't used protection. So what? They were

both clean and last night she'd told him that the only other person she'd been with was her husband. Besides, Hope had been on the pill back then, he knew that for a fact, and she never would have let him go bare if she wasn't. But . . . He frowned. Harrison was four almost five, and they'd been together . . .

Fuck Nate. He knew Hope and he would trust her with his life. She would never keep something like this from him. Never.

"How are you getting on?"

"I've been monitoring them, taking some notes. They're definitely close to being ready."

Chase nodded and passed her the bagel, then coffee.

"Thanks. Just what I needed."

Hope took a long, slow sip of coffee and he watched her, wondered how the hell he'd bring it up if he did decide to ask her.

"I've drunk more alcohol with you this past week or so than I've had in months," she said. "In fact, make that years."

"Head thumping?" Chase asked with a laugh.

"I'm not a seasoned whiskey drinker like you." She took another sip, then set her coffee down and reached for the bagel.

"And I'm not exactly sure that it's something I should be proud of." Chase followed her lead and took a bite of his bagel, swallowing it down as he stared at the herd. They were in the field closest to the yards, grazing on long grass and looking content, just how Hope had wanted them.

They stood in silence while they ate. Hope moved a few steps farther down the fence line, her eyes trained expertly on the cattle, and he let her study them without interfering.

"We'll start with the first lot soon, and from what I'm seeing I think they'll all be ready within twelve hours."

Chase nodded. "You tell me when and where you want me. I'll do what I'm told."

Their eyes met and they both laughed. "I'm glad it's not just me with the filthy mind," Hope said.

"Takes one to know one." Chase stared at her, could see the gentle rise and fall of her chest as she breathed deep. He shoved his hands in his pockets to keep them out of trouble; what he wanted was to grab hold of Hope and take her right there on the grass, but she was in work mode and what they were doing was too important.

"I think I'll head back to the house soon and take Harrison home. We could be a few hours down here once we start, depending on how things go, and I need to get him dressed. I brought clean clothes in case we stayed."

"He'll be fine up there with Nate," Chase told her. "Ryder and Chloe will be hanging around, so there'll be plenty of people to keep him entertained. I'll shoot Nate a text and tell him your overnight bag's in my room."

Hope looked relieved. "You're certain? It will be kind of hard to get someone at short notice on a Sunday, so I'd sure appreciate it."

"I'm sure." Chase did reach out for her this time, catching her hand. Her surprised eyes met his, but she didn't pull away. "Hope, Nate said something to me this morning that's kind of playing on my mind."

Her fingers tightened against his. "What's that?"

"I don't even want to ask you, but he had this stupid idea that Harrison could be my son."

Hope pulled back from him, letting go of his hand. Her smile was long gone, her arms folded across her chest as she put distance between them.

"I shouldn't have said anything," Chase muttered, reaching for her again only to be rebuffed. She angled her body so he didn't connect when he tried to wrap an arm around her, wanting to draw her in. Why the fuck had he listened to Nate? "Can you forget I even said anything?"

She let him draw her into his arms, but she was stiff. The night before, she'd molded into him, making it impossible to tell where his body ended and hers began, her body like a snake wrapped around his. Now it was like hugging a corpse.

"I'm sorry."

Hope pulled back. "Chase, it's been great seeing you again. We've had a lot of fun. But once I'm done here . . ."

"What?" he demanded, refusing to release her hand. "You're going to leave and I'll never hear from you again like last time? Is that it?"

"It's been fun," she said, never meeting his gaze. The electricity between them was palpable, but it was no longer fuelled by desire; now it was anger. Pure, raw anger.

"Yeah, it's been fun," he barked. "And there's no way I'm letting you run away from me this time. Not again."

"Let go of me, Chase," she commanded, yanking her hand away from him. "You're hurting me."

He released his fingers, never taking his eyes from her face. "You're angry at me, I get that. I should never have asked about Harrison. It's none of my business."

"What we did back then? It was just sex." She shrugged, finally raising her blue eyes. "We were great friends and we did the wild thing. Just like last night. It doesn't mean anything."

"To hell it doesn't." If he'd been angry before, now he was pissed.

Hope started to walk and he followed, hot on her heels. He strode past her and then ground to a halt, blocking her path. Chase stared down at Hope, not giving her the chance to look away. His body was so tense he was certain he was about to start trembling, the desire to grab hold of her and just shake some sense into her almost overwhelming. He balled his fists at his sides, moving closer up into her space. Maybe he shouldn't have said anything, should have kept his mouth shut instead of letting what Nate had said get to him, but he'd started it now and he wasn't going to back down. Hope had rocks in her head if she thought for a second he was going to just let her go.

"Don't make out like us sleeping together was just some random act," Chase growled out. "We both know it was way more than that, so don't even try to pretend otherwise."

Hope's eyes filled with tears as she blinked, turning her head slightly away from him. But Chase was having none of it. He reached out and cupped her chin, forcing her head up so their eyes were locked again. He didn't want to hurt her, and touched her just firmly enough so she had to do as he commanded, because he wasn't letting her walk away from this discussion, not this time. It was time they had it out—the way they'd behaved back then had been idiotic, but they'd been young. They didn't have that excuse anymore.

"We were friends and we did something stupid. Is that honestly what you believe?" Chase ground his teeth together, trying to keep his anger in check. "You don't think there was anything more to it than that?"

The tears had started to fall now, plopping down her cheeks. Chase refused to acknowledge them—she wasn't the only one hurting just because she was the one crying. When he'd finished with Stacey, he'd been pissed off, but the way he felt right now about Hope? Blood was pumping through his body, his heart was pounding, the anger welling inside of him only matched by the pain of actually giving a damn about Hope.

"Nate was right," she whispered, taking a visible deep breath before pushing him away. She planted her hands on his chest and pushed back, forcing distance between them. She looked like she was struggling to breathe.

"What did you say?" Anger, visceral and burning hot, started to pound through him. What the fuck had she just said?

Hope started to turn and he grabbed her by the arm, moving around so he was directly in front of her again. "You don't say something like that then just walk off."

She kept her eyes downcast, her body shuddering as she cried.

"Hope?" Chase bellowed. "What the hell are you trying to tell me?"

"Harrison is yours, Chase. He's your son." The tears stopped, replaced by a hollow, glassy-eyed look. "You want to know what I've been doing all these years? I've been pretending that your son belonged to another man, because I knew the last thing you'd want to do would be settle down and have a family. I kept this from you because it seemed like the right thing to do at the time, so don't you dare look at me like that."

Chase let go of her, heart pounding. All he could see was red—burning anger, *fury*, as Hope stood there like she hadn't just changed his whole fucking life in less than a minute. *How dare she?* What the fuck made her think she could just make a decision like that?

"Bullshit," he muttered, more trying to convince himself than accuse her of lying. "You've got to be fucking kidding me. I don't believe for a second that you'd keep something like that from me." He'd trusted Hope like she was family. *Always.*

She shook her head, slowly, her shoulders falling forward. "He's yours, Chase. Now you know the truth." Her arms were folded around her body, like she was trying to stave away the cold. Only the day was warm, the sun shining brightly down on them.

"I trusted you," he ground out, angrily running his fingers through his hair. "I fucking trusted you, Hope. I always goddamn trusted you and that's how you repay me? By keeping from me the fact that I had a *child* with you?"

"I didn't want to get pregnant, Chase," she whispered. "You think I wanted to find out that our one night had ended up with me pregnant and alone when I was so excited about my career? I didn't plan any of this, and I did what I thought was right to protect everyone. You, me, our families . . ."

"Don't you dare." He turned, spinning on his heel to get as far away from her as possible before he did or said something he'd regret. He stormed off a few paces before marching straight back at her, fists bunched again. "Don't you ever put words in my mouth again, Hope. I sure as fuck didn't want a family and a white picket fence back then, and I don't now, but I wouldn't have turned my back on you or my son, and don't you ever fucking *dare* pretend otherwise."

Chase left her standing there, tears streaming down her cheeks now. She dropped to the ground as he turned, walking away from her, her cries audible as he put as much distance between them as possible. Hope had been the one person outside of family that he'd have trusted with his life, the only woman he'd ever let close to him. And she'd betrayed him like no one in his life had done before. Hope had done this to him. *Hope.*

And he had a son.

Fuck. He was a goddamn father and had been for the past four years without even knowing it.

Chase slammed his fist into the door of a stable as he

passed, opening his palm and smacking it again. "Fuck!" His yell echoed through the barn, startling the horses inside.

There was only one thing he knew for sure; he would never trust Hope again, and there was no way he was ready to be a dad, no matter how cute the kid was. Even after the fun night he'd had with him.

He was an idiot for not putting two and two together the moment he'd met her son—of course she hadn't left college, met a man, and ended up barefoot and pregnant within weeks or months of them parting. This was Hope—top of her class, driven, passionate Hope. She'd had a plan, and that plan hadn't involved becoming a mom at twenty-six. Just like his had never been to be a father before he was good and ready.

He stopped walking, his breath ragged as he tried to process what had just happened. Chase leaned over the railings that bordered the cattle yard and shut his eyes, wishing to hell Hope had never walked back into his life.

But there was only one thing running through his head right now: Did he want the kid or not? Harrison might not have been raised as his son, but he was a King, and that meant he was Chase's flesh and blood, that he deserved everything the King name meant. It wasn't the poor kid's fault that he was born a bastard, and Chase couldn't exactly live with himself if he ignored him, knowing that his own son was out there in the world.

"Chase."

Chase ground his teeth together when Hope's soft, familiar voice washed over him.

"Leave me alone," he barked out.

A hand closed over his shoulder. "Chase, please."

His lips curled back as he dug his fingers hard into the railings beneath them. "Back the fuck off, Hope. I mean it."

Her hand disappeared, the softness of her touch gone as quick as it had arrived. Chase listened to her move away, waiting, not wanting to so much as see her traitorous face.

"You know what, Hope?" he said, changing his mind and furiously turning around, looking into eyes the color of the ocean, eyes that he'd once wished he could look into every single night. "Back then, I fucking loved you." There, he'd said it.

He watched as she gulped, her throat moving as she hugged her arms around herself even tighter than before, looking more fragile girl than strong, successful woman. "And now?" Her voice was barely audible.

"Now?" He laughed, a cruel noise that cut deep between them. "I don't know you at all, Hope, so I sure as hell can't love you. Because the Hope I thought I knew wasn't such a complete bitch. But then I never really knew you, did I?"

Chase knew he'd hurt her, but whatever pain he was causing her was nothing on how he was feeling right now. She'd made a decision for him that she'd had no right to make, and the only way he could take control was to figure out how the hell he was going to deal with Harrison.

Harrison King.

His own son had been living in Texas for weeks, and he hadn't had a fucking clue.

Chapter 12

There was nothing she could do. Hope stood and watched Chase walk away, her hands shaking as she curled her arms even tighter around herself.

She'd never wanted to keep Harrison a secret from him, but telling him had seemed impossible at the time, and then as time went on it had become even harder. But his words cut deep. He was Harrison's father and she shouldn't have kept it from him, but if she had her chance all over again? *Damn it.* Maybe she would have done the same. She could say, hand on her heart, that her son was the best thing that had ever happened to her. Her marriage, losing the ranch, everything she'd been through—it was nothing compared to the thought of not having Harrison. She loved him more than anything, and she'd never wanted Chase to have to be a dad, feeling forced into playing a role he didn't want. So she'd come home, reunited with a guy she'd known since they were kids, let him think she'd gotten pregnant straightaway, and everything had seemed okay. Like she'd made it all work. Until the day Harrison had been born, hardly a month after their wedding, and she'd blurted out the truth to him. She shook her head, hating going back in time, to the day her husband had started to treat her like the liar she was.

She reached into her pocket for her phone, stared at the screen as her mom's number ran through her head. Hope bit down hard on her lip, staring into the distance and refusing to shed more tears. For the first time in her life, she was alone. Her mom was no longer on the end of a phone line, waiting to hear from her only daughter; her dad was long passed now, and her husband had betrayed her. She'd slowly lost contact with most of her friends except one, been busy being a working mom trying to make a future for herself and Harrison. And her former best friend? She shook her head and stared after him. She'd just lost him, too. Chase had once been her rock, the one person in her life she'd truly loved and trusted, and instead of repaying that trust he'd given her, she'd betrayed him.

She pushed her phone back into her pocket, determined to deal with the situation on her own, allowed herself a few deep breaths as she wiped beneath her eyes to remove any trace of her tears, and forced her feet to move. She had a job to do. A job she loved. She had a son to care for. A son she loved. That's all she needed.

Hope walked through the barn and emerged into the bright sunshine, tilting her face to let the heat wash over her. Being back in Texas and reconnecting with Chase could have been amazing. Instead it had only made her heart break all over again.

Her phone rang and she yanked it out, eyes still shut as she answered.

"Hope?"

The gruff, deep voice on the other end shocked her eyes into popping straight back open. *Chase?*

"Yeah, it's me."

"We have a problem. Meet me in the office."

Chase hung up before she could answer, leaving her to square her shoulders and make her way back to the main building. Whatever it was must be urgent, because she was certain she was the last person he had any intention of talking to ever again. Although, personal feelings aside, he still had a business to run, and she doubted the King empire would ever grind to a halt. Not for anything. Nate would never drop the ball when it came to ruthlessly acquiring property and balancing the books, and Chase would be riding his land and breeding top-quality cattle till his last breath, of that she was certain.

"Chase?" Hope called out, still uncertain about coming face-to-face with him after what had happened between them. His words still echoed through her mind, the feel of his anger, almost tangible, like a metallic taste in her mouth she couldn't get rid of. It was even worse because she was starting to second-guess what she'd done all over again.

"In here."

She followed his voice and found him with his arms spread, palms planted on the table in front of him.

"What's going on?" she asked.

"Look," he said, voice so low that it sounded even more angry now than it had earlier.

Hope followed his gaze and saw two canisters lying on the ground. *Shit.* Any other time it might have been amusing to see the ground covered in sticky cow semen, except for the fact that each canister had cost King Ranch a small fortune. And it was the same semen she was preparing to inseminate his cows with. *Now.*

"Who did this?"

"Fucked if I know," Chase muttered, standing up to his full height and raking his hands through his hair. Now that he wore it longer she noticed that he did that a lot, especially when he was stressed about something. "But when I find the son of a bitch I'm gonna kill him."

Hope took a deep, shuddering breath. The look in his eyes was wild, the menacing way he was staring at the turned-over canisters enough to tell her that he might just do exactly that when he found the culprit. Chase was big by any standards, his shoulders wide, biceps thick; there was no man alive who'd want Chase pissed with him. And the fact that she'd already infuriated him meant he wasn't in a mood to be crossed.

"Let's be practical here," she said, stepping closer and seeing that each cane of semen had been smashed so that there was nothing usable left. Not that she'd be able to use something that had been compromised anyway, but she was frantically trying to figure out how to salvage the situation. "Who would even want to do this to you?"

Chase smacked his fist against the table, then folded his arms, walking toward the open door and staring out in the distance. She had the distinct feeling of being a caged animal, ready to bolt through the door the instant she felt trapped. Only right now his anger wasn't directed at her, which meant she was safe. Temporarily.

"We've employed the same guys for years here, and hardly any of them even know what we're doing, or how goddamn valuable the canisters even were."

Hope shut her eyes, played back all the workers she'd met so far on the ranch. His brothers? No chance. They might like to play jokes and give each other shit, but they wouldn't compromise something so important, not to mention valuable. When she opened her eyes, she cringed before speaking her mind.

"I know you trust him, but have you ever considered your foreman?"

Chase turned around, laughter dancing in his gaze. "Randy? You've got to be kidding me."

"Sometimes it's the ones we least expect," she muttered. "Who else knows?"

Chase raised an eyebrow, his mouth turning downward into a frown. She knew exactly what he was thinking—that maybe he had no idea who to trust anymore. "I trust Randy. Believe me when I say it wasn't him." His laugh was hollow. "Although I would have said you'd have my back, and I couldn't have been further from the truth."

"Look," she said, folding her arms, "who did this doesn't matter right now, Chase. What matters is what we do next. We have a limited window that we need to use to our advantage, so the next few hours are crucial. Agreed?"

Chase grunted. "You stored the other canisters at the lab at your work?"

"Yes," she replied. "I tested one straw out of each canister in the lab, so we still have enough to proceed with a smaller herd of heifers." Hope found herself nodding, calculating. "It's better than nothing, and if I leave now I can be back without us losing any time."

He turned away again, but his body was rigid, the muscles of his arms visible as he folded his arms tight across himself. Her fingers itched to touch him, to comfort him, wanting to feel her skin against his and go back in time. She should never have told him the truth. Or maybe she should never have hidden it from him in the first place.

She took a few steps closer to him, near enough to inhale the faint tanginess of his cologne, her hands at her sides. They hovered, then she dropped them, knowing the last thing he would want was her touching him now.

"Are you going to contact anyone from law enforcement?"

He grunted. "And tell them some semen from King Ranch has been tampered with? They'd think that was damn funny, I'm sure."

"It's a valuable product," she affirmed.

"I'm going to go tell Nate, let him and Ryder know what's going on," Chase said, heading out the door. "I'll call in law enforcement if and when we need it, but we have our own way of dealing with assholes who fuck with our stuff, if you get my drift."

"Chase . . ." she began, not sure exactly how to say what she wanted to tell him, or whether she should be scared of him, too.

He paused and half turned back toward her. "Don't," he said. "We talk business and that's it. Got it?" He ran his fingers hard through his hair again. "As far as I'm concerned, once this is done, we're through."

"I'll take Harrison now."

"No, you won't. He can stay here."

Hope raised her chin, stared him in the eye. "He's my son, Chase. I'll leave him here to keep playing, but don't go telling me what to do."

They stared at each other, neither giving in. "Just leave him here and come back when you have the straws."

She nodded, bottom lip snapped firmly beneath her teeth. She got it loud and clear. Trouble was, if she knew Chase, then she knew he wasn't going to just forget what she'd told him. He had a son, and there was no way in hell he was okay with having a child out there who didn't know the truth about his dad.

She watched him walk away from her for the third time that day. Chase King had broken her heart into a million pieces five years ago without even knowing it, and it was starting to splinter all over again right now. She didn't blame him—he'd had no idea that she'd fallen pregnant, so it wasn't like it was his fault—but still. There had only ever been one man capable of truly hurting her, because she never let anyone else close. Her husband had stung her financially, but he hadn't been even close to shattering her heart.

Hope grabbed her phone and speed-dialed work, walking briskly back toward her vehicle. It was a Sunday, but she knew the place wouldn't be empty and her call would be redirected to the after-hours mobile.

"Hey, it's me," she said when Kate, one of the other vets, answered the phone.

They chatted for a second, laughing about something Kate's new dog had done, before Kate got around to asking her what she'd phoned in for. They'd both been involved in all the lab work this week, so Hope knew she'd be able to help.

"I need you to check on something for me, just for peace of mind," Hope said, speaking more quietly when she spied Chase's foreman tying up a horse near her vehicle. She lowered her voice again. "Just a second, Kate."

Hope waved to Randy and smiled, jumping behind the wheel of her truck before continuing her conversation. As far as she was aware, the only two people on this ranch who knew about the additional canisters were her and Chase, and that's the way she wanted it to stay. Chase might trust his second-in-command, but she wasn't convinced.

"I have two canisters stored in the lab," she told Kate as she started the ignition. "They're both clearly labeled King Ranch, and I need you to do a quick check to make sure they haven't been tampered with in any way. I'll be back within the hour, but it's kind of urgent. Can you call me back as soon as you can?"

She said good-bye and drove slowly past the main homestead, admiring the immaculate post-and-rail fencing and a herd of mares with foals grazing together. She'd had a ranch not so different from this back home, a ranch that she'd always dreamed of owning, and of raising her own children in the home and on the land where she'd grown up. Now she'd lost it all—she was more in debt than flush with money, a single mom to a gorgeous son. And her son could have had all this. If only she'd stayed in Texas, things might have turned out differently. Maybe her family ranch would still be hers, too.

She shook her head and reached forward to crank up the music, looking straight ahead instead of reminiscing about the scenery. *What if*s were dangerous thoughts, she knew that better than anyone.

Nate was looking after Harrison, and she owed it to the whole King family to do what she could. Their empire was the biggest in Texas, but she wanted no part in them sustaining any kind of financial hit, not if she could help it. The stakes were too high, and the sooner she could walk away, the better.

Chase stormed into the house, searching for Nate. He couldn't find him. His hands were clenched into tight balls, desperate to punch something, *anything*, but he fought to keep his cool.

"Nate!" he called.

He took a look outside and spotted him, with Ryder and Chloe, by the little corrals they'd used when they were kids. He jogged straight down to them, stopping before he got too close. Harrison was sitting up on their old pony, Whiskey, a grin on the boy's face so wide Chase was certain he'd see all his teeth if he was in the corral with him. *Damn it!* Nate was supposed to have waited for him to get back.

"Nate!" he called, not wanting to think about Harrison yet. He had to figure out what the hell had happened under their noses first, right here on King Ranch. "Ryder!" They both looked up and he waved them over, yelling out, "Chloe, can you look after the little fella a bit longer? His mom will be back soon and I need these two for a sec."

She waved, smiling as she passed Ryder, kissing him before trading places and ducking through the railings so she was in the corral with Harrison. Chase could have stared at Harrison all day. He'd been so goddamn stupid. How the hell could he not have seen the similarities himself and worked out the time line?

"What's so urgent?" Ryder asked.

Chase frowned and dug his toe into the dirt. "Some asshole stole from us."

Nate's face was like a thundercloud, his dark brown eyes turning a stormy shade of black. "Stole what?"

"The imported semen. It's all gone, dumped on the damn floor."

"That's half a fucking million dollars' worth," Nate growled.

"Someone did this, on our land?" Ryder was shaking his head, hands fisted tighter than Chase's. "Who the hell would have the goddamn balls to walk in here and do that?"

Chase shook his head. "No idea. Hope had some stored at the lab in town, so it's not a completely lost cause yet. We're gonna make each one count."

Nate's arms were folded tight as he leaned closer, like he was trying to keep their conversation confidential even though there was no one within miles who could eaves-drop. "When we find the motherfucker who did this, there'll be no holding back. You two hear me?"

"Damn right," Chase muttered at the same time as his younger brother.

They all stood, silent, the only noise Harrison's laughter from the corral. Chase couldn't help it, couldn't fight the pull to look at the boy and watch his every move.

"Cute kid," Nate said with a chuckle.

Chase cleared his throat, pushed his hands into his pockets. "About what you said earlier."

Nate laughed and slapped him on the back. "I was just fucking with you. I should have kept my big mouth shut. You know how I get."

Chase blew out a breath. "You were right."

"What?"

"Sorry, can you guys fill me in on whatever the hell you're talking about?" Ryder asked.

Nate looked pissed when he moved to stand in front of Chase, forcing him to drag his gaze away from Harrison. "You're telling me that Harrison"—he paused, looking over his shoulder and hooking his thumb in the direction of the corral—"is your son?"

"What the fuck?" Ryder's eyes widened when Chase glanced at him.

"Yep. It seems that the one that got away was pregnant when she disappeared." Chase almost laughed, it sounded so insane. "So do I tell her to fuck off and take the kid, or do I man up and do the right thing?" He was talking like an asshole but the truth was the boy was his and there was no way he was going to let her go away, let alone tell her to.

Nate moved back to stand beside him. They were all staring at Harrison again.

"You know what you've got to do."

"About Hope?" Chase doubted he'd ever be able to forgive her, not after what she'd done.

"No, about the child," Nate said. "What you decide about Hope is your business, but if this boy is yours? Then he's a King, and there's no way he's not gonna be a part of our lives. He's staying in Texas and that's the end of it."

Chase knew his brother was right. He just had to deal with one thing at a time, and right now that thing was catching out the asshole who'd stolen from them.

Chapter 13

Hope watched the last cow walk out of the crush. Everything had gone completely to plan, except for the volume of inseminations. The herd was settled and relaxed, they'd happily munched on hay, moved through while she'd worked on them, and now she was standing alone as they started to graze in the small adjoining field.

She rolled her shoulders as she stretched her neck out, yanking out her ponytail. There had been plenty of times in the past couple of months that she'd felt alone, but none so acutely as right now. Chase was nowhere to be seen, and she was preparing to head over to the house to collect Harrison. She just needed a few moments to herself to think, to try to figure out a plan. Being in Texas was great for now, it gave her the chance to earn enough money to build up her finances again, but staying wasn't her long-term plan. She wanted to go back to Canada when she could, once she could take out a big-enough loan to try to buy her ranch back.

"Hi, Hope."

She turned around and found Randy walking over, his gaze trained on the heifers. A couple of younger ranch hands who'd been with him disappeared into a barn, and she wished she wasn't alone with the man she suspected.

"Hey. How you doing?"

He nodded, thumbs looped into his belt as he came closer. "Not bad," he replied. "You been doing inseminations?"

Hope didn't care what Chase said; there was something about Randy that told her not to trust him as far as she could kick him.

"We've done some of the herd," she said, not sure whether she should elaborate or not. "Everything went pretty smoothly."

"Huh." Randy stared at her, too long for her liking, before turning his attention back to the livestock. "When Nate said the canisters had been tampered with I thought this'd all have to be put on the back burner."

Hope wanted to extract herself from the conversation. And fast. "Hey, it was great seeing you, but I'm beat," she said, holding up her hand to stifle a very real yawn. She *was* exhausted, her body weary from working and her eyes burning from the tears she'd shed earlier. Not to mention she just needed some time alone, away from anything to do with the King family or ranch, to just figure everything out. "I'll catch you when I'm back tomorrow."

Randy nodded and she left him standing there, one leg hitched on the fence rail. "See you later."

Hope collected up her things and went over to her vehicle, systematically putting everything back in place and then jumping behind the wheel. She would usually have just walked over to the house, but she wanted to get Harrison and go.

As she was pulling away she saw Chase. He was standing by the barn, a solemn expression on his face as he stared in her direction. Tears burned like acid against her eyeballs, but she swallowed hard, pushed them away. *No more tears.* She'd promised herself that the day Harrison had been born, and the last thing she needed was to go back on her word now.

Hope raised a hand, staring at Chase as she drove past. There was nothing left to say—he'd worked silently alongside her until the last couple of heifers, then disappeared awhile, and he knew she was coming by again in the morning to check on them.

It only took a couple of minutes to reach the house and she jumped out, retrieving the boots she'd borrowed from Chloe before heading for the front door. She left them under the eaves so they wouldn't get wet if it rained and let herself in.

"Anybody home?"

Nobody answered but she heard voices and laughter and headed down the hall and into the kitchen. She paused at the doorway. Harrison was sitting on a barstool, his legs dangling as he drained a glass of chocolate milk, a half-eaten sandwich discarded on a plate beside him.

He was laughing at something Nate had said, and it wasn't until she moved farther forward that she saw Ryder had his head in the fridge, the three of them hanging out together. An all-too-familiar sensation of guilt passed over her, an icy haze washing through her body.

"Hey," she said, forcing herself to walk into the room.

The laughter on Nate's face died, his stare cold as the Antarctic Ocean. "I was just giving the little guy a snack."

"He'll eat you out of house and home if you give him the chance," she joked, clearing her throat when Nate's expression remained unchanged. She put a protective arm around her boy, suddenly terrified at what she might be up against.

Nate had seemed like a big teddy bear the night before, tough on the outside and like marshmallow on the inside, but she was fast seeing why he was so damn successful in business, why he was so naturally capable of taking over the running of his grandfather's company. His stare was making her knees knock, and that was without worrying about the sheer size of him towering over her as he moved closer to them. Hope did a quick glance at Ryder—up until now his blue eyes had shone with laughter, his grin infectious, but that smile was long gone.

"We'll be seeing you again real soon, Harris," Nate said, leaning over to ruffle his hair. "Today was fun."

"Today was so cool," Harrison said, eyes dancing when he spun around and almost toppled off his chair. "Chase came over before and took me outside, showed me some puppies. He said I could even pick one and choose a name and everything."

Hope swallowed, her throat catching. She was finding it hard to breathe with Nate so close, and it was becoming clear to her that it wasn't just Chase she needed to be worried about. He'd obviously told his brothers the minute she'd confessed, and they weren't about to let their nephew walk out of their lives. And giving him a puppy? She got the hint that the puppy was going to be living here, which meant Chase was expecting to be seeing a whole lot of their son.

"Harrison, can you go grab your stuff? Double-check you haven't left anything around the house."

"But, Mom . . ."

She touched his shoulder and dropped a kiss to his head before jumping him down from the stool. "No arguing, sweetheart. We have to go. You can tell me all about today in the car."

She kept her shoulders back, refusing to be intimidated by the two men standing before her. So they were wealthy and powerful. So what? She was Harrison's mom, and if there was one thing she could never be criticized of it was being a damn good mother.

"I take it Chase told you guys," she started.

Nate folded his arms across his chest and Ryder leaned back, both of them never taking their eyes off her for a second.

"He's a King," Nate said. "Pure and simple, he's one of us."

"And he's my son," she said. "When Chase is ready to talk, we'll talk, but until then . . ."

"We all make mistakes and I know that better than anyone," Ryder said, shaking his head when Nate gave him a sharp look. "Give Chase some time to cool the hell down, then work it out. This is between the two of you, and the only solution is to fix what's broke. Got it?"

"Bottom line is there's no way you're bringing that boy up without him knowing our family."

Hope bristled at the commanding way Nate spoke to her, but she could see that Ryder was more compassionate than his older brother and she needed to keep her cool while he was giving her a lifeline.

Just as she was about to answer him, Chase walked into the room. He ran a hand across his stubbled jaw as he first looked at her, then walked straight past. Harrison came running into the room at high speed at almost the same time.

"I've got everything, Mom."

She reached for his hand and took one of his Transformers so he didn't have so much to hold. "Thanks for having us last night," she said, ignoring Chase and looking between his brothers instead. "Tell Chloe I'm sorry I didn't get to say good-bye."

"See ya, Chase," Harrison called out, waving to the

others and breaking her heart all over again. "Can I come back and see the puppies again soon?"

Chase turned, dropping to his haunches. "You sure can, bud. I reckon you can come here whenever you want."

"And play Transformers?" Harrison asked innocently.

"And play Transformers," Chase said, his smile genuine as he reached out to touch Harrison's shoulder. "Definitely Transformers. I'll brush up on all the names so I can play better next time."

"And ride Whiskey?"

Chase chuckled and Hope just stayed silent, heart breaking.

"We can do anything you want. I bet that old pony had the best day ever with you playing with him."

"Come on, sweetheart," she said, squeezing Harrison's hand and walking him out, forcing him to go past Chase.

She could fall to pieces later. Right now, she had to be strong for her boy.

"How you doing?"

Chase shrugged and pulled open the fridge door, staring at the contents and then shutting it again. "Is it too early to get rotten drunk?"

Ryder glanced at his watch. "Yeah, kinda. But then again you've just found out you're a dad, so maybe not."

"I'm not a dad," Chase muttered, opening the fridge again and pulling out a beer. A beer he could justify at this time of the day. He'd wait to start on the whiskey until after five. "I'm the kid's biological father." Their dad hadn't deserved the title, and Chase was a firm believer in not taking that kind of term lightly, not without earning it. Their granddad had been their dad—maybe not technically, but by the way he'd taken over their care and raised them.

"He's a really nice kid," Nate said, taking Chase's lead and grabbing a couple of beers. Chase watched as he opened them both and passed one to Ryder.

"I know she really pulled one over on you, bro, but I think you should hear her out. Try to figure something . . ."

"She fucking lied to me, Ryder. Am I supposed to just forget that?" Chase was pissed but he knew it wasn't his brother's fault. "Sorry, I just . . . I don't even know what I'm thinking."

Nate grimaced, his face drawn into a frown as he stared at his beer. "My gut instinct is to hate her for what she did, Chase, but she's the mother of your son. And you guys used to be pretty close."

"Yeah, but maybe I didn't know her as well as I thought."

"Or maybe she knew you better than you realized," Ryder said.

"Hey, whose fucking side are you on?"

Ryder held up his hands in surrender. "Yours. But I'm just sayin', maybe she had her reasons. I just don't want you to cut this kid out to spite Hope." Ryder shrugged. "We know what it's like to grow up without a dad, but we were lucky to have Granddad. Who's this kid got except his mom?"

Chase knew Ryder was right, but it still didn't make it any easier.

"I loved her," Chase confessed for the second time that day, only telling his brothers was easier than telling Hope had been. "I never told her, but I did."

"So make things right," Ryder said.

Chase looked at Ryder, his barely noticeable nod telling Chase that both his brothers thought he needed to at least listen to what she had to say.

"And what if I can't forgive her?" Right now, Chase didn't even want to see her face again. What Hope had done was unforgivable as far as he was concerned, no matter her reasons.

"Then don't," Nate said. "But remember that nothing is the kid's fault, this is on her. We're here for you, and the boy deserves to know that he has a dad and uncles. He might have lost his mom's ranch, but he'll always have a place here. He's a King."

"Can we just get drunk and forget all about this for the rest of the day?" Chase asked.

"Damn straight we can," Ryder replied, holding up his beer bottle and clinking it against Chase's.

"Yeah, and while we're at it we can try to figure out how the hell we're gonna catch us a thief," Nate said. "I've organized cameras to be installed, but I doubt whoever it is will be coming back anytime soon."

"We gonna install them ourselves so no one knows what's going on? In case it was an inside job?" Chase asked.

Nate nodded and took a pull of his beer.

"Hey, did I tell you guys that Hope had this weird theory about it being Randy?"

Ryder laughed but Nate's face remained impassive.

"What?" Chase asked. "You believe her? I reckon it's one of the younger guys. One with nothing to lose. I saw a couple of them hanging around the barn today, and one stuck to Randy like glue the day before yesterday, when Hope was here."

"I don't know what I believe," Nate said. "All I know is that there are only three people on this ranch right now that I trust without question, and you guys are two of them. The other is Chloe. As far as I'm concerned it could be anyone else."

Chase finished his beer and headed over for another. If he wanted to forget about Hope, he needed to start drinking faster.

* * *

Chase rolled out of bed and cringed when he opened his eyes. Drinking away his troubles had seemed like a great idea at the time, but he was going to pay for it this morning. He kicked his shirt out of the way and reached for his jeans, keeping his movements slow so he didn't aggravate the steady thumping in his head, and pulled them on, heading first into the bathroom to splash some cold water on his face, then straight downstairs for coffee.

"You look terrible."

Chase ignored his brother and pushed the button on the coffee machine.

"Want something for the pain?" Nate asked.

"Yeah, that's why I drank whiskey last night." Chase glanced around, saw that Nate had already tidied up. "What's the time?" Maybe Mrs. T had already been in and tended to their mess.

"It's nine. You slept in."

Chase glared at Nate, not needing to be called out on having a late one. He was usually back inside after doing the rounds, sipping his second coffee of the day by now—one morning behind the eight ball wasn't gonna kill anyone.

"So what are you thinking this morning?"

"Fuck, Nate, I've just woken up," Chase grumbled, staring at the thick black liquid pouring in a steady stream into his cup. "I haven't even had time to think about her." This was why he'd have been better off surrounded by people who didn't know anything about Hope the night before.

Nate's laugh only annoyed him more. "I actually meant about finding the thief, but you wanna talk about Hope, no problem."

Chase resisted the urge to swear at his brother and blew on his coffee, burning his mouth when he took a small sip. Once he'd downed a good strong dose of caffeine he'd start to feel human again.

"You're drinking it black again? You must feel like shit," Nate said as he reached for an apple and took a bite.

A phone ringing took his mind off the grating sound of Nate eating and he looked around, realizing it was his. It was vibrating on the counter and he grabbed it, staring hard at the screen when he saw Hope's name displayed.

He didn't give Nate a chance to ask him who it was. "Yup," he answered.

"Hi, Chase. I just wanted to check in."

He cleared his throat. "They're all looking good this morning. I'm heading out to check them over again shortly."

Chase turned his back on Nate, hoping Hope couldn't hear his brother's snigger. She didn't need to know he'd been drowning his sorrows in alcohol and hadn't even made it out yet.

"Okay. Well, I'll be over later on to check them myself, but it'll be forty-five days before we ultrasound."

Chase took another sip of his coffee. Just hearing Hope's voice was pissing him off. "Will you be doing that yourself?"

She cleared her throat. "I could get another tech to do it. If that's what you'd prefer."

"Fine. Thanks for the call."

Chase hung up and spun around to find Nate shaking his head, looking at him like he was idiot.

"Thanks for the call? What the fuck was that about?"

"I was being polite," Chase muttered, draining the dregs in his cup and putting his cup in the dishwasher.

"You can't just bury your head in the sand."

"I reckon ignoring her is the best thing I can do right now. I'm not gonna turn my back on the kid, but I'm through with Hope. She screwed me over and I'm not giving her the chance to do it again."

"And if she's right about Randy?" Nate asked.

"She won't be. And if she is, then what? It doesn't change what she did to me." Chase opened the drawer where they kept medicines and found something for his head. He turned on the faucet and stuck his mouth under, taking a big gulp of water and swallowing the pills down. "A bottle of booze and a night's sleep haven't changed anything, Nate, and don't give me that look either."

Nate raised his brows. "And what look would that be?"

"That goddamn look on your face right now. Don't go acting like you'd be behaving any different than I am if you'd just found out someone you'd trusted had fucked you over. She had my child and she never told me. She let the boy think her husband was his dad."

Nate shrugged. "Maybe she didn't."

Chase met his gaze, glared into eyes that were as dark and stormy as his felt. "Okay then, maybe she didn't. Bottom line is I'm done with her regardless."

He left his brother and ran up the stairs, ignoring the pain in his head. Chase found a clean shirt, did up the buttons, and headed for the back door. There was plenty for him to do around the ranch, and the busier he kept himself the happier he'd be. He wanted to be in the saddle or working with livestock. What he didn't want to do was talk. Not to anyone.

"Wait up," Nate called out, catching up to him. "Ryder just phoned and told me the cameras were just delivered. We can set them up ourselves and monitor them from my iPad."

Chase grunted and pulled on his boots. "You thought about what we'll do when we find the son of a bitch?"

"No. You?"

"If anyone's throwing any punches, it'll be me. Got it?"

"Yeah, I got it."

"We telling Granddad about this?" Chase asked.

"The old man doesn't like anything being kept from him, so yeah. How about we go pick him up today, bring him back here for the afternoon if he's up to it."

"Sounds good." Chase walked alongside his brother, falling into an easy rhythm. "I miss having him around."

"Me too. And it's only gonna get worse."

They both knew the inevitable was coming. He might be the strongest man they'd ever have the privilege of knowing, but even someone like their grandfather could only fight cancer for so long. The last thing they needed was one of the newer guys, or all of them if they were working together, pulling one over on them and getting away with it, and then their granddad hearing about it.

"Are you gonna tell him about Harrison?" Nate asked, waving to Ryder as they approached.

"How about we just focus on how the hell we're gonna convince the nurses to let us take him out for the day," Chase said, eyes on his herd as he approached the field they were in. They were grazing near the fence so he was able to get close to them straightaway. "But yeah, if we bring him back, I'll tell him." He might be stubborn, but if there was one person who could always talk sense into him it was his granddad, and right now he could probably do with his perspective.

Hope arrived back at King Ranch, driving slowly past the house and heading toward the yards. She was hoping the herd would still be nearby, giving her the chance to look them over and go before she had to run into Chase or his brothers. She stopped and sat, immobile, not wanting to get out. Her eyes were still burning, like there was no moisture left around them, her pupils sore from a long day of work, then lying awake the night before, eventually crying herself to sleep. Not to mention the thumping headache she'd had all afternoon. It was times like this she just wanted to go home, only then she'd remember that home wasn't there anymore.

Hope forced herself to push the door open and dropped her feet onto the hard-packed ground. She straightened and stretched, glancing at her wristwatch and seeing that it was almost seven. Harrison would be so upset if she wasn't back to put him to bed—she was usually firm about being home early, he always came first, but today had been a disaster from the moment she'd rolled out of bed.

She stood and surveyed the cattle. They were a quiet mob, happily grazing and flicking their tails in the last moments of sunshine. She almost envied them—not a care in the world, only thinking about shelter and food.

"They're looking pretty good."

The bottom dropped out of Hope's stomach, her entire body breaking out in goose pimples just hearing Chase's voice.

"Yeah." She hadn't wanted to run into anyone, and yet here she was about to be face-to-face with Chase again.

"You'll be pleased to know we've set up surveillance," he told her, standing a few feet away, his eyes averted, focused on the cattle.

Hope was pleased. The last thing she needed was his dark gaze settled on her, those beautiful eyes all tortured and angry like they'd been when she'd told him. Her stomach did its impersonation of being home to a kaleidoscope of butterflies, batting their wings with fury.

"Any idea who did it?"

He shook his head and she studied his profile, wondered if she'd ever be close enough to him again to touch him, to run her fingers across his cheek, to feel his soft, strong lips against hers, his stubble teasing her skin. Hope turned away, stared at one of the black-as-night cattle instead.

"You're wrong about Randy." Chase's voice was flat, his mind made up. "We don't know who, but it's one of the younger ranch hands. We're fairly certain, just have to find out which one."

"Hey, maybe I am wrong," Hope said, shrugging and turning back to look at Chase. She straightened her back, squared her shoulders, and faced him. So she'd kept something from him and he hated her for it—it wasn't like she'd set out to hurt him, nothing could have been further from the truth, and she wasn't going to be some shrinking violet around him just because of who he was. Chase was powerful and attractive and rich, but that didn't make him better than her. "I don't trust him, there's just something not right about him that I can't put my finger on."

"So you want me to accuse a foreman who's worked on this ranch for over twenty years of vandalism, based on a hunch?" Chase shook his head. "Not a chance. Not when I know in my gut that you're wrong."

"Fine, don't," she said, shrugging like it was no big deal. "Do whatever the hell you like, Chase, but all I'm saying is don't rule him out. If I were you I'd be keeping that video surveillance to myself and not breathing a word to him."

"And what else would you be doing," he asked, a cruel edge to his voice cutting straight through her, *"if you were me?"*

Hope's body wanted to wilt like a flower in the burning hot sunshine, but she refused to let Chase have that kind of effect on her. He might be able to easily intimidate other women when he wanted to, but he'd never been able to do it to her before and she wasn't going to let him now. She also wasn't going to take the bait and end up engaged in a fight about Harrison. If he wanted to talk about their son then she would, but she wasn't going to let him be a bully about it.

"If I were you I'd treat everyone as a suspect. Who knows why someone would do this unless they had a reason to want to hurt you financially?"

"It's hardly going to break the bank," Chase said dryly. "And for that matter, maybe it's you?"

"Don't be an asshole," she snapped, sick of his attitude. He might be pissed with her, and for good reason, but now he was just being rude. "Besides, your favorite foreman is headed this way. Now."

Randy was crossing over from the big barn, his hand raised in a wave that she returned. Maybe she was wrong, maybe she was overthinking the situation, but she still didn't trust him. Or anyone right now for that matter.

Chase fixed his steely gaze on her. "Tell me then."

"Let me mention that I've just delivered more canisters. I have some empty ones in the truck that I can put in there. Just see if he takes the bait."

Chase scowled. "Fine. Do it." He shrugged. "At least it'll prove your theory wrong."

"Hey, Randy," she called out, throwing Chase a fake smile and taking a few steps backward. "I've just had a quick look at the girls. They shipped frozen semen to us already, so I'm just gonna store it and then I'll leave you guys to it. It'd be great to have your help tomorrow when I'm back."

"Sounds good," Randy replied, raising his eyebrows as he reached his boss. "We'll be good to inseminate the rest soon?"

"Sure will. Nothing's gonna stand in our way this time around."

Hope made her way back to the truck, fished out some

canisters, and put them in her freezer bag, making it look like she genuinely had the frozen goods with her. She headed straight into the storage facility beside the office and put them in the small upright freezer, taking care to remove the existing labels on them.

When she emerged, Randy was still talking to Chase, so she took her chance to leave, heading back to her truck. She wanted to get home—to give her boy a cuddle and be the one to put him to bed. And a nice big glass of red wine was sounding good too. In fact, it was about time she invited Kate from work over. They always got on great, but she never seemed to have any time to socialize—it was either work or mom duties—but it was time she focused on building some friendships.

"Hope! Wait up."

She groaned. Just when she thought she'd gotten away.

Chase was beside her almost immediately, falling into step alongside her before moving in front of her so she couldn't ignore him.

"Hope." His voice was deep, commanding.

She stopped walking and looked up at him. Now she could see a different side of him—the fun, easygoing guy who'd always made her laugh was long gone. He'd been replaced with a confident man used to getting what he wanted, and it was a side of him she'd always known about and had seen, only that attitude had never been directed at her before.

"I don't want to argue with you, Chase. Not now." She was tired and she just wanted to get home.

"You can't just walk away from me, Hope." He blew out a big breath and shoved his hands into his pockets. "You come here, act like nothing's happened, and then bam! I've got a goddamn son I never knew about."

Her skin prickled, like there were physical spikes

pushing out from her body. She stared at him, long and hard. "I never wanted to hurt you. Don't make out like I'm the bad guy here."

"Never wanted to hurt me?" he scoffed. "Fuck, Hope, that's bullshit if ever I've heard it." He laughed. "And if you're not the bad guy, then who is? Because it sure as hell ain't me."

Hope refused to be consumed by guilt. She'd been through so much and she wasn't going to let Chase make her feel like a bitch for making a mistake. So she'd made the wrong call? She was only human, and she'd only ever tried to protect everyone she loved.

"I've had to live with what I did all of Harrison's life," she told him, hands on hips as she stared at him. "Do you think that's been easy?" Tears burned in her eyes but she refused to let them fall.

"I don't know what to think," he said. She watched as he pulled his hands out of his pockets and put them behind his head, shutting his eyes for a second as he turned his face up to the sky. "All I know is that I'm a father and I don't know what the fuck to do about it. I don't know how to *feel*, Hope, and it's killing me."

"I need you to know that I didn't do this to hurt you, Chase." It was the truth, and it felt good saying it after keeping it to herself for so long. "We both had our futures all mapped out, and settling down with a baby wasn't part of that picture for either of us."

"You should have let me decide whether Harrison was part of my future or not." He shook his head. "And what happened to you being on the pill?"

Hope bristled. "I didn't lie to you about that."

"I never said you did," he countered straight back.

"Remember how I'd been really sick with a chest infection?" she asked. "Turns out the antibiotics I'd been on must have counteracted my pill. I didn't find out until I was about four months' pregnant, and by then it was too late to do anything about it, even if I'd wanted to."

"You thought about aborting?" he asked, the shock in his voice palpable.

"Yeah," she confessed, "I did." Hope sucked in a deep breath, still battling tears, only this time it was at the guilt and pain she still felt whenever she thought about the termination she'd once considered. "But life without Harrison, it's"—she swallowed, hard—"not even worth thinking about."

"Hey, at least you got to make that decision."

Anger swelled within Hope, burned her skin and blurred her vision. "Don't, Chase," she snapped. "Just don't."

"What? Point out that you got to make all the decisions about our child while I went about my life without a clue that I was a father? That you were pregnant?" He ran his fingers hard through his hair. "Geez, Hope. You didn't have the right."

Her breath came out as a big, ragged sigh, anger turning to sadness. The reality of what she'd done was huge, the weight on her shoulders almost unbearable. "Do you honestly think this was easy for me? That I meant to hurt you?" She shook her head and started to walk. "I did what I thought was right, and five years ago it seemed like the best decision."

Chase's hand shot out fast, grabbing hold of her wrist and forcing her to stop. "The best decision for you or for me?"

"For you." She didn't fight him, waited until he let go of her. "I did it for you, Chase, because I didn't want to be the ball and chain that ruined your life."

The silence between them was almost unbearable, the only noise the odd moo of a cow or whinny of a horse.

"Not a day has gone by since I found out I was pregnant

that I haven't thought about you, Chase, or the fact that I've kept Harrison's father from him. But I was twenty-six and pregnant. We'd just graduated and we had our whole lives ahead of us. I knew what you wanted, and a baby wasn't part of that plan."

"Was it part of yours?" he asked, no longer fierce, his expression softer all of a sudden.

"Don't you dare," she fumed. "Of course it wasn't part of my plan, but I've done the best I could and I'm a damn good mom." Hope stared at him, wishing she'd never come. Her boss had asked her to make the trip over—the King family were big-time clients by anyone's standards—but she should have made up an excuse not to come. "The ball's in your court, Chase. I did what I did because I actually gave a damn about you, and I didn't want to ruin your life." *I loved you.* That's what she should have said, but she didn't. Instead she dug her fingernails into her palms and faced him. "I have to go."

Chase stood in her way again, but this time he didn't look like he was filled with the full fury of Neptune. "Can I ask you one thing?"

She shrugged. "Sure."

"If you hadn't ended up coming here, if Nate hadn't said anything, would you ever have told me?"

Hope wished she could sink into the earth below. It was a question she asked herself constantly, and she didn't truly know the answer.

"Honestly? I don't know." She shook her head, looking back at Chase and wishing she were anywhere but here. "I kept telling myself I would, as soon as I was finished working here, but I'm not sure. I just wish you could understand that what I did wasn't to hurt you."

"Yeah, yeah," he muttered. "I heard you the first time you tried to make me believe that bullshit."

Hope bristled, but she didn't react. "I'll see you around, Chase."

"Did Harrison think your husband was his dad?"

So much for only one question. She inhaled deeply. "No. He knew he was his stepdad. When we first got married I let my husband think I was pregnant with his child, but the moment Harrison was born I had to tell him the truth. He hated me from that moment, I think, but what I did to him didn't mean it was okay for him to take everything from me. Not for a second."

She stepped around him when he didn't say anything else and headed straight for her truck, jumping in and buckling up before he could even think about stopping her. Hope bit down hard on her lower lip and blinked repeatedly, focusing on turning the vehicle around and driving away. It wasn't until she reached the road that she pulled over, her shoulders heaving as her entire body started to shudder, big sobs bursting from her mouth. Tears poured down her cheeks, tears she'd held in check for so long finally releasing. Hope slammed her palm into the steering wheel over and over again before collapsing forward, her forehead against the relative cool of the leather.

She'd loved Chase so hard it hurt. The kind of love that made a girl do crazy things, like pretend she didn't like him, push him away and then be repulsed at seeing him with other women . . . and the kind of love that finally let her give in to one long, lingering night of passion. And when she'd found out she was pregnant, she'd been too proud to come after Chase and let him know. Because she'd hoped, even before she knew, that he'd come after her anyway. That he'd decide that nothing was more important than them being together after flirting for so long, being best friends for years, and then only having one night together.

But he hadn't come and she hadn't been about to chase after a guy like him—he was used to women flocking after him, and she didn't want to play the part of desperate wanna-be girlfriend. And she sure as hell hadn't wanted to be the sad girl who'd snagged a guy like Chase just because she was knocked up. Chase had called, sent her a few texts to say hi, but he'd never once said anything about wanting to be with her.

So she'd raised Harrison the best she could, with a husband she'd thought loved her enough to get past what had happened, when in reality all he'd wanted was her money.

She raised her head and wiped her face, reaching up and angling the rearview mirror so she could deal with her panda eyes. Nothing had worked out as planned in her life, nothing. But crying over spilled milk wasn't going to help her any.

Hope pulled herself together, took a few sips of water, and cranked up the radio. Everything would seem better in the morning, or at least she hoped so.

Chase arrived at the hospital the next morning to collect his granddad alone. He'd already spent his entire drive there on the phone, organizing his temporary release, and he was looking forward to seeing him. If there was one person who could give him some perspective, it was his granddad.

He knocked and then pushed open the door to his room, grinning when he saw the old man sitting on the edge of the bed, dressed in a checked shirt, sleeves pushed up, and a nice pair of trousers. The thing about their granddad was that no one would ever guess he came from money if they just saw him walking down the street. He dressed like a rancher and acted like a rancher—the only thing that gave him away was the expensive watch glinting at his wrist or the even more expensive cars he liked to drive.

"Looking good, Granddad." Chase hugged him when he stood, taking care to support him without making a big deal about it. He kept his arm around the man's shoulders as he grabbed the bag from his bed.

"The nurse is meeting us there," he said, nodding and pointing toward the door. "Now let's get out of here."

They made their way down to the car after Chase had signed him out, checking they had the medication they needed and confirming when he'd have him back. He'd brought his SUV so it was easy for his granddad to get in instead of him having to bend down.

Chase closed the passenger door, then ran around and jumped in. It was quiet for a few minutes until his granddad made a soft grunting sound and turned so he was staring straight at him.

"Out with it."

Chase raised an eyebrow. "Out with what?"

"Whatever's on your mind. You're not saying a word."

"There's been a development."

"Bloody hell, if it's about the ranch just come out and say it."

Chase chuckled. "If it was about the ranch I'd have told you over the phone."

"Then what the . . ."

"It's about Hope."

"Who's Hope?" They were both silent a moment, then his granddad turned back to him. "Not Hope from college? The one I told you . . ."

"That I should have married? Yeah, that Hope," Chase finished for him.

"You've been talking to her?"

"She's the AI specialist we've been using. Long story short, she's here and we have some unfinished business."

His granddad laughed. "As in you want to sleep with her, or you want to take my advice and try to marry her?

I always told you that one was a keeper, the way she kept you in line back then. Only reason I didn't have a damn heart attack wondering what the hell you were up to while you were away."

"We have a son."

The laughter died from his granddad's lips and when he could, Chase pulled over. He turned the engine off and dropped his head to the steering wheel for a moment, taking a deep breath.

"You're telling me you have a son with this woman?"

Chase dragged his head up and nodded. "Yep." He hardly believed it himself. "She kept it from me all this time."

His granddad was silent, stared out the window a long time. "Did she tell you why?"

"Some bullshit about not wanting to be a ball and chain to me and ruin my life. Raised him on her ranch in Canada. Now her parents are gone and she's here working."

"So I'm guessing she didn't want you, or your family, insisting she raise the boy in Texas. Wanted to stay on her own ranch with her own family."

"And you're trying to tell me that's a good enough reason to lie to me?" Chase asked, exasperated.

"I'm telling you that if I'd have known I'd have made damn sure we saw the boy, made sure he was raised a King from the day he was born." He started to cough and reached into his pocket for a handkerchief, holding up his other hand to wave Chase away. He didn't like to be helped unless he actually needed it. "I think she's a smart girl who knew what she wanted, and the only way she could deal with the whole situation was to stay quiet, get on with her life, and not bother you about it."

"So it was okay to lie to me? To keep him from me?" Chase slammed his palm into the steering wheel. "Because either way I look at it she fucked up real bad."

They were silent again a long while. Chase didn't know if it was because his granddad was trying to think what to say or his breath was hard to catch.

"Did you give her any reason to believe that you wanted more from her?"

Chase shook his head. "We were friends. Friends who got carried away on graduation night."

"What do you want me to tell you, son? That you should fight for custody? That you should put a ring on her finger? That we should put the full force of our legal team to work to punish her?"

Chase started the engine again, not liking sitting idle. "I just want someone to help me figure out the hell of a mess I have going on. I hate her, but I don't. I like the kid, but . . ."

"You don't know about being a dad." His granddad shrugged. "I don't have the answers, Chase, but what I can tell you is that I've never lived my life with regrets. When I saw the way your father started treating you boys, I acted. Offered him money to clear out and he took it real fast. It was the best thing I could have done for you all, even though at the time it was damn hard after you'd lost your mom. I didn't want to look back and know I could have done something and didn't."

"So you followed your instincts, listened to your gut. That what you trying to tell me?"

"Damn straight." He coughed again, this time taking longer to stop, his breathing raspy. "I'm not gonna tell you what to do, but take your time. Make a decision with a clear head. Put all the bullshit behind you and look forward. Do what'll make you happy, because before you know it you'll be at the end of your life looking back like I am."

Chase reached for his granddad's hand and squeezed it, looking him in the eye.

"We're not letting you go yet," he told him, blinking away tears, the blinding stab of emotion one he wasn't used to.

"All I've ever wanted was for you boys to be happy."

"And we are, Granddad, we are."

"Then figure out how to fix your Hope situation real fast. Because I want to meet this grandson of mine before I kick the bucket."

Chase pulled back onto the road, grimacing at his granddad's choice of words. But there was no denying what was happening, they just had to enjoy every last minute with him while they had the chance.

Chapter 14

"So you're telling me that you boys can catch the god-damn asshole just from looking at this screen?"

Chase laughed. "God, I've missed you." He patted his granddad on the back and passed him the iPad. "You still getting that nurse to teach you about Twitter?"

They all laughed as Nate passed Granddad a small shot of whiskey in his favorite crystal glass.

"I tell you, boys, I might not have learned a whole lot about Twitter, but having that beautiful nurse lean over to show me what to do . . ." His granddad raised his eyebrows and took a sip. Chase noticed that his hand was shaking as he slowly brought the glass back down again, leaning back into the deep-buttoned leather sofa. They were in the library, Granddad's favorite room of the house, talking shit and taking turns staring at the iPad.

"Some things never change, huh, Granddad?" Nate asked, pouring them all another couple of shots.

"I'll appreciate a gorgeous woman till I take my last breath."

Chase stared at the man who'd raised them. All of them sitting around like this, it reminded him of growing up. He remembered sipping his first whiskey with Nate as their granddad had looked on, not laughing at them as the potent alcohol had burned their throats and left them coughing, gasping for breath. *And that's why you boys aren't ready to drink yet. When you can hold your liquor in here, then we'll talk about it.* It had been a lesson and a half, and one that they'd taken great pleasure in watching Ryder deal with a few years later.

"So, Granddad, ah, about Hope."

Nate and Ryder stayed quiet, sitting back and nursing their drinks. He already knew what they thought, that he needed to man up and just deal with the fact that he was a father, but he wanted to talk about it with all of them, now he'd had more time to process the conversation he'd had with the old man earlier.

"You decided what you want to do?"

Granddad's voice was shakier than it had ever been, but his tone was still deep, his presence commanding. Even at half the weight he'd once been and with shoulders that were starting to stoop, he could still command the attention of the toughest of audiences; there was no doubting he was the patriarch of a billion-dollar empire. But he was also their grandfather, and a damn good one at that.

"I want to know what you'd do. If you were me." Chase sipped his whiskey, savoring the velvety taste of the dark liquid on his tongue before he swallowed. "What decision would you make?"

"I think that life can throw a lot of curveballs at a man, Chase, but it's how we deal with those challenges that defines us."

Fuck. Why did he know his granddad would go and say something so goddamn profound as that. They'd already had that conversation, but he needed more from him.

"So I should just forgive her? Do you honestly think that's what I should do?"

He received a shake of the head in response. "No. But you need to remember that the boy, your son, had no part in this. If you want to be a man about this whole situation, then that's what I'd be telling myself."

"And Hope?" he asked, knocking back the rest of his drink. "What the hell do I do about Hope?" He ducked his head, shutting his eyes for a moment as he leaned into the leather. "I already know that I'm going to be the boy's dad, step up, but what about her?"

"Only you can decide what to do about Hope. Did you love the girl?"

Chase's eyes popped back open. Suddenly all eyes were on him, his brothers staring at him. But they weren't mocking him. A quick scan of both their faces told him they were waiting for his answer, that they were taking the whole thing as seriously as he was.

"Just thinking about what she did makes me want to . . ."

"Did you love her?" His granddad's deep voice silenced him as he asked the question again.

Chase stood up and took the bottle from the coffee table, pouring himself another nip and tipping it straight down his throat. When he finished he nursed the glass in his hand, staring down into it before raising his eyes. "Yeah," he finally said. "I fucking loved her so damn much, and I was too damn stupid to ever tell her." He shook his head. "You know what I did? I screwed every other woman I could to try to get her out of my system, and when that didn't work I thought I'd make her jealous. Look where that got me."

"So do something about it now," Nate said, twirling his glass and setting it on the table. "Make it right."

"Even after she lied to me?" Chase wasn't convinced. "You can't seriously tell me that you'd give her a second chance, Nate. I know you wouldn't."

"No," Nate replied, his eyebrows shooting up. "But I'm one stubborn son of a bitch, and I also don't have a kid out there in the world. A kid that's living right here in Texas who needs his dad."

Chase scowled. "So I should forgive her just like that? Just because I want to be part of the kid's life?" Part of him wanted to do exactly that, but he didn't believe that his brothers or his granddad would if they were in his shoes.

Ryder laughed, leaning forward. "No, you idiot."

Chase watched as his brothers exchanged glances with Granddad, pissing him off when they all chuckled.

"You need to man the fuck up because it's so damn obvious that you still love her."

Now it was Chase scowling at Ryder. "I don't trust her and I'm so angry with her that . . ."

"Hold up," Nate interrupted, taking the iPad from Granddad's lap and staring at it with an incredulous look on his face.

"What?" Chase asked, jumping up at the same time as Ryder so they could see the screen.

"Would you trust her if you knew she was right about Randy?" Nate asked.

Chase stared at the screen, watched as his foreman bent and removed the dummy canisters from the freezer. He steeled his jaw, grinding his teeth together as reality hit. *Son of a bitch!* He would have trusted their foreman with his life, wouldn't have suspected him for a second. Hell, even when Hope had voiced her concerns he'd as good as laughed her off.

"Randy? As in our foreman, Randy?" Granddad asked.

Chase nodded, meeting his granddad's furious, cold stare.

"Get my shotgun, boy. There's only one way to deal with shit like this."

Chase put a hand on his shoulder, not letting him get up. "I'll deal with this," he told him. "And we're not shooting him. The last thing we need is one of us holed up in jail for murder."

His granddad grunted. "I'd be dead before they locked me away. I say let me at him."

They all ignored him.

"What're we gonna do?" Nate asked, putting the iPad down and standing, fists balled at his sides. Ryder mirrored their older brother's stance.

"We're gonna teach the asshole a lesson, after we find out why in God's name he's double-crossing us."

"And what about the girl?" Granddad asked. "You gonna make that right, too?"

"She lied to me. She had my baby and she kept it from me all these years. I'm not just going to forgive her."

Granddad held up his glass for a refill and Chase watched as Ryder obliged before putting the bottle well out of his reach.

"Far as I can see and from what you've told me, she was a young woman doing what she thought was right at the time. She ever asked you for money?" Granddad asked.

Chase shook his head. "No."

"She asked you for anything at all?"

"No."

Chase watched his granddad, never broke his gaze.

"Then how 'bout you cut the lady some slack and think long and hard about what you want. Maybe, just maybe, she was in love with you, too. Don't be a fool, son, that's all I'm saying."

Nate placed a hand on his shoulder as he passed, squeezing his fingers against him. Chase took a big breath, watched as his brothers headed for the door. He turned back and nodded, knowing that no matter how pissed he felt right now, his granddad was probably right.

"I'll think about it," he finally said.

"Good." Granddad took a big gulp of Wild Turkey, clearly happy to be back home and able to get his hands on his favorite drink again. "Go easy on the girl, but teach that motherfucking foreman a lesson for me, you hear?"

Chase laughed and waved as he walked out of the room. "Good to have you back, Granddad."

"Son, it's damn good to be home."

"Come on," Nate called out. "Let's forget all about women and deal with this shit."

"Way too close to home," Ryder muttered as they all marched out the door.

It sure was. And now Chase was going to have to go apologize to Hope, because she'd been right all along, and if it hadn't been for her he would never have even suspected the one man on the ranch he'd have trusted with his life.

They ran silently, slowing down when they reached the barn where they'd been watching Randy only moments earlier. Chase took a deep breath and flexed his hands before balling them into fists, ears pricked as they heard a noise from inside.

"He's still in there," Nate murmured. "You still want to deal with him?"

It was dark out, but they were all standing together and he could see Nate's face. "Yeah, I'll do it. Just stick close in case I need you." Just his luck, Randy would be armed, and he liked to be prepared.

They moved with stealth past one side of the barn, then the floodlight flicked on, detecting movement, and Randy appeared, hurrying out.

"Not so fucking fast," Chase demanded, stepping out of the shadows, flanked on each side by his brothers.

"Chase?"

Randy looked panicked, his eyes darting left then right, before looking back at Chase. "Geez, you frightened the life out of me."

"What you doing out so late?"

Randy cleared his throat and took a few steps backward. "Just checking everything was in order. Making sure the, ah, horses that were in for the night had enough hay."

Chase just kept staring at him. "Seems like we just had another break-in."

He fought hard not to laugh at the expression on Randy's face. His foreman was trying to look surprised and failing miserably. "You need me to take a look around with you? We need to catch this son of a bitch."

Chase glanced sideways at Nate, then Ryder, before leveling his gaze on Randy, the security light still flooding the area with brightness. "Don't play games, Randy. You're the son of a bitch we just caught red-handed on camera."

He went to run, dodged sideways, but Chase was faster and grabbed him by the arm to pull him back before landing a punch to the man's jaw.

"You dare to think you could do this and get away with it?" He laughed, towering over Randy as he cowered. "No one fucks with us, Randy, you know that."

Chase pushed him hard, smiling when he hit the ground, sprawling backward. "Who did this with you?"

"Just me," Randy panted out. "No one else."

"You sure about that?" Chase asked, clenching and unclenching his fists. Randy spat out blood and stared up at him. "The quicker you talk the less likely I am to pound your face to a pulp."

Chase wasn't a fighter. He threw a good punch and knew how to look after himself, but he didn't get off on brawling. But Randy had betrayed them. They'd treated him like family for years, and he'd gone and done this to them.

"It was just me. I was paid to do it."

Nate stepped forward. "By who?"

Chase looked at Ryder, taking his eyes off Randy for a second, but it was one second he shouldn't have lost his focus. The foreman was on his feet like a man half his age, swinging a punch that clocked Chase in the eye.

"Fuck!" he swore as he threw a punch back, only managing to clip the side of Randy's head. It was Nate who took him down.

"Who was it?" Chase demanded.

"Larry Eaglewood," Randy finally uttered, nursing his head, blood pouring from his nose. "He paid me to sabotage anything on the ranch that he thought would hurt you. Wanted to see you boys knocked down a peg."

"Larry?" Nate echoed. "What the hell have we done to piss him off so bad?"

"He's hurting," Randy continued, clearly happy to talk if it saved him running into a fist again. "Ranching ain't profitable like it used to be, and he's got no oil to drill."

"Yet he had enough spare cash to pay you," Chase muttered. He didn't believe Randy for a second, certain he was just trying to get their neighbor in trouble to take the heat off himself. "I call bullshit."

Randy looked terrified, eyes wide. "I . . ."

"You want Nate to slam that fist of his into your face again?" Chase glanced at Nate, saw his brother flex his fingers again.

"Fuck! Fine, it was me."

"Why?" Nate asked. "We've treated you like family all these years and you just decided to betray us?"

"I was sick of seeing you boys drive around in your

expensive damn cars, making out like you own the world. I wanted to see you hurt, wanted you to . . ."

"Enough," Chase growled out. "I don't give a fuck what you thought or what you wanted, you're done here and I'm gonna make damn sure there's not another ranch in Texas that'll take you on."

"You should have just paid me that raise I asked for," Randy muttered.

"You're already paid more than any other foreman I know, a whole lot more, not to mention the house we gave you rent-free to live in," Nate snapped.

Chase took a step back, not wanting to deal with Randy any longer. There was somewhere else he needed to be.

"Clear out," he told Randy. "Grab your things and be off this ranch within the hour. Fuck off and don't come back."

Silence echoed around them. Chase ran the ranch, and that meant neither of his brothers would second-guess his orders.

"You still here in an hour, I'll call the sheriff and have you arrested. You hear me?"

Randy hung his head, nodded even though the movement must have hurt like hell.

"You guys okay if I clear off for a bit?" Chase asked, looking at his brothers.

"Go get her," Nate said, slapping his back. "And tell her she was bloody well right all along."

Chase touched his eye and wished he hadn't. "I'll see you soon."

Chapter 15

A noise at the door made Hope jump. She muted the television, put down her half-empty glass of wine, and listened, waiting to see if she could hear anything. A light knock echoed out again and her body froze—who the hell would be at her door at this time of night? *Shit*.

She bent and unplugged the table lamp closest to her, clasping it tight and walking toward the door. It might not be much of a weapon, but if she had to defend herself she'd rather have *something* in her hand.

"Who is it?" she called out, pleased that her voice sounded a hell of a lot braver than she felt.

"It's Chase."

Hope let out a big gasp of air, her heart pounding so loud it was in danger of beating straight out of her chest. She flicked the top safety lock and then the main one, swinging the door open and finding Chase standing on her doorstep.

"You frightened the life out of me," she said.

He grinned, the gorgeous smile of his that came complete with a heart-melting dimple and made her forget everything else. For a second at least.

"Were you planning on hitting me with that?" he

asked, his smile stretching even wider when she held up the lamp.

"Hey, it seemed like a good idea at the time when I thought an intruder was about to break into my house," she muttered.

"The kind of intruder that knocks on the door first?"

Hope scowled at him, but she had to admit that it was kind of nice to be joking around with Chase instead of arguing with him. "I'm kind of nervous on my own," she admitted. "And I have that seriously protective mamabear thing going on, so yeah, if I'd had to beat down an intruder with a lamp, I would have."

"He's lucky to have a mom like you," Chase said, moving closer so that he was standing under the porch light.

"Oh my God, what happened to you?" Hope put the lamp down and moved forward, reaching up to touch Chase's jaw and tilting his head down so she could inspect his face. The side of his eye was a mess, a dark red mass tinged with purple that would only go darker as the night progressed.

"How about you invite me in and I'll tell you all about it."

Hope looked up, took her hand from Chase's face, and stepped back. Earlier she'd wondered if they'd ever talk again, let alone touch, and now here she was standing with him on her front doorstep.

"Sure. Come in," she said. "How about I make us some coffee and get some ice for your eye?"

"Sounds good to me."

Hope walked ahead of Chase, stopping to return the lamp to its rightful place and plug it in. She switched it on, and collected her wineglass, leaving it in the sink and flicking on her coffee machine instead. She knew Chase was following her but she did her best not to overthink the fact that he was in her house. He might not look pissed with her anymore, or at least not like he had the day before, but he could be a wolf in sheep's clothing. What if he'd decided he wanted joint custody of Harrison? Or even worse, that he wanted him to live on the ranch full-time? The thought sent a shudder through her body.

"So are you here to hang out or . . ."

"I'm here to say sorry."

Hope slowly spun around, her hands resting on the kitchen counter as she leveled her gaze on Chase. "You are?" He couldn't have surprised her more if he'd tried.

"I'm still trying to process everything that's happened, Hope," Chase said, taking a seat on one of her barstools, his eyes locked on hers, not letting her escape.

She stayed still, remained completely immobile, waiting for him to continue.

"You were right?" he finally said.

"About what?" She had no idea what he was talking about, but she was grateful that he'd calmed down and they weren't fighting.

"We caught Randy stealing tonight."

"You what?" She shook her head. "I'm sorry. It was just a hunch and I wish I'd been wrong."

"Yeah, but you weren't." Chase shrugged. "And I should have listened to you."

"Why?" She turned away and reached up for coffee mugs. "I'm hardly on your list of most trusted people right now."

"Hey, do you still make those wicked hot chocolates?"

Hope burst out laughing. "You remember those?"

"How the hell could I forget them? I think I almost drank more of those than I did beer when we were studying."

Hope flicked the coffee machine off and crossed the kitchen, taking out a block of chocolate and a carton of milk. She set them down and opened a drawer, pulled out a small pan, and set it on the gas range.

"I make these all the time for Harrison," she said, breaking the chocolate into large pieces and dropping them into the pan. "It's kind of our thing."

Warm hands covering her shoulders made her freeze, Chase's touch like a bolt of heat through her body. Instead of turning around, she reached for a wooden spoon and started to stir, ignoring the fact that a man she'd once loved was standing so close to her that if she just rocked back . . .

"Hope," he said, his voice low.

She kept stirring, only stopping when his hand closed over hers and forced her to turn around. Chase was staring down at her, his eyes soft, crinkled at the sides as he watched her.

"I loved you," Chase said simply. "When we were in college, I was in love with you. I had a crap way of showing it, but I need you to know that."

She sucked back a lungful of air, finding it ridiculously hard to breathe. "I loved you, too."

He let go of her and she turned back to the pan, not wanting the chocolate to burn, and wanting even more to put some distance between her and Chase. Having him so close to her and saying those words—it wasn't what she needed right now. Hope slowly poured milk into the pan, still stirring, trying hard to concentrate on what she was doing.

"We need to talk."

She nodded, still not turning back around and breathing a sigh of relief when he moved away. When she glanced over her shoulder she saw he hadn't gone far, and was resting on the kitchen side of the counter, but it was enough to give her some space. She finished stirring and turned the gas off.

"I don't want to argue, Chase. I meant what I said yesterday." It was true—she'd beaten herself up for years over what she'd done and she didn't have the energy to fight with him.

"How about we drink some of that chocolate and I tell you all about what went down with Randy," Chase suggested, one eyebrow raised in question. "Then when you're good and ready you can talk me through what happened after college, and I promise just to listen."

Hope smiled at Chase, and this time she didn't have to force it. "That sounds like a good plan."

She grabbed the two mugs she'd taken out earlier for coffee and poured hot chocolate into them instead, passing one to Chase and then wrapping her hands around her own. There was something comforting about a sweet, warm drink, and right now she needed it.

"I'm pleased you came around tonight, Chase," she said, taking a sip.

"Me and my shiner of an eye?" he asked with a laugh.

Hope put her drink down and hurried to the freezer. "I forgot all about icing it!"

Chase chuckled. "Don't sweat it."

She ignored him and took an ice pack out, wrapping it in a kitchen towel and crossing back toward him. She reached up and pressed it gently to the side of his eye, grimacing for him.

"It must really hurt."

"Yeah," he grunted, wincing when she moved the ice pack slightly.

"So he just slammed his fist into the side of your face?" she asked.

"Not exactly. We confronted him, he tried to get the hell out of Dodge, and I took a punch."

"Double ouch." She took the ice away and inspected the redness, then pressed it back gently again.

"He's in worse shape. I think Nate broke his nose."

"And did he tell you why?"

Chase didn't say anything straightaway, but he did look at her, his dark eyes taking her prisoner and holding her captive. "He'd worked on our ranch for almost twenty years, and we'd paid him pretty darn well. But I guess he got bitter and twisted about our family money or something. Tried to pin it on another rancher paying him off but we got the truth out of him eventually. Probably hated that I was running the ranch and telling him what to do as well."

"It's hard to believe someone could betray you like that," she murmured, thinking aloud. "After so long."

"Yeah," Chase agreed, covering her hand with his and guiding the ice away from his skin. "It is. But we've got some great guys working for us, and we'll start searching for a new foreman straightaway. Someone with experience, someone who appreciates what we pay and how we look after our employees, and doesn't think he can betray us and get away with it."

Hope's heart started to hammer away again, her body betraying her as Chase's fingers stroked against her skin, still holding her hand. Suddenly she wasn't sure if they were still talking about Randy or not.

"I'm sorry," she whispered. "I'm sorry a thousand times over, Chase. You have to believe me."

"I don't know if I can forgive you, Hope. I really don't," he said. "But I do want to listen."

Hope couldn't help herself. She leaned into Chase, eyes still on his, completely lost to the power of his touch and his gaze, drawn to the powerful man standing in front of her. They stood like that for too long, until Chase took the ice from her and put it on the counter before placing his hands on her shoulders.

"Is it wrong that I want to kiss you?" he asked, head dipped down, mouth so close to hers.

Hope watched his lips as they parted, her breath ragged. "Yes." She wanted the same thing.

He dropped a slow, warm kiss to her mouth, his lips hardly moving. She wanted to wrap her arms around his neck and tug him closer, to rub her body hard up into his. But when he pulled back only a few seconds later, she stepped away instead of closer.

"It would be a whole lot easier to have make-up sex," Chase muttered. "But then tomorrow we'd be back to square one again."

She nodded, scooping her hot chocolate back up and focusing on the warmth against her palms. It wasn't the same as touching Chase, but it was better than nothing.

"I need you to tell me everything, Hope," Chase said. "Right from the start."

Chase gritted his teeth when he accidentally bumped the side of his eye. It was hurting like hell, but it was a damn good reminder of the fact that he hadn't been on form tonight. If he'd been focused there was no way Randy could have swung at him like that and managed to connect, but he had and Chase deserved the bruiser he'd received. Now he was sitting beside Hope, about to give her a second chance. Or at least that's what he knew he should do.

"So tell me again, how far along were you when you found out?" Chase asked, sipping his hot chocolate and remembering exactly why he'd missed the sweet drinks. Even Mrs. T hadn't ever been able to make them like this.

"Four months," she said, tucking her feet up beneath her on the sofa. "I couldn't figure out why I was so sick all the time, and it went on way too long to be a stomach bug."

He nodded and listened.

"I went to the doctor, laughed when she asked me to do a pregnancy test, and then laughter kinda turned to tears pretty damn fast when I found out how far along I was."

"Did you tell your parents then?"

"I took a few days to process it all, considered all my options, and then decided to keep it to myself for a while before finally breaking the news."

"They took it okay?"

"It's complicated. I didn't actually tell them until I was with my ex."

"So when did your husband enter the picture?"

"Harrison knows he wasn't his father, if that's what you're worried about," she said quickly, meeting his stare. Before that she'd been gazing into her chocolate. "I met him again when I was pregnant. I'd known him for years, and things moved fast and I let him think I was pregnant with his baby, that when I went into labor it was really early. But I confessed to him as soon as Harrison was born, told him the truth. I thought he loved me enough that we could get past it, but even though he let me think he could, I guess he never did."

"And you told your parents the truth?"

"Yes, the very same day."

Chase took her hand, linked their fingers, and squeezed. "He should have loved you anyway."

"Yeah, he did," she added, her voice a note deeper. "For my money."

"Hey, I've been there," he said. "I've had one serious girlfriend since college, the first woman I've actually ever let close to me other than you, and I've told you already how that ended."

"Chase," Hope said, leaning across to set her mug down and facing him on the sofa, both feet still tucked beneath her, "I need you to know that there was no one else. I mean, I hadn't been with another man in college, in case you were . . ."

"You kept something huge from me, Hope, but you don't have to explain yourself. You never slept around and it's pretty obvious from looking at the kid that he's a King." Chase laughed. "I was the douchebag who didn't put two and two together. I mean, he even looks like me."

"I want you to know that since I've been back, not a day has gone past that I haven't felt like the biggest bitch on the planet." She held his hand tight as she spoke. "Seeing you after all this time, watching Harrison with your brothers, it's been like a knife to my heart. I can see how much he's missed out on and it's killing me."

Chase was still pissed with her, it was impossible not to be, but he also got what she'd done. Hope had been young and scared, and she'd made a decision that she'd had to live with.

"Would you do it differently if you could?"

"Now that I'm here with you, yes." Tears welled in Hope's eyes and it hurt him to just stare at her, to watch and do nothing to comfort her. But he needed to hear this no matter how much it hurt her. "But I was only twenty-six back then, Chase, and I wanted so badly for you to just *want* me. Like you wanted all those other girls. But we had one night together and then . . ."

"I emailed you," he said, letting go of her hand. "I texted you, tried to check in."

"You didn't text me for a week after we had sex, and then like a month after that," she said, shaking her head and wiping at her face, brushing tears from her cheeks. "And I wanted more, Chase. I wanted you to love me. I wanted some big gesture so I knew that I meant more to you than just one night in a cheap motel. Not just a friend doing a cursory check-in."

He stood up and paced across the room. "You could

have called me. Told me how you felt, what had happened."

"And then I'd have been as desperate as the girls you bedded all the time. The ones you never called back." She sighed. "And then there was the fact that I was never going to relocate here, leave my family."

"Hey, I've always been deadly fucking clear," Chase growled. "I never pretended I wanted anything more than a night of fun, not with any of the women I was with."

"And me?"

"What happened between us meant something, Hope. You know it and I know it." He was pissed off again now, anger building deep within him and threatening to boil over. "But yeah, there was that whole geography issue."

"I didn't want you to feel trapped and I didn't want to be the desperate one." She wrapped her arms around herself, chin on her knees. "You were always so careful not to get yourself in a relationship, sure about what you wanted . . ."

"Did it ever cross my mind that maybe I was doing all that to get at you? That I wanted *you*?"

She smiled, but it was a sad upturn of her mouth, her eyes still swimming. "Part of me always hoped that was the case, but when so many weeks, then months, passed with nothing but the odd friendly text, I realized what had happened between us was just a drunken fling."

"It was more than a drunken fling," he growled, crossing the room again and dropping to the sofa beside her.

"I know that now, but I didn't then," she said, her voice barely a whisper. "Imagine me four months later. I hadn't spoken to you, I thought you'd moved on, but I still loved you and didn't want to burden you."

He put his arm around her, swallowing his anger and tugging her close. "And here we are. Two idiots who didn't know what was good for us."

"I don't expect you to forgive me," Hope said, turning her bright blue eyes up to him, her lower lip caught beneath her top teeth. "But Harrison needs his dad, more now than ever, even if it's just some weekend time with you."

"I'm not gonna shirk my responsibilities, Hope. Not now that I know." He stared at her. "Not when I've met him and can't stop thinking about what an awesome kid he is."

"And what about us?"

Her voice was deep and emotional. He'd never seen her like this before. Hope had been so strong, so unflappable in college. It hadn't mattered how much he'd tried to get under her skin, because she hadn't reacted when he'd slept around, when he'd teased her or tried to get her into bed, or when he'd brazenly tried to copy her notes or drink her under the table. Hope had always been his fun, beautiful friend, only he'd been so stupid that he hadn't seen how hard it must have been for her.

"When I was a dickhead back in college, all the shit I did when we were friends, did you actually not give a damn?"

She reached for her hot chocolate, cupping the mug again and not once glancing at him as he watched her. "Of course I gave a damn, Chase."

"Why?"

"Do you really need me to say it?" She shook her head and finally met his stare.

"Yeah, I think I do."

"Because I loved you," she whispered, blinking away tears again. "Because I wanted you to want me as more than a friend. And I wasn't going to spend one night with you just for the hell of it, to be one of those girls so desperate that I took my panties off in the heat of the moment and regretted it forever."

Chase didn't know what to say. He'd been a fucking idiot, he knew that, but he didn't even know where to begin.

"And then I did exactly that and regretted it for five years." She laughed, slamming her cup back down on the coffee table and shuffling farther down the sofa, away from him. "Hell, I still am."

"Well, I don't regret sleeping with you for a second."

"Of course you don't."

Hope didn't look impressed, but it took more than a pissed-off look to stop him in his tracks.

"I don't regret finally having you naked in bed with me," he told her, moving down the sofa until his thigh was hard against Hope. "I don't regret all the years of flirting that finally resulted in the best goddamn sex of my life, although I sure as hell regret not doing it sooner."

"And Harrison?" He watched as she swallowed, her eyes wide. "Do you regret what we made that night?"

"The only thing I regret is not jumping on a plane and telling you how much I missed you," Chase said. "And that's the most honest goddamn thing I've ever said in my life."

Hope ran her fingers through her hair and he watched until she reached the end. Then he reached to pull her forward, not letting her resist. Chase was happy once he had his fingers tugging gently through her long strands of blond hair, her head on his shoulder, her body finally, *finally* relaxing into his instead of being so hard and tense.

"We're going back to where it all began."

"What?" Hope wriggled and turned so she was staring at him.

He ran his tongue over his lips, chuckled as her eyes dropped to watch his mouth. "We're going on a road trip, Hope. And this time, we're gonna do things right."

She grinned at him, the smile kicking up one corner of her mouth before spreading to the other. "We are?"

"Yeah, we are." He might have thought he could never forgive her, but maybe he was wrong. Just like he'd been wrong five years ago when he'd let her walk away in the first place. "We've both made mistakes, so let's just be honest and admit that we've both fucked up."

She nodded. "Agreed."

"And this time we're gonna give it a go, no bullshit, no holds barred. We say how we feel when we feel it." Chase ran his eyes over her full mouth, her plump lips parted. He dropped a slow kiss to those very lips, was hard after only a moment of brushing their mouths back and forth, her tongue teasing his. "We do what we want, when we want it."

Hope's eyes were hidden from view, her dark lashes shielding her from his gaze as she stared down lower, maybe at his mouth.

"And when are we going to take this trip back in time?" she asked, grabbing hold of his hair before he had a chance to evade her hand. He only resisted a moment before yielding, only he did more than give in. Chase grinned and pushed her back onto the sofa, laughing as she tugged hard at his hair. She could pull all she liked—unless she actually told him no, nothing was going to stop him.

Chase forgot all about why he was in her house, what had gone down between them, his body covering hers as he lowered himself over her and planted his lips on hers again. There was nothing gentle about the way he kissed her this time, his mouth rough, loving that she matched him every step of the way, her body arching up to press harder into his. When Chase finally extracted himself, he had to jump back onto his feet, staring down at her. His breathing was ragged, his body begging to be jammed hard up to hers again. But he wasn't going to take her on the sofa.

"Sweetheart, I just promised you a trip down memory lane, and that doesn't involve me screwing you on your sofa."

Hope's lips were still parted, her chest rising and falling, fast, as she stared at him. "I thought we just agreed to let bygones be bygones?"

"No," he corrected her. "We agreed to a no-holds-barred trip down memory lane, and for the first time in my life I'm going to turn down a beautiful woman."

"You're telling me you've never actually said no before?" The look on her face told him she wasn't at all impressed.

"I'm saying that I'll pick you up Friday once you've knocked off for the week. Then we do this." He started to walk backward and threw her a wink.

"Have you forgotten about Harrison?"

"I want to see that boy every second I can, make up for all the time I've missed out on, but we need some alone time, too." Chase touched her hand. "His uncles can take him for a few days. Chloe'll be there and he'll have a blast hanging out with them, if that's okay with you?"

A look of terror washed over her face. "We can't tell him," she said. "Not without preparing him, without . . ."

"Relax. We'll tell him when we're good and ready. Just meet me at the ranch on Friday, okay? There's no pressure to tell him anything yet."

She nodded.

"Promise me."

She laughed. "I promise."

"Good." Chase changed his mind and marched back across the room, bending low and pressing one last, slow kiss to her lips, groaning when her tongue darted straight back to dance with his.

"Good night, Hope," he murmured against her mouth as he pulled away. "Sleep well darlin', because you're not gonna get much shut-eye come the weekend."

He backed away, a familiar current surging through his body, one he hadn't felt in a long, long time. Because he was suddenly playing to win something that wasn't his to take, and he never backed away from a challenge.

"Can I look in on him, before I go?"

Hope nodded and took his hand. "Come with me."

They walked upstairs and down the hall and Hope nudged open the half-shut door, standing back for him to move past. Chase held his breath as he stepped closer, looked down at the sleeping boy in the bed. His hair was all messed up, body out of the covers, mouth open as he breathed heavily. Chase bent low, traced a hand through Harrison's hair, gulping as he kissed his forehead.

The past was the past now. He was a dad, and nothing was going to change that. Hating Hope for what she'd done was only going to make him bitter and twisted— the only choice he had now was to move on and be the best damn dad he could be.

He pulled the covers up a little, covering Harrison, and turned around to Hope. The light from the hallway cast shadows into the room, pools of light that allowed him to see her face. He stepped closer and kissed her cheek, squeezing her hand.

He was going to fix what was broken between them. Starting now.

Chapter 16

Hope glanced in the rearview mirror at Harrison, a pang of guilt hitting her hard. She'd hardly ever had a night apart from the little guy, so an entire weekend was making her feel like the world's worst mom. She knew she deserved a break, but still. Nothing about leaving him was easy.

"You're sure you'll be okay?" She also shouldn't be asking him so many times, because the next time she asked him he'd probably say no.

"Do you think I can ride the pony again?"

Hope smiled, a weight lifting off her shoulders as they turned into the driveway. Something about King Ranch was very settling, calming somehow, and it reminded her a lot of home. Harrison had made the transition from home to living in Texas remarkably well. He hadn't been that close to his stepdad in the end, not after months of him being distant and spending little time with them before finally leaving. It was his grandparents she knew he missed terribly, because he'd been used to spending hours with them every day of his life, doing everything with them.

"I'm sure you'll be able to ride the pony," she finally replied, swallowing her emotion away.

"Awesome."

Hope pulled up outside the main house, putting the car in park and taking a moment to gather her thoughts. Part of her thought that agreeing to go anywhere with Chase was pure madness, but the other part was screaming the exact opposite. This was their chance, to go back in time and to deal with what had happened—maybe it would lead nowhere. Although the butterflies in her stomach were telling a completely different story. *Something* was going to happen, of that she was sure.

Chase appeared on the porch before she'd even gotten out of the car, running down the steps and opening her door for her. She tried to disguise her smile but it was impossible. The magnetism of Chase's gaze was like an infusion of confidence straight to her soul, just the way it always had been. She'd been more herself around Chase than with any other person, and having him close was reminding her of that feeling all over again.

"Thanks," she said as she stepped out.

He grinned and ducked his head back into the car to look at Harrison. "Southern manners," she heard him say. "You're never too young to learn to open a car door for a lady."

Hope couldn't believe the change in him. She knew he was probably still struggling to come to terms with everything, but she had to give him full points for trying.

"So you're ready to roll?" he asked, one hand trailing slowly up her arm, stopping just above her elbow.

Hope shivered, his touch ice cold and burning hot at the same time. "I'd be lying if I said I hadn't thought about turning around and driving the hell out of dodge."

He bent his head closer to hers. "And I'd be lying if I

said I wasn't freaking out about the whole being a parent deal. So I guess we can call it even."

"Mom!"

She spun around, emerging from Chase's web and opening the back door for Harrison. "Sorry, sweetheart." She unbuckled him and grabbed his overnight bag, swinging it over to Chase because she knew he'd insist on carrying it in for her.

"How about we hang out with Harrison for a bit, let me spend some time with him?" Chase asked. "Then we can settle him down with the others and wait till he's having fun before we leave."

Hope nodded and went to reach for Harrison's hand, laughing when he ran ahead, completely forgetting about his mom now they were at the ranch.

"Something tells me he's going to be just fine here," she said, letting Chase take her hand as they walked. He pulled gently, making her stop, and when he dropped Harrison's bag to the ground and circled his hands around her waist, she knew she was in trouble.

"Despite all the bullshit," Chase murmured, "I'm looking forward to starting over with you."

"Me too," she replied, leaning back in his arms and studying his strong, angular face. She was lost in his dark chocolate eyes immediately, caught in his web with no chance of release.

Chase cupped her face and dipped down, his big frame folding around her as he closed his mouth over hers. At first it was soft, so soft his lips were like feathers against her own, like he was waiting for her to do something about it. Hope moaned as he rocked his body into hers and she crawled her fingers up his body, loving the hardness of his chest and the muscles of his arms as she traced every inch of him. So much for holding back until they were on the road.

"Huh-hmm," came a loud, deep rumble. "Hands off the kid's mom."

Hope jumped back, eyes darting to the house and thankful Harrison wasn't watching, that he'd run on ahead. That was something she didn't need to explain to him just yet. Instead she met the amused gaze of Nate, his arms folded like he was the security at the door instead of the owner.

"Ah, thanks for having Harrison this weekend."

"Mmmm-hmmm," Nate muttered, before laughing and jogging down the steps. Chase put his arm around her protectively, hugging her against him.

"We'll hang around a while before heading off," she told him. "So don't go waving us off just yet."

"I'm just coming out to check the car for Transformers. According to your son, there's a few to come in still."

"You're amazing. Thanks, Nate."

"Just don't break my brother's heart, okay?" Nate said, heading past her and calling over his shoulder. "We'll forgive you once, but there's an old saying about never crossing a King twice."

Hope wasn't about to be intimidated, but she doubted Nate was actually trying to scare her off. She was just thankful that Chase's brothers had been so welcoming after everything that had happened.

"Come on darlin'," Chase drawled, his body hard against hers as he walked them toward the house. "Let's play before we roll outta here."

She glanced up at him as they walked, her hand looped around his waist and tucking into his pocket. His butt was rock hard. "Are we just going to hang out, or are we actually going back there?"

"We're going back to all our old haunts," he told her with a grin. "We're going to our favorite bar, our favorite restaurant, and we might even take a wander around campus." His chuckle was more of a low roar, a rumble befitting a lion. "And then we're going back to a certain motel."

Her cheeks were on fire, heat shooting through her. "We are?"

"Damn right we are."

Hope was in danger of losing her breath, every part of her screaming out for Chase, desperate to be back in that motel room and reenact everything they'd done so many years ago. And more. The other night in Chase's half-finished new house had been great, but an entire night of leisurely doing anything and everything they wanted to each other? "Mmmm," she murmured.

"What was that?"

Hope giggled. She hadn't realized she'd made that noise out loud. "Nothing. That was nothing."

Chase slapped her hard on the ass and she punched him in the arm.

"Didn't sound like nothin'," he grunted.

She shook her head and avoided his hands as he reached for her. Later she'd go out of her way to let him touch her, but right now she needed to stay in mom mode.

"Hey buddy, what are you doing?"

She sat down across from Harrison, happy to sit back and let Chase get to know him.

"Can we go riding?" Harrison asked.

"Now?" Chase raised an eyebrow and glanced at her.

"Yeah. Before you and Mom go."

He shrugged and looked back again. "Sorry, Mama. Think we'll be sticking around a while."

She just smiled, happy they were getting on. Letting Harrison get closer to Chase was hard and hurt her because she was so worried about things not working out and Harrison losing someone else from his life, but she just had to trust that everything was working out for the best. Even if it did scare her to half to death.

* * *

Chase put his foot down and accelerated, enjoying the power of the vehicle as they headed toward College Station at high speed. They had almost three hours of driving ahead of them, and he was pleased they'd taken his new truck. The leather seats were pure luxury, and he reached forward to flick on the heat for Hope's seat.

"I don't want to get used to this," she said, her body angled so that she was facing him. They'd had fun playing with Harrison before he left, but if she'd stayed there with him any longer she probably wouldn't have been able to leave him. She was still feeling terrible, even though she knew he was absolutely fine.

"Nothing beats a warm butt on a cold morning, that's for sure." Chase chuckled, settling back again with one hand on the wheel. "This one even has a heated steering wheel. Crazy the shit they come up with."

"One day," she murmured. "I'll get back to this one day."

"You don't have to worry about money," Chase said, glancing across at her.

"Yeah, I do."

He made a noise in his throat, a deep kind of grunt. "No. So long as you let me be part of Harrison's life, I'll make sure he has everything he needs. School fees, clothes . . ." He shrugged. "Hell, don't sweat anything, okay?"

"I didn't tell you about Harrison because I wanted your money, Chase," she said, her voice soft. She also didn't want to owe anyone anything—she wanted to make it on her own.

"I know," he replied. "And that's exactly why I don't mind giving it to you."

It was true. She'd pissed him off by keeping Harrison a secret, but it was blatantly obvious that she hadn't wanted or needed anything from him. She might have lost her family's fortune, but she was capable of earning good money in her own right.

"I know it's a sensitive subject, but why don't you tell me how you actually lost the ranch," Chase said, indicating before passing a slow vehicle. He had raw power beneath his foot and he wasn't scared to use it. "We can get all that depressing shit out of the way now, and then when we hit Northgate we can forget everything and just be us."

"We're actually doing Northgate? I honestly thought you were kidding, that we were just heading to a hotel somewhere."

"What, you thought I was going to drive you all the way back there and not take you for some Jell-O shots?"

"Jell-O? Man, that takes me back."

"Vodka in general takes me back," Chase said with a laugh.

"Hey, you didn't even like Jell-O shots! I still remember that look on your face when I used to talk you into them."

He shot her a look that was supposed to be fierce but only made Hope grin. Chase grinned straight back—he'd always worked his ass off to keep that smile on her face, and it was worth every effort. When she smiled it was like a pure shot of sunshine.

"They were disgusting then and I'll bet they still are. But this is a walk down memory lane, so we have to do them, right?"

Hope sat back in her seat and he kept taking his eyes off the road for a second to glance at her. She was wearing a low-cut T-shirt and with her leather jacket discarded on the backseat, he was finally getting the kind of view of her breasts that he wanted. Her hair was loose, falling over her shoulders just the way he liked it, her shampoo or perfume or whatever the hell smelling all berry flavored and only making him want her all the more.

"I thought my folks would be around for years," Hope said, her words taking him by surprise. "I should have been more savvy with my finances, but I loved Matt and I trusted him. Hell, one of the reasons I married him was because he seemed so damn dependable."

"So you didn't have a good prenup?"

He glanced over and saw her shake her head. "I didn't personally have a lot when we married, and the ranch was always going to be passed to me and any children of mine. I expected that to be decades away, and I also trusted that my husband was telling me the truth when he spoke about how he'd never compromise Harrison's inheritance."

"So how did he do it?" Chase was keeping his voice level, but inside he was fuming. He didn't even know the whole story yet but if he ever met this deadbeat ex of hers he'd like to wrap his hands around his neck and do the guy some permanent damage.

"He used my inheritance as security against a couple of risky real estate developments, without my knowledge," Hope said, her voice low. "I was grieving for my parents and trying to do my best by Harrison, and before I realized what had happened I was receiving phone calls from the bank about foreclosure. It all seemed to happen so fast, and then it became blatantly obvious how stupid I'd been not having a cast-iron prenup, letting him manage our finances. My parents had known him since he was a kid so they trusted him too, never pushed me to put anything in place to protect myself. Dad was a rancher, a man of the land, and he took people at face value."

"Son of a bitch," Chase muttered.

"What? For stealing my inheritance, going behind my back, or forging my signature?" she asked dryly. "Because the fact he'd practiced that to get it perfect was kind of disturbing."

"You know where he is now?" Chase asked.

She shook her head. "He disappeared real fast. And if I did know, the answer would be yes."

He gripped the steering wheel tight. "To what question?"

"To your fist." Hope had angled her body back toward his again. "If I knew where he was, I'd happily let you teach him a lesson. King-style. And then I'd sue his ass."

He grunted. If he ever did get the chance, the bastard would sure regret ever crossing Hope. "So how did you actually lose the ranch in the end? Did the bank foreclose?"

"His developments went belly up and they went down owing millions. The bank foreclosed on the ranch to make their money back, and I couldn't raise enough to save the place." She took a deep breath. "It was just before Mom died, but I managed to keep it all from her."

"Damn."

"Add to that a ton more debt that I didn't even know about, and I managed to lose everything. Dad had left everything to me, knowing that Mom was having health issues. It was all just one bad thing upon another."

"Then you somehow ended up in Texas to start over."

"Yeah, something like that."

Chase closed his hand over her thigh, wishing to hell he hadn't as soon as his fingers connected. The last time they'd been in his truck together they'd been in the backseat and he was about ready to try his luck again.

He took a deep breath and patted her before taking his hand back and placing it on the wheel. This was gonna be one hell of a long drive.

"You up for a game?" he asked. Hell, he'd do anything

to take his mind off Hope and the fact that within a few hours they'd be back in a certain motel that held a lot of good memories.

"You mean like the license plate game or something?" Hope asked.

He looked sideways for a second. "From the unimpressed look on your face, I'm gonna take that as a no." Chase bit his tongue. He could have always asked her for a blow job, then he *really* could have seen her look unimpressed.

He laughed and gripped the steering wheel.

"What?" she asked.

Chase shook his head. "Nothing you want to know."

Hope ignored him and turned up the music. "Were you serious about pretending we're back in college again? About starting over?"

"Sure."

"Good. Because I want to forget everything that's stressed me out. I just want to be the old me. Not a care in the world, nothing to lose and everything to gain."

When she reached for his right hand he let her link their fingers before raising it and pressing a kiss to the back of her hand. He hated to admit it, after so long being a bachelor and making sure he never got too close to anyone, but there was something about Hope that got under his skin enough to make him want her around all the time. He wanted her naked, but he also wanted to look after her. He wanted to do bad, bad things to her, but he also wanted to hold her close and kiss her, to protect her.

He was losing his fucking mind and he didn't even give a damn.

Chase pumped the accelerator a little harder, impatient to get there as fast as he could. How the hell he'd gone from walking away from Hope to not wanting to let her out of his sight, he had no goddamn idea. All he did know was that planning this dirty little road trip on a Monday and then having to wait four torturous days before seeing Hope again had slowly killed him.

"Are we going to pretend we're college kids?" Hope asked over the music. "You know, to make this whole get-away authentic."

Chase scowled. "Do I *look* like a freaking college kid?"

"Well," Hope laughed and squeezed his hand before keeping hold and dropping it into her lap, "no. Unless college guys come in sexy six-foot-three, muscled bodies wearing designer digs and a thirty-thousand-dollar watch."

Chase groaned as she moved beneath his hand. "First of all, I need you to stop doing that."

"What? This?" she asked, all innocent like butter wouldn't melt in her mouth as she wiggled her thighs.

"Yeah," Chase said through gritted teeth. "Like that."

"And what was second?"

"My watch only cost twenty-five grand."

Hope tucked his hand between her legs and then crossed them, her laugh wicked as she teased him. "You look just the same as you did back then, except now you don't give a damn about standing out. You were just as tall and goddamn sexy back then."

"Right back at you, sweetheart."

He glanced over and noticed Hope had shut her eyes, her head tilted back. She still had an ironclad hold on his hand. *Goddamn, Hope.* He'd never wanted a woman so bad in his entire life, and in a couple of hours, he was going to show her exactly why he deserved her.

Hope snuggled closer against the warmth, refusing to open her eyes. She was so tired and whatever she was cuddled up to was so nice . . .

"No," she moaned, reaching out as the warm thing was taken away.

A low, familiar chuckle made her eyes pop open. That something warm was a gorgeous, big cowboy, and he was hovering above her.

"Are we"—she pushed up onto her elbows—"on a bed?" She asked the question even though she already knew the answer. *Oh my God.* "We're on *the* bed?" Hope swallowed as Chase stood back, his arms hanging at his sides. "I can't believe I fell asleep in the car."

He shrugged. "Hey, your snore is pretty cute so I didn't mind."

"Chase!" she protested. "I do *not* snore."

She looked around the room, finding it hard to believe that she'd slept so soundly that Chase had managed to un-buckle her and carry her from the car before she'd woken. Hope squinted at a painting on the wall, a faded picture of a few horses galloping through a field. It could be a coincidence, or maybe they had the same painting in every room . . .

"This isn't the exact same room we were in . . ."

"Yes," he interrupted, a smug look on his face. "Room 69."

Hope shifted on the bed, eyes locked on Chase. There was nothing about the man that didn't scream alpha—even his eyes were predatory, the way he stared at her giving everything away.

"There are some things I'll never forget," Chase mur-mured, his eyes never leaving hers as he moved forward. "The number of this room, the look on your face after we first kissed, the smoothness of your long legs wrapped around my waist . . ."

"Stop," she said, her husky, low voice sounding foreign to her own ears.

"Why? Does it make you uncomfortable?" His grin

was a potent blend of confidence and raw sexuality, and it only made her body tingle all the more, aching for his touch.

"No," she said. "But it's time for you to stop talking and show me what I've been missing out on all these years."

"You sure about that?" Chase asked, ripping off his T-shirt to show off an impressive set of abs that never failed to excite her. Just as fast he was kicking off his boots and unbuttoning his jeans. "Because once I start, you'll have to beg for mercy to get me to stop."

Hope wriggled up the bed, moving away from Chase as he came closer. She was still fully clothed but he was almost naked, the only thing covering him a pair of boxer shorts that did nothing to hide his intentions. When he pounced she squealed.

"No!" she protested, play fighting him, pushing Chase back as he grabbed her wrists and held her down. She struggled against him, loving that he was so powerful, that he was strong enough to hold her down, his body large enough to crush her if he wasn't holding his own weight.

"You sure you mean *no*?" Chase asked, taking her hands above her head and holding them there with one hand, the other skimming down her chest.

"No," she whispered, her breath coming in short, rapid pants. "I meant yes. Yes, yes, *yes*."

Chase's wolfish grin was like a shot of pure adrenaline. One second he was staring at her, and the next he was stripping her, his hands working fast to get rid of her shoes and jeans as she struggled out of her top. They were both breathless as Chase threw her clothes off the bed, the moment of silence as they stared at each other sending goose bumps across every inch of her skin.

Hope stretched up, desperate to feel Chase's mouth

against hers, looping her arms around his neck and pulling him down toward her. He kissed her with as much desperation as she had building inside of her, his lips moving feverishly against hers. Chase's hands were as relentless as his mouth; one moment they were in her hair, the next they were trailing down her thigh.

"This is even better than back then," Chase muttered against her mouth as he pulled away, letting her catch her breath for a second as he stared down at her. Only he wasn't giving her a breather—he was pausing to flip her over, undoing the catch on her bra.

"Why?" she managed, breathing rapidly. "Because we're older and wiser?"

"No, because I haven't had anything to drink." He manhandled her bra off and slipped his fingers beneath the lace of her panties as he tugged them down. "And because I know I have all damn night to do to you whatever I please."

A shudder ran down her spine as he stripped her completely naked, his lips pressing a wet, seductive kiss to her butt that had her moaning and pushing it higher in the air. But it was his fingers pressing hard into her skin within seconds, not the warm wetness of his mouth. She went to protest, to turn over, but Chase had other ideas.

"I promise I'll pleasure you any way you want later," he muttered, as something a whole lot harder than his fingers and damn impressive rammed against her ass.

Hope laughed, reaching around to guide him inside of her. "How about we agree to some afterplay rather than foreplay?"

Chase didn't respond with words. He gripped her hips, his hands splaying across her skin as he slid straight into her from behind. Hope's muscles gripped tight around him, and she moaned as he pushed in deeper. She rocked back and forth against him, on all fours as he ran one hand down her back, the other still holding her in place.

"Chase," she gasped as he stopped touching her back and gripped her hair instead, pulling just hard enough to make her groan.

His mouth was wet to her neck, sucking hard as he pumped into her even harder. All these years she'd remembered her one night with Chase, and now here she was again, and it was even better than she'd remembered. Fast, hot, illicit, and . . .

"Baby, if you keep wriggling that ass back at me like that it's all gonna be over in seconds," Chase growled.

"What, like this?" she asked, laughing as he slapped her hard on the butt. *Lucky we've got all night.*

Chase pressed a kiss to Hope's flat stomach as she lay back on the bed, her eyes shut and her breathing shallow. He studied her smooth, golden skin and ran his fingertips around in circles.

"I can't believe you carried our baby in here and I never even knew," he said.

"Chase, don't."

"As far as I'm concerned we're past all that shit, Hope," Chase said, propping himself up on one elbow. "Let bygones be bygones, right?"

Her body relaxed again, her skin quivering as he stroked her. "Right."

"You don't even have a mark."

"I was lucky. Maybe it helped that I was so young."

"Still, this body carried our son, so it's more than just something beautiful to look at," he said, hardly able to believe the words he was saying. "I'm proud of you." He was. He just wasn't proud of himself for not chasing her hard enough back then, for not being honest about his true feelings.

"He was crazy in the last few months," Hope said, stretching out her arm and stroking his hair as he went back to plucking kisses across her skin. "He did gymnastics in there. Sometimes I'd swear I could actually see his foot or his fist stretching my belly out as he pushed against me."

Chase chuckled. "Sounds like a King for sure." He moved up her body, pressing gentle kisses as he went. He stopped when he reached her lips.

"He's your son without a doubt." Hope arched up and stole a kiss, her mouth moving in time with his.

"I think we need to stop talking about kids," Chase said. "Despite the fact that he's damn cute and a hell of a lot of fun."

"Weren't we going out tonight?"

He touched his forehead to hers. "We could. Or I could just do some more of this to you." Chase kissed her again, his tongue searching out hers before he dragged his mouth away and made his way back down her body again. There was no sense of urgency now, the edge taken off already. He was starting to get hard for her again real fast, but this time around he wasn't going to rush anything.

"About that *afterplay* . . ." Chase murmured.

"Mmmmm."

Chase ran his tongue past her belly button and pushed the sheets away. He closed his mouth over her sex, loving hearing her moan. He lifted his head for a second. "Maybe we'll do Jell-O shots *after* this."

Her laughter was short-lived as he used his tongue to delve inside her. Her moans only stirred his desire more, and he wasn't going to be satisfied until she was begging for him to take her again.

Chapter 17

When Hope woke up, she stretched and then nudged into the deliciously warm body against hers in the bed. She smiled as she turned and flung an arm over Chase, pressing her breasts into his bare chest as she snuggled up to him. There was no waking with regret this time, not like the first time she'd woken up looking at the walls of the cheap motel.

"Please don't run out on me," Chase mumbled, his eyes still shut. "I don't want to have to chase you and throw you over my shoulder in public."

Hope laughed and kissed him, her lips rubbing at the soft skin across his chest. When she reached his nipple she sucked it, running her tongue across the hardened nub, until Chase grunted and grabbed her by the hair.

"Ow!" she protested, even though he wasn't really hurting her.

"Come here," he ordered, and she obeyed, sliding up his body a little so she could kiss his mouth instead.

Hope ran her fingers across the dark shadow of his jawline, the bristly hairs rough against her fingertips, the exact opposite of his warm, soft lips.

"How late do you think it is?" she murmured against his mouth.

"I think we slept through any chance of joining in with the nightlife. Or getting breakfast anywhere for that matter." Chase pushed the sheets down, his hand stroking down her side and settling on her ass.

"As much as I don't want to ruin the moment," Hope said, pushing back so she was looking down at Chase, "I think I'm going to pass out if I don't eat something."

His laughter rumbled, his chest vibrating beneath her palm as she looked into his dark eyes. She'd wanted Chase for so long, and then she'd bolted when they'd finally spent the night together. But not this time. This time she wasn't going to feel guilty for having fun, even if it was only two nights of sex and nothing more.

"We can't exactly order room service here, can we?" He tugged her back down again for a final kiss before turning them both sideways and sitting up, his bare chest golden brown and chiseled. If she could have picked a fantasy body to explore for the night, Chase's would have been it, no exceptions.

"Maybe they do a mean grilled cheese?"

Chase reached for his jeans then stopped, turning back around to face her. "You wanna check in somewhere nicer for tonight? I'm starting to think my idea about being sentimental might have been stupid."

"We're not moving to a flashy hotel," she said, looking around at their dull surroundings and grinning anyway. "If it was good enough for us back then, it's good enough for us now."

"You do know I'm paying, right?" Chase dodged sideways as she tried to hit him.

"This place is just fine," she insisted, taking the sheet with her as she stood up, keeping it wrapped around her body. She shouldn't have been shy after all the wicked things Chase had done to her—he'd seen every damn inch of her body and then some—but old habits died hard.

"Want to come check out the shower with me? See if it lives up to our expectations?" Chase was stark naked, clearly not giving a damn about what he had on show. She dragged her eyes up and down his body. He had nothing to be ashamed of, not a goddamn thing.

Hope's stomach grumbled and they both laughed. "If I say yes, we'll have to make it a very, very quick shower."

Chase stalked toward her, back in predator mode. She shivered even though the room was warm, shuddering as his hands closed over her shoulders. Chase's eyes fixed on hers.

"It just so happens that I'm partial to a fun quickie."

"Oh really," she managed, her voice all breathy and husky.

"Yes, really," Chase growled, his body towering over hers.

He let her sweat it out; waiting, anticipating as she stared up at him, her hunger pangs no longer the dominant need surging through her body. Then Chase bent in one swift motion, yanking the sheet from her and swinging her over his shoulder. She giggled, dizzy as he carried her, stopping only when they reached the shower.

"Ouch!" He bumped her into the shower door when he leaned in to turn the faucet on.

"Shit! Sorry." Chase put her on her feet and gently touched the side of her head. He pressed a kiss to her cheek. "You okay?"

Hope reached up and grabbed Chase by his hair so he had to stay partially bent forward. "Don't go all sweet on me now, King. I preferred the rough caveman act just before."

She walked them back into the shower, thankful the water was already hot as it cascaded down her back and over her shoulders. Hope only stopped when they were completely under the water, not even noticing their surroundings, not caring about anything other than being with Chase under the hot stream of water.

"Oh you did, did you?" His voice was deep and dark, and if she hadn't known him so well maybe it would have been scary.

"Yeah," she exhaled.

Faster than she could react, Chase's fingers closed around her wrist, yanking her hand away from his hair and rendering her powerless. He grabbed her ass with both hands, lifting her up and slamming her back against the shower enclosure, his mouth hot and wet over hers as he stared into her eyes, his body still only for seconds, giving her time to snap her legs around his waist before he pushed into her, fucking her fast and furiously, her breasts bouncing with each hard thrust.

Hope moaned loud into his ear, his actions unrelenting as he pushed even deeper, his mouth closing over her nipple, sucking hard, until he swore softly against her skin. She smiled and dug her nails into his shoulders, not letting him slow down even for a moment, taking pleasure in pushing him to the edge so fast.

"Stop!" Chase commanded.

But she refused, her thighs holding him in a viselike grip. When his body finally went slack, she kissed his ear and whispered, "Now how about we get clean and go get that food."

Chase walked them back under the water again, finally letting her go. "You're a bad, bad girl. You know that?"

She just laughed and reached for the soap, rubbing it over his chest so he was covered in suds.

"Why thank you."

* * *

"I can't believe we slept for so long."

Hope almost choked on her burger. "Are you kidding me? I don't think I've ever had a workout like that. I probably could have slept for two days if you'd let me."

Chase had been drinking his soda through a straw, but he quickly pushed it away, his attention back on Hope. "You saying it's the best you've had?"

Hope laughed. "Easy, cowboy. I was just saying it was the most exhausting."

"That's what your insatiable appetite gets you."

"On that note, I think I need another burger."

Chase reached for the fries on the table between them, not believing her for a second. "You're serious?"

"Deadly."

He nodded and got up, pulling his wallet out of his back pocket. By the time they'd left the motel, it had been almost five. They'd slept the day away and then some, but he still hadn't been expecting her to be able to eat as much as he could. Chase ordered another couple of burgers and joined Hope at the table again, reaching for her hand and turning it over so he could stroke his fingertips in circles around her palm.

"You were never like this," she muttered.

He stopped, looking up at her instead of at her palm like he was about to read her future. "What do you mean?"

"With the girls I saw you with."

"I was always like this with you." He frowned. "Wasn't I?"

She shook her head. "No. I mean, yeah, we kicked around like this, but you never just, I don't know. Forget I ever said anything."

He closed his fingers around hers now, linking them together. "No way. You don't get to say something like that and not finish."

She looked uncomfortable, but he still wanted to hear what she'd been about to say.

"I don't know, just touching like this. Once you got them into bed you weren't . . ."

Chase grinned. "That was because I never had a girl-friend," he told her. "Once I got a woman into bed, the game was over. So was the fun."

"So what's happening here?" Hope asked.

Neither of them looked up as their second round of burgers was placed on the table. Chase kept hold of her hand, staring into her eyes and not giving her a moment to pull away. There was so much he knew he should be saying to her, but his words didn't come as easy as his actions.

"It was never about just getting you into bed, Hope. You know that, right?"

"And when we did . . ." she started, her voice trailing off.

"I was a lazy asshole, that's what," he admitted. "I should have made more of an effort, but you didn't return my texts, and the one time we spoke it seemed awkward, so I just guessed you'd moved on."

She sighed, her shoulders going from bunched up to low and relaxed. Chase watched as she unwrapped her next burger, her painted pink fingernails almost comi-cal against the greasy bun. He laughed and it made her look up.

"I'm such a fuckup where we're concerned," he said, reaching for his soda and draining the rest of the takeout cup. "I can run the biggest ranch in Texas, deal with any shit thrown my way in life, but when it came to you, I just dropped the ball."

"I think we're both to blame," Hope said, putting her burger back down without taking a bite. "We're all about coulda, shoulda, woulda, right?"

Chase shrugged. "Maybe. But I'm not gonna fuck things up between us again. And that's a promise."

He started eating his burger, wolfing it down as she took a few delicate bites of hers, clearly not ravenous any longer. When he finished he wiped his mouth with a napkin and bent over to plant a kiss on her lips.

"What was that for?" she asked, sounding surprised.

"That," he said, "is because I think I'm falling in love with you all over again, Hope."

She looked stunned, her mouth forming a perfect O. "You are?"

"Yeah," he said, smug as hell. "And for once, I'm not afraid to just come out and say it."

He was sick of playing his cards so close to his chest, of not letting anyone too close except for family. One woman had burned him, and he'd let it hold him back for too long. Sure, Hope had fucked up, but he'd told her he'd give her a second chance, and he'd meant it.

"Now what do you say we head to our old hangout?" he asked, holding out a hand and swinging her up to her feet.

Hope looked unconvinced. "You sure you don't want to act our age?"

"Not a chance." Chase grinned. "I promised the lady Jell-O shots, and that's exactly what she's gonna get."

"Hey, I'm not complaining. I just . . ."

"Forgot that they have a band playing live on Saturday nights?" Chase interrupted, hugging her body close to his as they headed back in the same direction they'd come from. "You want to head there now or go get changed?"

"I'm good. Besides, if we go back we might never make it out again," Hope said.

He glanced down at his jeans and worn tee. "Let's go."

"You sure about the live band?" she asked. "For all we know, the bar could have closed down by now."

Chase kissed the top of her head, inhaling her sweet shampoo smell. He'd always liked the fragrance, but now that he'd actually been the one to massage the stuff through her hair and see the suds wash down over her gorgeous body? He grinned as a strand blew up and across his face. Hell, he'd never smell it without thinking about her wet and covered in suds again.

"I asked at the burger joint, and it's still a crowd favorite." Plus he had plans to do more than just drink with her there.

Hope surveyed the bar. She'd never really felt old before, but surrounded by a bunch of college kids? She felt ancient.

"These girls are making me feel like I have crows'-feet and should have a walker or something."

"These girls? They're not even close to looking as good as you." Chase looked around like she was crazy. In reality, she knew he was lying. There was no way he didn't find any of the gorgeous young women, some wearing a whole lot of nothing, insanely attractive.

"Liar, liar, pants on fire," she said, bumping her hip into his. "You're not going to offend me by admitting how cute these girls are."

Chase shrugged. "So they're cute. So what? You're fucking gorgeous."

Hope reached for the drinks that arrived in front of them. Two Jell-O shots, four tequilas, and two beers. She wasn't convinced that mixing alcohol was their best move, but she wasn't going to be a party pooper, not with Chase.

"Jell-O first?" she asked, brow raised.

"Your choice."

She nodded and reached for hers, choosing orange and leaving Chase with the green one. He followed her lead and took his, grinning before sucking it down.

"Oh man, I forgot how good they were." Hope licked her lips.

"And I forgot how damn good you looked when you licked your lips like that." Chase moved up into her space, leaning forward and kissing her lower lip only, plucking at it, before kissing her mouth properly. "That's the reason I always bought you shots."

"Bullshit," she muttered, eyes on his mouth still, wanting more kisses.

"No shit," he shot straight back. "I fucking hate Jell-O."

Hope started laughing and found it almost impossible to stop. She dropped her head onto Chase's shoulder, leaning into him. "Seriously, Chase," she said, shaking off the stupid feeling that she didn't deserve to be standing beside him after everything that had happened. "How did we end up here, at our age, in a damn college bar?"

"Sweetheart, look around. We're the hottest things in this place."

Chase slapped her ass and she squealed, only no one heard her over the music, the as-promised band so loud she had to stay pressed against Chase to hear him speak. Not that she minded.

"So, tequila?" she asked, shouting over the sudden screaming of a group of girls behind them.

Chase nudged her glass toward her, and then grinned and slid the salt closer, too. Hope took a deep breath, wishing they were just sticking to Jell-O. She kept her eyes on Chase as she raised her hand and sucked the soft skin between her thumb and index finger, making it nice and moist and loving the fact that Chase was groaning. Even without hearing him she could see the strain on his face.

Hope poured the salt over her hand as Chase bent closer.

"You're killing me here." His voice was as slick and sexy as liquor pouring over ice.

She ran her tongue over her lips again, slowly this time, playing the game, sucking the salt off her skin. She knocked the shot back in one big gulp, powered by the glint in Chase's eyes, the desire she saw reflected in his gaze. As soon as the shot was down she sucked the lime slice, shutting her eyes as the citrus hit her senses.

"Your turn." Hope did her best to sound like she wasn't spinning from drinking a shot like that, and kept her head held high.

"No problem," Chase said, voice as smooth as silk.

He did what she'd just done, except at rapid speed, then he reached for his beer.

"I guess there's some badass left in you after all."

"What made you ever doubt *that*?" she asked, pulling her best offended face. "And please don't tell me the fact that I'm a single mom holding down a job."

Chase winked at her. "How about I tell you what made me realize I was wrong?" His smile was naughty as he ran his fingers up and down her back. "It might have been when you wrapped your legs around my head last night, or when you . . ."

"Whoa! Enough!" she protested, grabbing the next shot and knocking it back faster than she should have.

"I love the fact that I can still shock you."

Chase followed her lead for the second time in minutes, downing his and then almost knocking her off her feet with a smacker of a kiss.

"What was that for?" she asked, arms slung around his neck as she pulled him back for more.

They were both happy drunk now, or at least she was both and Chase was definitely the happy part. His lips were warm, the alcohol was buzzing through her, and the only thing she was thinking about was getting Chase back to the motel. They only had one more night alone together, one more night of her pretending to be a woman with zero responsibilities, and she didn't want to waste a second.

"Hey, you remember how I used to sing?" Chase asked.

Hell, did she ever. If there was one thing he'd done that had made her stir-crazy, it was pulling out his guitar and singing just for the hell of it. Every woman in a two-mile radius had probably gone weak-kneed from seeing Chase sing, his soulful voice a perfect match to his large frame propped against a wall, one knee up to rest the guitar on, his dark head bent as he plucked at the strings. And the first time she'd heard him play had been in this very bar, the first time they met, when she'd decided not to be another notch on his belt.

"Why? You going to join the band?" He had a big enough head as it was without her boosting his ego any more by telling him how much she used to love it.

"It just so happens that I'm going to serenade you."

Hope made a coughing kind of sound, her words catching in her throat like she'd just swallowed some tequila down the wrong way. "You're what?"

But with one dimple fueled grin, Chase was backing away and then disappearing into the crowd, leaving her alone at the bar. The band was still playing, and she took her beer and turned her back to the bar, wondering what the hell Chase was up to.

She sipped her beer and waited, half expecting Chase to just rock back up to the bar and tell her it was a joke. But he didn't, and when the band finished their song and the speakers went silent, the only noise the rowdy crowd of students, she knew he was doing exactly as he'd threatened.

The microphone squeaked. "Ah, we're gonna take a

quick break and let ah"—there was a muffled noise before the voice came back on—"Chase King take over for one song."

Hope laughed, raising her beer bottle to her lips and smiling into it. She didn't doubt that he'd just slipped the band a wad of cash to turn a blind eye and let him sing, but she couldn't have cared less how he did it. She was just happy to sit back and hear him sing, refusing to feel embarrassed—no one here knew them, so what the hell did it matter?

"Excuse me," Chase said, but he may as well have been talking to himself for all the attention it got him. The tap he made on the microphone helped more. "Free drinks!" he yelled. "Ahhh, that got your attention. I want you all to stay quiet for the next three minutes, okay? Then I'll put free Jell-O shots on the bar for all of you!"

There was a round of cheers and Hope smiled. He always did have the uncanny ability to win over a crowd, usually by offering them what they wanted.

"This song is for a special girl," Chase said. "She was my first love, my last love, and she's my baby mama."

Hope slowly pulled the bottle away from her lips. Everything else blacked out; every other sound and distraction just faded away. She pushed her way through the crowd, beer held tight in her hand as she fought to get close enough to see Chase. Her heart was racing as he struck the first chords, as she recognized the song. His head was down, his eyes hidden. All she could see was his dark, unruly hair as he strummed, pinging each note.

"She's a good girl, loves her mama. Loves Jesus, and America too . . ."

Chase looked up as he sang, his eyes locking on hers like he knew exactly where to find her, like he'd known she'd be standing in that exact spot.

"Free Fallin' " had always been her favorite song and

Chase knew it. He'd sung it to her when he was drunk once, something she'd never forgotten, and now he was singing it to her to serenade her.

If he wanted her in his bed tonight, he'd sure as hell sealed the deal.

Tears filled her eyes as she listened, but she blinked them away fast, refusing to get emotional. Only she couldn't help it, because the man she'd always loved, the man she still loved, was perched on a barstool singing to her like she was the only person in the room, and all she knew was that she didn't want to lose him again.

Chase strummed the last few chords before setting the guitar down carefully and standing. Applause sounded out, loud and only getting louder as the rowdy bunch realized their free shots were on the way, and Chase jogged down the steps of the makeshift stage, high-fiving the guys he'd bribed to let him up there. It had only taken a couple hundred dollars, probably more than they got paid in some of the dives they performed at.

He scanned for Hope, finding her standing in the same spot he'd seen her when he'd been singing.

"Can I buy you a drink?" he asked, putting on a deep drawl as he moved closer to her.

"No," she said simply, one corner of mouth tilting up into a sexy smile. "You can take me back to your place."

Chase raised his eyebrows and whistled low. "Geez. If I'd known you were that easy I wouldn't have dusted off my vocal chords like that."

Hope's fingers locked around his when he took her hand, leading her back to the bar. He threw some money down as promised to buy the rounds, tipped the bartender, and pushed through the crowd to the exit. He'd forgotten what college was like, and he was pretty sure if they hung around any longer they'd end up wishing they hadn't.

"I didn't know you still sang," Hope said as they emerged from the packed bar, the fresh air like a blast of reality as their feet hit the pavement.

"Neither did I." Chase let go of her hand to pull her closer against him, wanting to keep her warm and protect her from the idiots yelling and staggering around them. He couldn't remember the last time he'd sung, either.

"Did you mean it?" she asked, forcing him to stop walking when she did.

Chase turned, staring down at Hope. "What part?"

"The part when you said I was your first love." Her gaze was filled with something he hadn't seen before, like she was finally opening herself up to him.

"I only say what I mean," Chase said, cupping her cheek and never taking his eyes off hers. "I do love you, Hope. I loved you then and I love you now, the only difference is that I'm not scared of telling you this time around."

She didn't say anything, but she did lean into him, her face pressed to his palm.

"I don't think I needed so much to drink tonight," she murmured, leaning forward and into him, her head bumping into his chest.

"So you'd rather go back to the motel than head to another bar?"

She groaned. "You betcha."

Chase threw his arm around her and pressed her body back against his, his lips on her hair as they walked. "I do love you, Hope," he said.

"I know you do," she said back, her voice low.

What she didn't know was that she was the only woman he'd said those words to. They were three little words that he'd always choked on with anyone else, even Stacey, but not Hope.

"I love you, too, Chase," Hope whispered, her arm wrapped tight around him.

"Why do I feel a *but* coming?" he joked, wishing he hadn't tried to be funny when he should have been screaming from the rooftops that she'd said it back to him.

"No buts, Chase," Hope said, kissing him as they walked, her lips skimming the side of his mouth. "I just can't believe we're finally here. Like this."

"Well, believe it, baby," he said, slipping his hand into the pocket of her jeans. "And just in case you don't, I'm gonna spend all night proving to you just how real this is. Okay?"

Hope's laughter was muffled against his chest. "You're a bad, bad influence on me, Chase King."

He nipped her lower lip and made her squeal. "That's what all the dads say when I date their daughters."

Chase hadn't thought he'd be able to, but tonight all he cared about was replicating their one night together, which he'd fantasized about for half a decade.

"I forgive you, Hope," he muttered into her hair.

"You do?" Hope squeezed him harder.

"Yeah," he said, realizing that forgiving her was the only way for them both to truly move forward. "I do."

Chapter 18

"So are we going to tell him now?"

Hope had that feeling like she was being suffocated, like there wasn't enough oxygen in the car for the both of them. Being away with Chase had been amazing, like existing in a perfect bubble, but the reality of telling Harrison was like a shot of cold ice to her veins. They'd partied and played, the latter over and over again, but arriving back in Dallas was a dose of reality, pure and simple. Life suddenly seemed complicated all over again. The bubble was bursting.

"Um, yes," she managed. "I mean, if it seems like the right thing to do at the time."

She saw Chase's frown, his mouth fast hovering from a smile into a downward turn. "So you do want to tell him or you don't?" he asked.

"I do, Chase, but I just want it to be right." She sighed. "I know that I said I wanted to tell him, but after all this time it's . . ." Hope couldn't think of the right word.

"Scary," Chase finished for her. "I get that. But you need to see it from my perspective, Hope."

She fidgeted in her seat, wishing she wasn't screwing up the end to what had been an amazing weekend. "I deserve to have you hate me, Chase. I know that, and I know how amazing you've been."

"So what's the problem?" he asked. "Because for the record, after the weekend we've just had? 'Hate' is the last word I'm thinking. I thought I'd made it well and truly clear to you that I forgive you."

"Oh really?" Trust him to turn the situation around and make her smile.

"I mean, you could always make it up to *me* by doing something dirty while I drive the rest of the . . ."

"Chase!" She slammed a punch into his arm, pleased when he howled in pain.

"Hey, it was just a suggestion."

"On a more serious note . . . ," she started.

"Oh man." Chase groaned. "What the hell have I done now?"

"Nothing," she reassured him, closing her hand over his thigh and resting it there, trying to remind herself that this wasn't some sort of weird flashback, that she was actually in a car with Chase after a dirty weekend away. "I just wanted to say thank you. Being together again, just the two of us, it was nice."

"Darlin', it was way better than nice." His hand slid over hers.

She knew Chase would never understand, that he couldn't possibly get how she felt, but she needed to try to tell him. The last couple of days had been incredible, like there was nothing else in the world to worry about except what to drink and eat after glorious hours between the sheets, and after the year she'd had, it was nice to feel that way.

"We had a blast in college, didn't we?" she mused.

"We sure did," Chase replied. "But this weekend tops anything we did back then."

She refused to blush, thinking of *all* the things Chase

had done to her. Before she could think of anything else
to say, they were turning into the driveway of King Ranch,
trees waving them in, like a canopy of green on each side
forming a line all the way to the first bend. From there
they passed the first guesthouse, then the main homestead came into view. They'd called ahead and told Chloe
when they'd be back, and Harrison burst from the house
almost the minute they pulled up, like he'd been watching out the window for him.

Hope went to throw her door open straightaway, ready
to leap out and race toward her son, but Chase's hand
stopped her. He grabbed her arm, looked deep into her
eyes when she turned back to him, and placed a soft,
warm kiss on her lips before leaning over and opening
the door for her.

She hesitated, wanted to say something to him but
didn't know what, and then Harrison had reached the car
and she was landing on her feet and wrapping her arms
around him as he jumped up and locked his legs around
her. Hope glanced over, saw that Chase was out of the
truck, but saying hi to Harrison took over from everything
else.

"Hey, baby boy." She kissed his cheek as he hugged
her tight. "Did you have fun?"

"Nate is so awesome," Harrison said, his voice all
squeaky and excited. "And Ryder. He's way cool."

"That's because you haven't spent enough time with
me yet," Chase grumbled, appearing from around the side
of the truck. "'Cause if you had, you'd know that I'm way
more fun than those two."

Hope came over all hot again, her head spinning. She
looked at Harrison, at his innocent, sweet little face, then
focused her attention back on Chase. They were so similar now she had them side by side, but the thought of

Chase telling Harrison the truth? It sent an ice-cold shudder down her back. She'd shielded her little man for so long, and . . .

"Can I show you what we've been doing? Please, Mommy, please!"

She nodded, braving a smile at both of them and nodding toward the house. "Let's go. Show me what you've been up to. And let's take Chase with us."

Harrison ran on ahead, jumping up the porch steps and disappearing into the house. Hope followed, just at a slower pace, with Chase holding her hand as they walked in. What she wanted was to grab her things, put them in her car, and speed away, because she was scared of change and what might happen, now that it was so real. Instead, she sucked it up and put on a brave face. She could do this.

Or not. Hope looked around the room, fear lacing every sense she had her words froze in her mouth, her hands started to shake, and she could hardly figure where to look first.

"Hey, Hope," a warm female voice called out from the kitchen. Hope stared around, snapping back to reality and turning to see Chloe. She was a familiar face and a kind one, not intimidating like the other three staring at her from the opposite side of the room.

"How was your weekend?" Ryder asked with a chuckle from where he lay sprawled on the floor.

Harrison suddenly appeared from beneath a large blanket that was draped over some chairs. "Mom, we made a tent! I even got to sleep in here with Nate last night! We had sleeping bags and chocolate and . . ."

"Whoa!" Nate exclaimed, jumping up from his spot on the sofa and grabbing Harrison, planting a hand over his mouth. "What happens in the tent stays in the tent, buddy. Remember?"

Harrison laughed and struggled as Nate first hung him upside down then put him back on his feet. Hope smiled, but inside she was dying. A very, very slow death. Because no matter how funny Nate might have been, it was the more serious, older gaze across the room that was worrying Hope.

"Hey, Granddad," she heard Chase say, going over to give his grandfather a hug. "What are you doing here?"

"Nate got me out of there again," the old man said, slapping Chase on the back with what appeared to be a lot more strength than Hope would have expected a man his age to possess. His steel-gray eyes sought out hers over Chase's shoulder, his expression kind if not curious. "Besides, I had to meet the woman who had you all in a bother, didn't I?"

Hope had never been so pleased to see someone when Chloe came to stand beside her, passing her a cup of coffee and bumping her shoulder gently against hers, as if she was trying to reassure her.

"Granddad, this is Hope. Hope, this is my granddad, Clay King."

The old man nodded and straightened, pushing Chase's hand aside as he considered her and moved forward. Hope sprang into action, crossing the room toward him and holding out a hand, the other clasping her coffee.

"I'm pleased to meet you, sir," she said.

"Clay," he corrected, firmly shaking her hand and meeting her gaze without missing a beat. "I remember hearing all about you a long while back. When that boy over there was dumb, young, and full of—"

"Granddad!" Chase interrupted. "Hope knows exactly what I was like back then so there's no need to explain."

Clay laughed. "Oh, I'm sure she does, son. I'm sure."

Hope was a wreck; she didn't know whether to laugh or cry, her body wound tighter than an old-fashioned clock.

"So tell us about the weekend," Chloe asked, clearly trying to break the ice and take some of the pressure off. "You visit some of your old haunts?"

"It was fun," Hope said, trying to relax when Chase casually slung an arm around her like it was the most natural thing for him to do in the world. "We, ah"—she cleared her throat—"would you believe we did Jell-O shots and Chase sang to an almost-full bar?"

"He what?" Nate roared with laughter.

"Yeah, I did," Chase admitted, "but I had something to prove so I didn't have much choice."

Hope stared at the three men, wondered what they really thought of her, if they were just being nice to be polite, because they knew she meant something to Chase. Did they resent her? Did they despise her for what she'd done?

She glanced at Chloe, saw the concern on the other woman's face. And then she looked at her son. He was busy playing with a rope, working on a knot, and it broke her heart to think that he could have had this kind of upbringing from the very start, that she should have found a way to divide her time between here and home. But it also killed her to think that he might get used to being surrounded by the King men and then have it all taken away if Chase didn't want to commit to something long-term. He'd said he loved her, but they hadn't exactly talked about the future.

"Hope, why don't we take Harrison for a walk? Maybe head out to see the cattle you worked on?" Chase said.

The room was silent until Chloe spoke up and started

talking about something trivial, the other men suddenly engaged in banter about the weather as Hope stood and stared at Harrison.

"Hope?" Chase's voice was deep, full of concern.

"Mom, let's do it!" Harrison enthused.

Hope opened her mouth to speak and ended up just shaking her head. "I'm sorry, but we have to go."

Chase reached for her hand, his eyes searching her face. "But Hope, aren't we going to . . ."

She pulled her hand from his, reaching down for Harrison's instead. "Sweetheart, show me what room your things are in. It's a pre-K day tomorrow and we need to get back home."

"But . . ."

She kept her eyes trained on her boy, giving in to the terror consuming her, the worry over what she had almost done, what she'd planned to tell him.

"No buts, Harrison. Let's go."

Chase steeled his jaw, staring at Hope's retreating figure. He balled his fists, then released them, trying damn hard to diffuse his anger.

"Hope," he said, keeping his voice as level as he could, not wanting to alarm Harrison. "How about we go for that walk first? It won't take long."

She edged away from him when he reached for her, eyes wide like he'd just asked her to commit a crime. "Not now, Chase. I just can't do it right now."

Hope was talking about a lot more than a cancelled walk. Telling Harrison terrified her. "Hope." He repeated her name, taking a step closer to her as she walked backward again, keeping her distance. "Don't do this."

"I'll call you, Chase. Thanks for an amazing weekend."

"Hope . . ."

She raised one hand in a wave before pushing Harrison toward the front door when Chase reappeared, not letting him near.

"See ya, Chase," Harrison called.

Chase forced himself to reply, to not let the kid see how pissed he was. "Yeah, I'll see you again real soon, okay? We can hang out and have way more fun than you've ever had before."

Hope gave Chase one last fleeting, apologetic look, then the door was shut behind her and she was gone. Chase waited, focused on each breath, on sucking back enough air to fill his lungs until he heard Hope's vehicle start up and pull away from the house. What the hell was going on? How in God's name had they ended up with things going back to this?

"Fuck!" he yelled, marching back toward the kitchen, fists balled at his sides, a wave of fury building like a tidal wave within him. *"Fuck,"* he swore again, this time slamming his fist straight into the wall, pain arrowing through his knuckles and straight up his arm.

Chase stood, shoulders heaving as he extracted his hand. *Damn.* He was pissed, but he hadn't exactly meant to trash the place. He walked into the kitchen, shoulders hunched as he took out a glass and crossed the room to get the bottle of whiskey he wanted.

It wasn't until he'd drained the glass that he realized the room was silent, that all eyes were on him.

"You gonna fix that wall in the morning, son?"

His granddad's deep, steady voice calmed him. There was nothing they'd ever done that had managed to faze the old man, and he doubted anything ever would.

Chase nodded, tipping the bottle to give himself another generous pour, and hastily raised the glass to his lips. "I will." He should never have done it in the first place. *Damn idiot.*

"How about pouring another few glasses and telling

us what your Hope did to get you all in a pickle? Why the hell was she in such a hurry to leave?"

This time Chase had to laugh, his brothers joining in. Nate winked as he passed him, getting three more glasses and setting them on the table. Chase poured, pleased to have something other than his sore-as-a-motherfucker knuckles to think about.

"We were supposed to tell Harrison. About me being his dad," Chase ground out after downing the rest of his second drink.

"And?" Nate asked.

Chase looked up and saw that Chloe was watching him, her brown eyes kind as she listened.

"She just got the hell out of dodge, in case you hadn't noticed."

"It was kind of hard to miss the sound of your closed fist connecting with the wall," Nate said dryly.

"Fuck you," he snapped.

"Did it ever cross your mind that she's just trying to protect your son?" Chloe asked in a quiet voice, her hand resting protectively over her stomach.

"I'm not exactly a threat to the boy," Chase replied.

Every man stayed silent as Chloe spoke, her soft voice low yet commanding. "You've probably told her how you feel about her, Chase, but have you told her how you feel about Harrison? Told her what you actually want?"

"I'm not following." He put down his glass, feeling like a dumbfuck for not even getting what Chloe was trying to tell him.

"Chase, she needs to know that you want her son as much as you want her. She's protected him all this time, so she's hardly going to let him get hurt by getting close to you, unless she's absolutely sure, is she? She's a two-for-one deal, Chase. And she's not exactly giving me the vibe that she wants to play things casual with you."

Chase stared at Chloe. How could he have been so stupid that his sister-in-law had had to spell it out for him?

"You're right," he said, slowly pouring himself one more shot of his favorite liquor and drinking it, savoring the slow burn as it traveled down his throat. Chase discarded his glass and made his way over to Chloe, slinging an arm around her and pressing a smacker of a kiss to her cheek. "She wants me to prove myself? Then fuck it. I'm up for the challenge, just you watch me."

He backed away from Chloe when Ryder as good as bared his teeth at him, warning him off his woman. Chase just laughed, dropping into the sofa opposite Nate and kicking his boots off so he could stretch out with his feet up.

"So how about you guys tell me all about Harrison."

His granddad took a sip of whiskey then coughed, holding up his hand to stop any of them from rushing at him. Chase slowly took his feet down, ready to move if he had to but respecting his granddad enough not to treat him like an invalid before he actually was one. It broke his heart to see him coughing, hacking away like it might never stop. They all stayed silent and waited him out.

"The boy's just like you lot were," Clay said quietly. "A heart like a lion and a mind so damn curious it'll get him in trouble one day."

"So there was no doubt in your mind he was a King, Granddad?" Chase asked.

"Not a doubt, son. Not a single doubt."

Chase held his granddad's gaze and then eased back into the sofa. From the moment Hope had told him, he'd never once doubted her, not for a second, but it meant a lot to hear his granddad reiterate what he already knew.

Harrison was his son, and Hope was the woman he'd let get away once, and he sure as hell wasn't going to let it happen again.

She wanted a grand gesture? Chase grinned to himself. Then he'd damn well give her one.

Chapter 19

"Chase?" The look on Hope's face was priceless, a combination of confusion and what he hoped was happiness at seeing him. "What are you doing here?"

Chase shrugged. "Aren't I allowed to just swing past and say hi?"

"No," she said, leaning into the door as she watched him. "I'm already running late and I have to get Harrison to pre-K and . . ."

"No, you don't." He'd tried phoning her and she'd screened his calls, which is why he'd decided that coming by was the best option. Now that he was here, he wasn't giving her an option but to come with him. Both of them.

Hope placed one hand on her hip, eyes narrowed. "What are you up to, Chase?"

"Let's just say that your boss isn't expecting you at work today." Chase laughed. "And I may have called in and told Harrison's teachers that he wouldn't be in today, too."

"You what?" She looked angry, and angry wasn't the reaction he was going for today. "Chase, what are you playing at?"

"I need you to grab a day bag, Hope. Put whatever you need for you and Harrison for the day. We'll be back before bedtime."

"Chase . . ." She still had her hand on her hip, but her expression appeared less angry and more curious now. "Is this because of what happened the other day? Because I just needed some time to think."

"Just trust me, darlin'," Chase said with a wink. "It's gonna be fun. And I'm not planning on holding the other day against you." He'd been pissed at the time, but he got it. She was Harrison's mom and she was super protective over her boy—it was frustrating, but it was also understandable. As far as he was concerned all it meant was that he had to work a little harder to prove himself.

Hope held her arms out and blocked the doorway. "Give me a hint or I'm not moving an inch."

He leaned in and gave her a kiss, hands to her hips as he lingered longer than he needed to, smiling against her mouth as she groaned and kissed him back.

"Let's just say we're *leaving, on a jet plane*," Chase said in a singsong voice, manhandling her aside as she protested.

"Chase, get back here!" she called, following him down the hallway as he jogged into the kitchen.

"Hey buddy!" he said when he saw Harrison, holding up his hand for a high five.

Harrison slammed his palm into Chase's. "Whaddaya doing?"

"I'm here to take you and your mom somewhere fun for the day. What do you say to an adventure?"

"Chase, where are you planning on taking us?" Hope asked, standing behind him.

"Canada," he said simply, like it was the most sensible answer in the world, even though he knew he'd as good as shocked the pants off her. "I've got the jet fueled up and waiting for us."

"You have *your plane* waiting?" Hope's eyes were wide, her hands back on her hips like she was about to tell him off.

"You have your own plane? For real?" Harrison asked, jumping up and down on the spot.

"Yeah, we have a plane. It's pretty cool." Chase held his hand out to him. "Want to come for a ride in it this morning instead of going to pre-K?"

"Yeah!"

Chase turned, hand in hand with Harrison and putting on his best sad-puppy-dog expression. "What do you say, Mama Bear? Can we go?"

"Canada?" Hope asked, like she was more stuck on where they were going than the fact he had his family's jet waiting. "Why Canada?"

He let go of Harrison's hand and crossed the kitchen, staring into her eyes as he reached for her. Chase touched one hand to her cheek, wishing he could tell her everything he felt for her and not even knowing where to start.

"Just trust me, Hope. I'm doing this for you."

He watched her take a breath, her chest rising, then falling.

"Do you trust me?" Chase asked.

"Of course I trust you," she replied, smiling up at him. "I just don't understand why we have to go to *Canada*." Hope laughed. "I mean, take us on your jet if you want to impress us, but couldn't we have gone to New York or somewhere more exciting?"

"It's not just about impressing you with the plane," Chase told her. "When we get there it'll make sense. Trust me."

"I'm just not sure about going back, Chase. I don't want to keep thinking about what we lost there."

He looked into the only pair of eyes that had ever had the power to truly captivate him, and gave her what he hoped was a reassuring smile. For the first time in his life he was ready to give up everything for a woman, and it scared the crap out of him.

"Just trust me, Hope. You'll be happy you did, okay?"

Harrison slapped at Chase's leg just as Chase was about to kiss Hope.

"Hey, Chase? Do you mean like a real *real* plane or a pretend one?"

Chase looked at Hope and they both burst out laughing. "A real *real* plane, Harris. Now let's give your mom a minute to get ready. You like video games?"

"Yeah!"

"Then how about I make a call and check we've got some good kids movies and games on the plane, huh?"

Chase ruffled Harrison's hair, something inside of him turning to mush as the kid smiled up at him. He'd never been a soft touch, *never*, and all of a sudden he wanted to bend over backward just to make the boy happy. Not to mention the fact that he'd warned his brothers they might have to make some changes around the ranch. It'd break his heart to leave Texas, but if it meant keeping Hope and Harrison in his life, then there was nothing he wouldn't do. He protected what was his and fought for what he wanted, and there was no battle too big when it came to family. *Not one*.

"I still can't believe it," Hope said, nose pressed to the glass as they landed at Grand Forks International Airport. "You didn't have to make some grand gesture to impress me." He didn't have to, but he sure as hell *had* impressed her.

"It's nothing."

She resisted the urge to roll her eyes. "Yeah, 'cause just anyone could fire up their private jet and whisk a girl to off for the day."

"Hey, if you want me to get the pilot to turn back around . . ."

"No!" Hope pried her eyes from the window and turned her focus on Chase. "I just can't believe that when I woke up this morning I was prepping for a day at work, and now I'm here. The last time I was in GFK, I was a mess."

Chase was sitting beside Harrison, who was too busy playing games on the screen that was attached to his chair to even notice that they'd just landed, and she was sitting across from him.

"These past couple of weeks seeing you again have been like . . ." Her eyebrows pulled together as she tried to find the right word. "Like a dream, I guess. Part of me still thinks I'm going to wake up one morning and I'll have just imagined it all."

Chase leaned forward and took her hand in two of his, turning it over so he could stroke her palm. "And the other part?"

She shook her head, refusing to cry even as emotion bubbled up in her throat. Hope took a deep breath and smiled as Chase brought her hand up to meet his mouth and pressed a gentle kiss to her wrist.

"That part is telling me just to stop overthinking everything for once and enjoy life."

"I'd listen to that voice, if I were you," he told her.

She smiled as the flight attendant approached them now that they'd landed. "Mr. King, is there anything you need?"

"No, thank you. We'll be wheels up before dark, so please be prepared to leave again within a few hours."

"If you were me, Chase, what would you be thinking right now?" Hope asked, still completely at a loss to figure out why he'd whisked her away from Texas on such short notice.

"I'd be wondering if I was going to visit my family's old ranch."

Her heart started to beat faster than it should have. She'd sworn never to go back there, to never torture herself by dreaming about what she'd never be able to have again, and now here she was desperate to head straight there.

"And if I asked you that?"

Chase leaned over and carefully took the headphones off Harrison, and it made Hope worry all over again. She loved seeing Chase with their son. The only trouble was that Harrison still didn't know and she was terrified of telling him in case it all turned to shit. After so long of everything going pear shaped on her, she didn't have a whole ton of confidence about the world suddenly throwing her a lifeline.

"We're here, little man," Chase said.

Harrison looked up. "We're home?"

Hope forced a smile when all she wanted to do was frown. "We're almost back in Canada."

She looked up at Chase. He'd never answered her question and she needed to know.

"It just so happens that we're heading to Rocking R Ranch as soon as we get off the plane," Chase was telling Harrison, but he was staring at her. "If your mom says that's okay."

"But the new owners . . ." she protested, torn between wanting to go back and hating the thought of seeing new owners on the property where she'd grown up.

"Were investors and have never moved in," he told her. "There'll be no one there."

Hope's heart started to pound again, heat spreading

across her body. "So no one's moved into the main house?" She wasn't sure whether to be angry or happy.

"They're all questions you can ask the realtor," Chase said cryptically. "So I take back what I said before. There will be one other person there."

If they'd been alone she would have leaped on him and begged him to tell her what the hell was going on, but with Harrison listening to every word they were saying, his eyes on theirs, she just squirmed in her seat.

"It seems like you know more than I do about the ranch," she said, raising an eyebrow and reaching for her bag. "I presume the realtor is doing you a favor?"

"Everyone has a price, Hope," Chase said. *"Everyone."*

The drive from GFK to Rocking R seemed to take forever, but Hope didn't want to give Chase the satisfaction of begging him for information. Harrison had fallen asleep, the journey on the plane taking it out of him. He was a great kid, but he was only four, and he was absolutely exhausted.

"We're here," Hope said, leaning forward as the property came into view. Two massive rocks marked the entrance a wooden sign hanging high and bearing the ranch name, a sign that her granddad had made for her dad when she was just a kid.

Chase grinned and took the turn slowly in the rental car, driving at a snail's pace as they made their way toward the house. Tears welled up in her eyes as she watched the trees waving in the wind, the large specimens planted all the way up on either side of the driveway.

"It's beautiful, Hope," Chase said, taking his eyes off the drive and reaching for her hand. "I didn't realize how amazing it would be."

"You don't have to be in Texas to see an incredible ranch."

Hope blinked away tears and when Chase stopped the car he turned to face her, brushing away a few that had escaped before they could fall right down her cheeks.

"I know this is hard, but you needed to come back."

She shook her head, biting down on her bottom lip. "So I could remember what I'd lost?" She was trying not to be angry with him, her excitement turning to dread now they were here, but it was hard not to be pissed off with him.

There was a tap on the window and she turned away so the woman standing there couldn't see her tears. Chase never took his eyes off her, she knew because his body didn't move an inch, and he reached for her hands, taking both of hers into his.

"Just trust me, Hope. I'm doing this for you, and it's supposed to be a happy day, not a sad one."

Hope nodded and let Chase kiss her. She craned her head to look at Harrison in the backseat, still asleep, and followed Chase's lead, pushing open her door and stepping out. Familiar smells hit her straightaway; a rush of feelings that almost took the breath from her lungs.

She could hear Chase talking, but she wasn't listening. Instead she was looking around her, taking in the house that still seemed like home to her. The wooden exterior was in perfect condition, but it was nothing fancy from the outside, just a beautiful ranch house full of beautiful memories. Farther away were more trees, their branches covered in vivid green leaves, the fields a more parched shade of yellow stretching farther than the naked eye would ever be able to see.

"Hope?"

Chase's voice pulled her from her thoughts. "Sorry, I was a million miles away."

She noticed the realtor had returned to her car, was standing beside it and tapping at her phone.

"You want to take a look around?" Chase asked.

"No," she said, shaking her head and wishing to hell she'd never set foot on the place again. "I don't think coming back was such a good idea."

"Can I ask you something then?"

She let him take her hand and turn her around. "Sure." She wasn't in the mood to play, but Chase had obviously thought he was doing something nice for her in bringing her back. It wasn't his fault she couldn't deal with it.

"Come on, I want to ask you somewhere more private."

The husky note of Chase's voice surprised her. The last time she'd heard him sound like that they'd both been naked—it was his seriously sexy, deep-in-thought voice. The one that usually sent shivers down her spine, anticipating what might come next.

"I don't want to go too far," she said, glancing back at their vehicle. "Just in case Harrison wakes up."

"Neither do I. Just come over here by this tree."

She followed. "Chase, I . . ."

"Just stop talking," he ordered, grabbing her hand. "This will only take a minute."

"What will?" she asked.

"This," Chase said, his face lighting up as he grinned and dropped to one knee.

"Chase . . ." Her hands were shaking, her breathing shallow as Chase looked up at her, his dark eyes tinged with gold as he watched her.

"Hope, I let you walk out of my life almost five years ago, and it was the stupidest thing I've ever done."

She let him take both of her hands, tears filling her eyes again as he smiled and gripped her fingers.

"I don't want to make that mistake again, which is why I have something to ask you."

Chase let go of one of her hands to reach for something, but he never once broke their gaze.

"Hope Walker, I love you. I can't believe it took me so long to admit it, but it's true." He laughed, and she realized he was nervous—it was the first time she'd seen him look even remotely unsure of himself before. "Hope, will you marry me?"

"Marry you?" If she'd thought she couldn't breathe before, then now she was positively being strangled. A rush of warmth through her body made her hold Chase's hand even tighter, worried she was about to faint.

But Chase had other ideas. He let go of her hand and held it out instead, slipping something cold against her skin, something . . . *Oh my God*. The something was the biggest diamond she'd ever seen, a single solitaire on a plain platinum band. She looked from the ring to Chase and back again.

"What do you say?"

"Chase, you don't have to do this," she mumbled, shaking her head, trying to wake up from what had to be a dream.

"I don't *have* to do anything," he said, his voice strong and confident, as self-assured as she was nervous right now. "I want to marry you, Hope."

"If you're doing this to try to stay in Harrison's life, because you think it's the right thing, because . . ." He silenced her jumble of words when he stood, staring down at her with a determined look on his face that she'd never seen before.

"Hope, forget all the crap you worried about when Harrison was born, okay?" he said, cupping her face with both hands and looking into her eyes, his touch so tender, so soft it was almost painful. "I love you, and I want to spend the rest of my life with you. *And* with our son. Is that so hard to believe?"

"I'm not even officially divorced yet," she muttered.

Chase's eyebrows shot up. "Need me to track the bastard down and kneecap him so he signs the papers?"

Hope sighed, but she wasn't even sure if Chase was kidding or not. "No."

"You sure about that?" His eyebrows were raised, a determined look on his face as he waited for her reply.

"Maybe you could just hurt him a little," she said with a laugh. "Although knowing you, you probably won't stop at one punch."

"Done. A black eye but no broken bones," Chase said. "Now I'm gonna do this again, and this time you need to give me an answer." The no-nonsense look on his face was replaced with a softer, more loving expression.

Hope reached for Chase's hands and held them tight when he dropped on bended knee again, his smile warming her like no other man ever could have. His eyes were bright and so full of kindness, so far removed from the man who was capable of protecting her in a rowdy bar, who she knew would have no qualms about physically dealing with her ex if she asked him to.

"Hope, will you marry me?"

"Yes," she said straightaway, unable to contain her smile any longer. "Yes, yes, yes!"

Chase was back on his feet and scooping her up into his arms within seconds, his lips closing over hers in a kiss that was almost as dizzying as the way he was twirling her.

"I love you, baby," he whispered against her mouth.

Hope looped her arms around Chase's neck and kissed him again. "I love you, too."

When he finally set her back down on her feet, he kept hold of her, his arm locked around her and keeping her snug against his body. They stood like that, staring out at the land, land that was a part of Hope's soul, that she would never forget for as long as she lived. It was so surreal that she was convinced she was about to wake from a dream.

"Chase, why did you bring me here?" He could have proposed to her anywhere. "Why here?"

His smile was mischievous.

"Chase?" she asked, pushing away from him so she could try to read his face.

"This is your home, sweetheart. It should belong to you."

She stared at him, eyes wide. "What have you done?"

"I found a very helpful realtor, and even though the new owners were very happy with their purchase, I worked out that magic price that made them reconsider."

"Chase, you didn't . . . ."

"You want your ranch back, it's yours," he said simply, like he'd just offered to buy her a trinket or a piece of art, not something that cost tens of millions of dollars. "And there are no strings attached. If you'd rather be here with just Harrison, it's yours. But given what I just asked you, I think I've made my feelings very clear. About both of you."

Hope took a few steps back, needed some space from Chase for a second as she tried to digest what he'd said. She felt her eyebrows pull together as she tried to comprehend what he'd offered her. What he'd just agreed to.

"So you're saying that we can live here? That you'll leave your family behind, that you'll give up running King Ranch to be here with us?"

Chase nodded. "I understand what it means to feel a connection with the land you love. But the only thing stronger than that is family, and you and Harrison are my family now."

Hope couldn't hold back her tears any longer. She

gasped as emotion choked her, tears rushing down her cheeks at the enormity of what Chase was offering her.

"No," she finally said, cocooned safely in Chase's arms as she cried, pulling herself together. *"No."*

"What do you mean *no*?" Chase asked gruffly.

"I'm not letting you leave your family or your ranch for us," she said, feeling even more certain about her words as she said them, empowered by what she was about to tell him. "Your home is our home, and that means we all belong at King Ranch." She reached up to touch his face, stroking down his cheekbone and to his jaw. "You're building a new house there and I'm not going to be the one to make you leave your family. They mean too much to you."

"So do you." His words were simple. "I love you, Hope. Always have, always will."

She smiled, blinking away tears that were bittersweet. "And I love you more than I love this place. Here"—she gestured around them—"is a place of memories. Beautiful, wonderful memories, but they're in the past. You?" Hope stood on tiptoe and kissed him, indulging in the feel of his full, delicious lips against hers. "You're my future, Chase. I'll choose you every single time."

He wrapped his arms around her, held her in a bear hug so tight she could hardly breathe. "I love you," he muttered, "and for the record, I'm still buying you this place."

"But . . ."

He released her and slung his arm around her, turning them back around so they were facing the house. The realtor was nowhere to be seen, but she was probably just giving them their space.

"It's a good investment, and you have history here," he told her as they walked, hips bumping as they made their way back toward the car. "Who knows? Maybe one day Harrison will want to run a quarter horse stud here like his mom wanted to? All I care about is making sure it's here for him if and when he wants it. It's his legacy." He grinned. "Hey, we found a new foreman for King Ranch easily enough, so we can appoint someone great to run this place, someone who knows what they're doing. You pay enough money, you usually get the best."

"You would do that for us?" she asked. "For our son?"

"Abso-fucking-lutely," he replied. "But there is one condition."

Hope groaned. "What?"

"No more keeping the truth from Harrison. We tell him," Chase said, kissing the top of her head, "today. On the land he grew up on, with both of us together."

Hope took a deep breath, knowing it was the right thing to do even though it terrified her. "Okay. But just because I'm letting you buy the ranch doesn't mean I don't want my own independence still."

He raised an eyebrow. "Darlin', I wouldn't have it any other way. So long as you're mine and everyone knows it."

"I love my work, and I want to keep practicing," she told him.

"Promise to keep doing our insemination work on the ranch and it's a deal."

"Damn you, Chase," she muttered, leaning in for a kiss.

"Baby, you can punish me any way you see fit."

"Okay? Just like that?" Chase asked, unable to hide his grin.

"I just didn't want to tell him without knowing we were going to be a part of your life," Hope explained. "Long term."

"So you've been waiting for me to propose?"

Chase intercepted Hope's punch and dodged out of her way, stopping only when a bold voice called out to him.

"Hey! Leave my mom alone!"

Chase jogged over to Harrison, laughing at the boy standing with his fist bunched and raised beside the car like he was about to take Chase on for play fighting with his mom. His little face looked happy though, mouth stretched into a massive smile as Chase ran and scooped him up, swinging him through the air.

"Hey! Put me down!"

Chase obliged when they were in front of Hope, putting Harrison down and bending so he was on the same level as his son.

"We've got some exciting news," Chase said, one hand on his shoulder.

"Are we going to get ice cream?"

Chase laughed. "No."

"Did you buy me a pony?"

Chase cleared his throat and made a straight face, glancing up at Hope. "Do you want a pony?"

"Yeah."

"Hmm, well, it just so happens that I gave your mom a gift today," Chase told him, reaching for Hope's hand. "I gave her this beautiful ring and asked her to be my wife. We're going to get married."

Harrison looked confused and Hope dropped to her knees, too, so they were all on the same level.

"Mommy loves Chase a lot, and we're going to go live with him at King Ranch. In his new house?" She touched Harrison's shoulder. "If that's okay with you."

Harrison was wide-eyed.

"I might move in with you guys for a couple of months until my place is ready, and by then it might be about time to give you something," Chase told him. "I mean, since I gave your mom a present, it'd only be fair to spend the next few weeks or so looking for a pony for you. Whadda you say, kid?"

"Yes!"

Chase held his hand up for a high five and received a little body being hurtled against him at full speed instead, Harrison's arms tight around him.

"Harris, there's something else we need to tell you," he said, an unfamiliar nervous sensation passing through him. Chase sat down on the grass, the boy still in his arms. He gestured for Hope to do the same, and he recognized what he saw reflected in her face as the same worry that was coursing through him. He'd never been responsible for anyone else before, never cared so badly about not hurting another human being, about protecting someone from harm. He smiled as he looked down at Harrison. He finally got what it meant to be a dad, to love so fiercely that it hurt.

"Some kids, like me, we had to grow up with a dad who didn't really love us. Not like a dad should love his kids. But I was lucky, because I had two pretty awesome brothers and a really great mom, just like you. And after she died, my grandparents looked after us."

"I don't have a dad either," Harrison said. "I had a step-dad, but not a real one."

Chase watched as Hope took Harrison's hand, and Chase ran his fingers down her back as he took a deep breath and prepared to say the hardest thing he'd ever said in his life.

"The difference between you and me, Harris, is that you do have a dad who loves you. I'm just sorry that you've had to wait so long to find out. To have me in your life."

"I don't understand." Harrison looked from Chase to Hope and back again.

Chase smiled at him. "I'm your dad, Harris. And from this day forward, I promise to be the best darn dad in the world. Okay?"

Harrison stood dead still, not making noise, unblinking as he stared at Chase. "You?" he asked. "You're my dad?"

Chase grinned. "Yeah, son, I am."

There was silence, none of them saying a word until Harris suddenly threw his arms around Chase again like he'd just received the best news of his life. Tears streamed down Chase's cheeks, emotion clogging his throat and making him cry like he'd never cried before. He didn't cry, *not ever*, but today he was in pieces.

Hope's arms went around both of them and he leaned over to kiss her.

"Can we all just go home now?" she asked.

"No," Chase said, clearing his throat a few times and rising with Harris still in his arms. He swiped at his face, getting rid of any evidence that he'd actually given in to his emotions. "I've got a deal to close, and you," he said, reaching into his back pocket for his iPhone and throwing it to her, "need to call Chloe and tell her that you said yes."

"Chloe knew about this?"

He laughed at the bemused expression on Hope's face. "Chloe knows everything. That's just something you'll have to get used to."

Chase strode forward and stole one last kiss, his lips lingering over Hope's for longer than he'd planned.

"And you," he said to the grinning boy on his hip, "are gonna have to get used to me kissing your mom. All the time."

"Gross," Harrison protested, but he was still smiling.

Chase left Hope and headed back toward the house, waving to the realtor when he saw her. He appreciated that she'd given them some privacy when she must have wondered what the hell was going on.

"You still like this place?" Chase asked his son.

Harrison nodded, arms around him as they walked. "Yeah, but I like your place, too."

"Good," Chase said. "I'm gonna buy this place for you and your mom anyway though, so you always have somewhere to come back to, the place where your granddaddy ranched long before your mom was even born. It's important to understand your history."

He doubted the kid cared about all that kind of stuff yet or even really got what he was saying, but one day he would.

"Now it's time for me to teach you how to negotiate a deal. You up for it?"

"Can we get ice cream after?"

Chase had never laughed so hard in all his life. "Yeah, we can get ice cream afterward."

He stole a quick look over his shoulder at Hope. She was walking slowly, her hand held out in front of her as she looked at her ring—he knew it would be sparkling like crazy in the bright sunshine. Chase couldn't wipe the grin off his face as he turned back, taking in the mountains still tipped with snow, the dark green of the fields around them. It was a hell of a place to have as a second home, and Hope was going to make one hell of a wife.

Epilogue

"We really need to get downstairs." Hope stretched out, flexing her toes against Chase's leg. He just grunted, his lips moving lazily across hers.

"Why can't we just stay here?" he mumbled.

Hope finally pushed him away. He'd sidetracked her once and if they stayed upstairs any longer it was just going to be embarrassing. "Up," she ordered. "We can't pretend like we don't have guests any longer."

"Nate can entertain everyone. How about we just stay here?"

"And when our son comes looking for us and finds you doing wicked things to his mommy?"

Chase groaned, releasing her wrist and stroking down her leg as she moved. She'd come back upstairs to find a necklace she'd forgotten to put on, and Chase had ambushed her before she'd left the bedroom. It was only his family and Nate's friend Sam there right now, but still, she didn't need them all knowing what her insatiable fiancé had been doing to her.

She crossed the room and disappeared into the adjoining bathroom, sighing when she saw how disheveled she was.

"You need to go back down. I'll just be a minute."

Chase appeared behind her, his arms looping around her waist, chin resting on her shoulder as she stood in front of the mirror.

"Have I told you how beautiful you are lately?"

Hope smiled, already finished touching up her foundation and now reapplying her lipstick. "Hmmm, yes. But you can tell me again."

He dropped a kiss to her shoulder and stepped back, tucking his shirt back into his jeans. "I'll see you down there, gorgeous."

Hope finished tidying herself up, retrieved the necklace she'd come looking for in the first place, and slipped her shoes back on. She smoothed down her dress and headed downstairs, excited about finally having all their friends and family over. They'd waited to have their engagement party until the house was finished, and they'd been in a week now. Hope smiled as she looked around—it already felt like home.

"Hey, beautiful," Chase murmured, taking her hand and grinning, the mischievous look on his face making it impossible for her not to return it. "I was starting to wonder where you'd gotten to."

"Oh really?" She laughed and linked their fingers. The doorbell rang just as they started to walk, and she pulled Chase in for a quick kiss before letting him go. "I love you," she whispered.

"I love you, too, darlin'," he replied, pressing another kiss to her hand before leaving her side.

"I still can't believe it, seeing Chase like this."

Hope turned when Chloe spoke. She took the champagne flute her sister-in-law-to-be was holding out for her.

"You say it like he was an ogre before."

"No," Chloe said, her smile infectious, "I say it because he was always so damn hotheaded about not ever wanting to settle down. Then, poof, along you come and he's a different man."

"How's that baby?" Hope asked, turning the conversation away from her and touching Chloe's rounded stomach. They'd become close over the last couple months, and she loved Chloe like she was her own sister.

"Moving way too much. I can't believe we're having a girl." Chloe made a face. "I'm just thankful it's not another Y chromosome though. It's not like there's a shortage of them around here."

"Hey, I know exactly what it's like to carry an acrobat in there." They both laughed. "And for the record, there's nothing wrong with any of the Y chromosomes around here, but a little girl will be so nice."

Chloe giggled. "Honey, you don't have to tell me."

"Can I steal my beautiful fiancée away from you?" Chase asked, slinging his arm around her and tugging her against him.

Hope gave Chloe an apologetic smile and followed Chase, pulling away from him only when she saw Harrison running a hundred miles an hour through the house.

"Harris—" His name died on her lips. She'd been about to scold him for running through the house when she saw that he was in pursuit of one of his uncles.

"Ryder's going to make one hell of a dad, don't you think?" Hope said into Chase's ear as they walked.

"Yeah. He's like a big kid himself."

The house was filling fast, friends steadily arriving and making themselves at home. They'd invited family, friends, the guys who worked on the ranch—everyone who they cared about—and now it was time to welcome everyone to their home for the first time.

"Are we going to wander around and say hi?" Hope asked.

Chase gave her the smile of his that told her he was up

to no good again, his dimple doing nothing to convince her otherwise. He ran a hand through his hair, dark locks that she'd convinced him to leave unruly and slightly too long.

"I think I need a glass of champagne," Chase said, stealing a quick kiss before leaving her for a few seconds and returning with a flute the same as hers.

"Chase, what are you up to?"

He just shrugged, giving her a sexy wink that made her belly swirl with anticipation. She hated the way her body reacted to him sometimes; even when she was trying to be angry with him, she couldn't stop thinking about stripping him naked to see his gorgeous, big, muscled body.

She watched in horror as he slipped her ring off her finger and used it to tap against his glass repeatedly until he had everyone's attention. The jazz music that had been playing just loud enough to be heard stopped, and suddenly everyone had turned toward them. Chase smiled as he placed the ring back on her finger, held her hand up, and kissed it in front of their audience, then turned back around.

Hope had no problem talking to a room of people at a veterinarian conference, but standing as the center of attention, surrounded by people they knew and loved, was all of the sudden overwhelming. She kept her eyes trained on Chase, amazed all over again at his confidence. He could have charmed the pants off every girl in the room, she was sure of it—right now he was his dazzling, sparkly-eyed, handsome-as-hell self—and she knew there was no way she could ever resist him. She'd fallen hook, line, and sinker and she wouldn't have it any other way.

"I just wanted to say a few quick words to thank you all for being here tonight," Chase began, smiling at the crowd gathered listening to him. "This was originally going to be a plain old housewarming party, but as you all know things have changed a little in my life lately."

Laughter rippled through their guests and Hope found it impossible not to join in. What had happened between them had been painful at the time, and they'd kept the actual details completely private between them and Chase's brothers, but everyone standing in their home right now knew they'd rekindled their romance after a long separation.

"I wanted to take this moment to tell this beautiful woman standing beside me how much I love her," Chase continued, turning to face her, his eyes locked on hers as he spoke. "Once upon a time I was too proud to admit just how much, but thank God I came to my senses. She's the love of my life and I'll shout it from the rooftop if I have to." He cleared his throat, smiling at her. "And not only has Hope made *me* happier than I can express, she's also helped us to establish a promising organic beef venture. Thanks to her, we now have all of our new heifers in calf, so tonight is a double celebration."

Hope shook her head, tears brimming as she listened to him. It was all too much, hearing what he had to say to everyone.

"So I'd like you all to join me in a toast," Chase said, giving her another toe-curling wink before turning back to their friends and raising his glass high. "To Hope, my beautiful bride-to-be, and our son, Harrison. I couldn't imagine my life without them."

"To Hope!" everyone called out, raising their glasses.

Chase turned back toward her, taking her hand in his and holding his glass out to clink against hers before taking a sip.

"To us," he murmured.

"To us," she repeated, sipping her champagne as she

stared at the man she'd loved longer than she could remember.

"Mommy, can I have more lemonade?"

Hope laughed as Harrison tugged on her leg, completely oblivious to what was going on around them.
Chase bent down to scoop their son up, hoisting him up
into the air and then letting him settle on his hip.

"Do you know how much I love you?" Chase asked
Harrison.

Hope bit her lip as she watched them together, trying
not to laugh at the expression on Harrison's face.

"Hmmm, this much?" he asked, holding his little arms
as far apart as he could.

"All the way to the moon and back," Chase told him.

"*Now* can I have more lemonade?"

"Sure, kid. You go tell Uncle Nate that I said you can
have it, okay?"

They both watched as Harrison ran back through the
house, a blur among the adults in the room.

"He's a great kid," Chase said, drawing her into his
arms.

"And you're a pretty great dad," she replied, standing
on tiptoe so she could kiss him, her arm around his
neck as she pushed her body against his.

"I wouldn't do that if I were you," he murmured, kissing her again before pushing her away.

"Why?" She faked a frown.

"Because unless you want our friends to see me throw
you over my shoulder and march you upstairs to our bedroom like some kind of caveman, you need to ease off."

"Ah, Chase," she said, running her hand down his muscled arm. "Just one of the reasons I love you."

He slung an arm around her shoulder. "You can toy
with me later, woman. Now it's time to go be social."

She walked with him, their bodies pressed together as

one as they made the rounds, clinking champagne glasses and chatting. It had taken five years and a whole ton of heartache along the way, but she finally felt like she'd found her way home.

Hope glanced down at the massive diamond on her finger, hardly able to believe that by the end of the year she'd be Mrs. King.

"You okay, baby?" Chase asked.

Hope pressed an impromptu kiss to his cheek. "You betcha."

Coming soon . . .

Stay tuned for the next novel in the spectacular
Texas Kings series

I Knew You Were Trouble

Available in June 2016 from St. Martin's Paperbacks